*H*

## She hadn't gone far
## when she saw him coming...

...a man hunched into his winter coat, a broad-brimmed hat pulled low over his face.

She let her pace falter as her heartbeat quickened. The furtive figure watching her apartment—could this be the same man?

Shelby couldn't decide if she should go on, go back the way she'd come or cross the street. On, she thought, tired of being afraid. She wrapped the shoulder strap of her bag around her hand so that she could use it as a weapon if necessary. Her adrenaline pushed her boldly forward, on to her apartment, through the double set of glass doors to the inner hallway.

She stopped short on the threshold, and her mouth went dry. It couldn't be. But it was. The pine branches were laden with flowers. The small banner read To the Dutchman.

Someone had left a wreath from Dutch's wake on her apartment door!

## ABOUT THE AUTHOR

Patricia Rosemoor began creating romantic fantasies while in grade school, never guessing she would someday share her stories with more than her best friends. A native Chicagoan, she supervises the television production facility of a suburban community college. Patricia finds time to write because her husband helps with the research, her four cats assist with the computer work and her dog guards against unwanted interruptions. She also writes with a partner as Lynn Patrick.

### Books by Patricia Rosemoor

HARLEQUIN INTRIGUE
38–DOUBLE IMAGES
55–DANGEROUS ILLUSIONS
74–DEATH SPIRAL

# Crimson Holiday

**Patricia Rosemoor**

## *Harlequin Books*

TORONTO • NEW YORK • LONDON
AMSTERDAM • PARIS • SYDNEY • HAMBURG
STOCKHOLM • ATHENS • TOKYO • MILAN

To my aunts:
Jean, Penny, Stell, Lois and LaVerne.
Happy holidays.

Harlequin Intrigue edition published January 1988

ISBN 0-373-22081-2

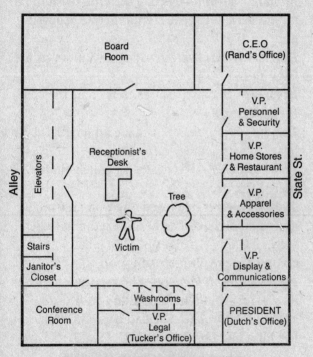

**WESTBROOK'S EXECUTIVE SUITE
9th FLOOR**

# CAST OF CHARACTERS

*Shelby Corbin*—Was she responsible for Santa's *last* Merry Christmas?

*Randall McNabb*—He had seen the swish of red tafetta leave the scene . . . but no one believed him.

*Dutch Bertram Vanleer*—Playing Santa was his last role.

*Iris Dahl*—She had aspired to become the next Mrs. Vanleer.

*Loretta Greenfield*—She made no qualms about her deal with Dutch.

*Frank Hatcher*—His deal with Dutch almost succeeded, except . . .

*Tucker Powers*—He loved one woman from afar . . . and Dutch had become a threat to her.

*Edgar Siefert*—In his eyes, Dutch had committed the ultimate sin.

*Pippa McNabb Vanleer*—She was determined to be set free—but Dutch wouldn't let her go.

*Althea Westbrook*—She had trusted Dutch, but her faith had been misplaced.

## Chapter One

Colors danced through darkness—glowing, haloed beacons cutting through the night.

*"Twinkle, twinkle, little star... how I wonder..."*

Shelby Corbin ordered her sleep-drugged mind to focus so she could see the stars more clearly. No, not stars. The seductive twinkle of Christmas lights shone on the wood of the open door, their syncopated shimmer reflecting off its polished surface. Red. Green. Blue. She concentrated on the splashes of color that hypnotized her back to the warm, safe, waiting void. She closed her eyes and let herself float. Colors lingered, smudging her thoughts. Something had disturbed her, making her leave this peaceful inner sanctum, but it required too great an effort to figure out what.

Quick footsteps and the sound of a closing door nearby made Shelby open her eyes. This time she realized her nocturnal surroundings were foreign. She struggled to sit up, then grabbed for support when her head threatened to explode. A cold, smooth surface rather than the soft texture of her down coverlet met her hand.

A leather couch rather than her bed.

Where was she?

Shelby waited until her inner world righted itself with a dull thud that started at the roots of her hair and bounced its way down to her toes. Trying not to taunt the gremlins who would wreak havoc inside her at any provocation, she moved . . . oh, so carefully. The rustling of her taffeta dress pounded through her head.

Crimson taffeta. The company Christmas party. She remembered now. She was still at Westbrook's, in the store's executive offices. During the evening, she'd come in here to lie down for a minute. . . .

As she set her sandaled feet on the floor, Shelby knew she was in for one doozer of a hangover. Her head felt so odd, and the taste in her mouth that reminded her of the punch she'd tried was sickening. Normally she stayed away from hard liquor; a glass of wine was enough to make her giddy. But the occasion had been the department store's Christmas party and the punch had seemed so innocent. And Santa Claus had given the drink to her, she thought wryly.

How could anyone refuse Santa Claus anything?

Well, *she* should have. She put her hands to a head that seemed larger than the rest of her. No, it hadn't grown. Smoothing her cap of black hair away from her round cheeks and broad forehead, she felt for the pressure points at her eyes that would alleviate the pain. Her fingers fumbled awkwardly, uncooperatively. Shelby sighed in exasperation. She'd never been good at acupressure, anyway.

Work would be pure hell unless she found some aspirin. Her assistant, Zeke, had a bottle in his desk downstairs; she'd look for the aspirin before she left for home. Getting to the window-display office in the dark would be a challenge. While she might be able to find the light switch once she got there, she expected the hallway would be in total darkness.

Shelby rose with caution, telling herself that as long as she didn't make any sudden movements, she'd be okay.

Odd that no one had noticed she'd passed out in this office. She'd heard someone leave, so the party must have ended a short while before. She followed the glow of twinkling colored lights into the main reception area. That they'd been left on at all was curious, but she wasn't about to question her good fortune. The Christmas tree would be her guide. Finding her way out of the executive suite and into the hallway would be half the battle won.

No, wait! She could call Edgar Siefert. The older security guard who usually worked afternoons and evenings had taken over the graveyard shift this week because the regular guy was on vacation. Edgar would have a good laugh at her predicament, but she preferred being teased to having her neck broken by a fall down the stairs in the dark.

The phone—where was it? Shelby could see the bulky outline of the reception desk. Relieved, she was heading straight for it when her foot tangled with something on the floor. She tried to catch herself, but her other foot got caught as well and she flew forward, landing with a jolt on her hands and knees. The room tilted crazily. She shook her head to clear it, then squeezed her eyes shut when pain exploded through her temple. Wrong, wrong, wrong! It took a moment for her equilibrium to adjust.

Crawling around to see what had tripped her, Shelby froze, the breath caught in her throat.

"Oh, Lord!" she croaked hoarsely, unwilling to believe her eyes. For before her, the Christmas lights danced across a ludicrous scene: Santa Claus lay sprawled on his back next to her, eyes open and staring, mouth slack behind the fake beard and mustache. "Hey, Santa, wake up."

As her pulse rapidly scooted through her, Shelby told herself the actor playing Santa Claus must have been sampling the punch, too. He'd passed out as she had.

"Come on, wake up! The party's over!" At first she shook the actor gently to wake him, but when he didn't respond, she pushed harder at his chest with both hands. A piece of mistletoe pinned to his suit tore free and fell to the floor. Her voice echoed hollowly through the spacious reception area as she still tried to deny what she'd found. "It's time to go back to the North Pole—Mrs. Claus is waiting!"

His Santa suit was sticky-wet and her probing fingers found a hole ripped through the fabric—and through his chest. Her forefinger made a sucking sound as she pulled it free. Her head went woozy and her stomach threatened to revolt. Her hands came away coated. Hazel eyes blinking in disbelief, Shelby stared at her palms as the holiday lights lit them, the changing display camouflaging the color of clotting blood.

"You're still alive—you've got to be!" she choked out, her fingers now fumbling for the pulse in his neck. She ripped the beard from the man's face only to make another startling discovery. "Dutch!" This wasn't the hired actor who'd played Santa at the party.

Dutch Vanleer, one of Westbrook's two controlling stockholders, the president and figurehead of the department store, stared up at her blankly.

And he had no pulse, was already stiffening to the touch.

Dead! She was trying to find the pulse of a dead man, for God's sake!

"Aah!" Shelby slid away from the body as bile rose to her throat, threatening to choke her. She swallowed with difficulty and stared down at her blood-covered hands.

Repulsed, she wiped them on her dress over and over until she'd removed the blood. The horror of finding a dead body muddled her mind. An accident. Dutch had had some kind of accident. But accidents didn't leave a hole in the chest like the one she'd found, did they? She looked around for some sharp object he could have fallen on. Nothing. No weapon of any kind.

Weapon...murder... Dutch must have been murdered!

What the hell was she going to do now?

Throw up, that's what. Though the room whirled around her, Shelby somehow managed to get to her feet and head for the bathroom next to the office where she'd passed out. If she didn't act quickly, she'd retch on the corpse. Stumbling into the bathroom, she spent the next agonizing minutes clutching the toilet bowl. Only when her stomach was empty and she was rising from the floor did she notice dull winter light seeping through the cracks of the closed blinds. It was morning; she'd been passed out for hours.

Light shafted over streaks of blood where she'd held on to the porcelain bowl. Horrified, Shelby found a sponge and frantically scrubbed at the fingerprints as if she could wipe away not only them, but the murder as well; then she washed her hands until no trace of red remained. Teetering back into the reception area, she avoided looking at the corpse and headed for the telephone to call the police. Her hand stretched toward the receiver, but stopped halfway there.

She'd been left alone with a dead man—her employer, who'd been after her to go out with him since she'd been hired as the manager of window display six weeks before; with whom she'd had several witnessed arguments on that very topic. Zeke and Dana had heard her threaten Dutch with a sexual-harassment suit only a week before.

She shuddered and let her arm drop to her side.

In addition to being alone with Dutch, her dress was covered with his blood. And if the police found out about that other work-related incident when she'd defended herself from being molested by hitting a man with a beer bottle, she'd be a prime suspect, for sure.

No, she couldn't call the police.

Shelby pressed a trembling hand to her stomach, which felt as if it had been squeezed in a vise. Someone had been in this room only a few minutes ago. That person—the real murderer?—might have killed Dutch while she was trying to struggle out of sleep. Maybe the murderer was still around and she herself was in danger....

Backing toward the door, she looked around wildly, as if the murderer would spring from one of the darkened corners of the room.

RAND MCNABB ENTERED Westbrook's rear entrance feeling like hell. Who wouldn't after a sleepless night like the one he'd just had? He'd rushed back to his Lincoln Park town house long enough to leave his bag, change his shirt and shave. He had to look decent for the board meeting later that morning. As CEO of Westbrook's, he had an image to maintain.

He passed the security office, noticing it was empty. The video monitors were on, but the man who was supposed to be watching them was nowhere in sight. Maybe the security guard was in the washroom. "Edgar?" No answer.

Frowning, Rand turned and headed out into the store proper. He checked the State Street side, but there was no sign of the man. Then he spotted Edgar coming from between two banks of escalators in the middle of the store.

"Hey, boss, you're back!" Edgar said with a broad smile. As he approached Rand, he jerked his trousers, lifting them from where the waistband rested under his middle-aged paunch. "You missed one terrific wingding last night."

"It couldn't be helped." His reason for missing the Christmas party was the last thing Rand felt like talking about. "Edgar, is there something wrong out here?"

"Nah, no problem. Maintenance is late this morning—the party and all—so I decided to turn everything on for the boys. That's what I was doing when I heard a noise over by the fire stairs. I checked it out. Nothing. Must have been the rats."

"Doesn't maintenance have the rodent problem under control yet?" Rand asked, irritated that Dutch couldn't even take care of the small problems.

"Listen, boss, when you been in the department-store game as long as I have, you'll realize there's some problems you never get rid of." Edgar shook his balding head and adjusted his pants again. "And in a city the size of Chicago, and with this store being over the subway system and only a couple of blocks from the river and all, rats are gonna be a fact of life."

The facts of life of running a large department store were piling up on him, Rand thought. Maybe his early retirement from football had been premature; dealing with the real world was taking its toll on him. Of course, if he had a partner who actually did half the work, Rand was sure he'd be in a different frame of mind. But his disgust was only natural, since Dutch had decided he wanted the glory of being Westbrook's quarterback without having to run with the ball. Well, Dutch wasn't going to get away with it anymore.

"Hey, I gotta go, boss. My shift is almost up. My reports—"

"Go ahead, Edgar," Rand said, heading for the elevators. "I need to do some paperwork before the board meeting myself."

On his way up to the ninth floor and the executive suite, Rand couldn't help thinking about the mistake he'd made when he'd let Dutch talk him into buying the failing store from Althea Westbrook two years before. But his kid sister had still been trying to work out her stormy marriage with Dutch, and Rand had figured the partnership was a way to ensure Pippa's future. He hadn't realized the burden of bringing Westbrook's back to its former prominence would be almost completely on his shoulders. His brother-in-law had been good for public relations, but not much else.

That was about to change.

The elevator doors opened. He stepped out and was heading for the executive offices when he heard the creak of hinges behind him. Turning toward the sound, he caught sight of shimmery red material swinging through the fire-stairs doorway. He craned for a better look, but only managed to get a split-second impression of the back of a slender, dark-haired woman before the door closed and cut off his view.

Dutch never had been subtle about his infidelities, Rand thought with disgust, sure the mystery woman was his partner's latest paramour, one whom rumor said worked at Westbrook's. It was obvious she'd just come out of the executive suite, a fact that didn't surprise him.

Rand grabbed hold of the knob before realizing the door was open a crack. He pushed and it swung wide. The Christmas tree was the only thing lit in the room. He stepped inside, his eyes drawn to the body on the floor. Rand walked to it calmly, stooped down, then felt for a pulse to make sure Dutch Vanleer was really dead.

LUCKILY, Shelby had gotten safely into the stairwell without being spotted. Thoughts of escape pounded through her head as she finished descending a flight. She'd worried that she'd be caught when she'd heard the elevator stop while in the process of leaving the executive suite. For all she knew, the murderer might have returned to the scene of the crime. After taking a steadying breath, she opened the door a crack and peeked out to make sure no one was wandering around on this floor.

All clear.

Shelby sneaked out of the stairwell and quietly tiptoed along the hallway until she reached the window-display office. Her hand was on the doorknob when she heard the soft sound that made her catch her breath. A shoe scuffling against the marble floor? A quick look around assured her no one was in sight. Maybe she'd imagined it, or maybe the eighty-year-old building was merely crumbling with a sigh.

Breathing normally once more, she let herself into the office. A glance at the clock told her it was eight-fifteen, barely a quarter of an hour before the office employees were expected. She headed for her work area where she'd left her clothes the night before and tried to undo her dress as she went. The zipper caught halfway down.

"Damn!" The word exploded off her lips as tears of frustration stung the backs of her eyes. She had to change before someone else got there and saw her or she'd be held suspect for a murder she didn't commit. She knew running instead of calling the police made her look guilty as hell. But then, she'd had past dealings with the police in which she'd fared badly. Though it had happened a little more than two years and two jobs ago, the memory was as fresh as if the incident had happened yesterday.

The zipper still wouldn't budge, so Shelby grabbed the material with both hands and tugged until it ripped free. No matter. She'd never wear the dress again, anyway. Cold air met her half-naked body as she slipped out of the torn taffeta. The crimson that remained on her torso made her stomach clutch. Frantically she used the dress to scrub the blood off her skin, then threw the garment on her drawing board. She wore only a pair of sparkly holiday panty hose and her sandals, and the rest of her crawled with goose bumps.

Shelby ignored her discomfort as she tried to figure out where to hide the dress and how to get it out of the office. She spotted her art portfolio in which she took work home. The leather case now held nothing more than a sketch pad. Grabbing the dress, she panicked when it seemed to catch on her drawing board. She tore the garment free, then folded it as flat as possible and stuffed it into her case. She slipped out of her sandals but, realizing they'd leave a bulge in the large, flat portfolio, hid them in the bottom of her big shoulder bag that she'd later lock in one of her desk drawers.

Shelby felt as cold as ice by the time she got her things down from the pegs on the wall behind the drawing board, but she wasn't sure if the reaction was due to being half naked or to finding Dutch the way she had. She was still unnerved. Getting through the workday without giving herself away would be a miracle.

She quickly pulled on the forest-green slacks and turtleneck she'd worn to the office the day before, praying no one would wonder why she'd worn the same outfit two days in a row. Remembering the multicolored scarf she'd stuffed into her coat pocket, she pulled it out and draped it around her neck to give the ensemble a different look.

She checked the clock. Eight twenty-one.

Shelby hurriedly slipped into her dark green flats, grabbed her coat, portfolio and purse and headed for the ladies' room where she'd wait until she heard the sounds of other people arriving. This was one morning when she'd report to work late rather than early as she usually did. Thank goodness managers didn't have to punch in a time clock as did the general office and sales people, so no one would be able to prove she'd been in the building all night.

Hopefully, the first woman to arrive wouldn't come into the ladies' room, but just in case, Shelby decided as she entered, she'd lock herself into a stall.

Time dragged and the early morning's horror rolled over and over in her mind as she counted the minutes. She felt so alone. She couldn't tell anyone about what she'd found or how she felt. The idea of being accused of murder made her head throb. She wanted to run outside and disappear into the State Street crowd, but voices and the sound of the elevator at work told her the store was coming to life. Glancing at her watch, Shelby realized it was eight-thirty-four. She'd waited long enough. She got her things together but hesitated when she heard the ladies'-room door open.

"So what do you think those police cars are doing outside?"

The question issued by a strange voice made Shelby stay where she was. Someone must have discovered the body.

"I dunno, Loretta. Think we got robbed?"

The flippant words came from Iris Dahl who worked in cosmetics. Running water made Shelby strain to hear.

"Robbed? In the morning? Come on, Iris. Any street jerk would know yesterday's receipts have already been deposited."

The water stopped. In her most theatrical whisper, Iris said, "Maybe someone is being held hostage for a huge ransom!"

Shelby shifted and her portfolio banged against the stall's wall. She flushed the toilet so the women wouldn't get suspicious, then pressed her ear to the door to listen.

"More than likely, some little punk made a prank call to the cops," Loretta answered. "Well, I have to get going. I have an early appointment with Dutch."

A slight pause later, Iris asked, "You do?" She sounded odd.

"I have to talk to him about the latest order. Not nearly enough bathing suits. When the women of Chicago see my new line, they'll be storming Westbrook's doors."

"Oh, yeah. Save me one of everything as usual, huh? Well, I'd better be getting down to the cosmetics counter myself."

Sales staff didn't have to report to work until nine, so Iris was early. Curious, Shelby thought as the women's heels clicked across the marble floor. Iris had a reputation for being late. Some of the employees had complained about it, wanting to know why the blonde was so privileged. But now was not the time to think about it. The door opened and closed again, and Shelby had to get out of the rest room—hopefully unnoticed—while the going was good.

Grabbing her things, she left the stall and almost ran out of the place, setting her jaw against the dull throb at her temples. She was entering the window-display office when her assistant, Zeke Newburg, caught up with her.

"How's the head doing this morning chief?"

Surprised by the teasing manner Zeke usually reserved for the staff, Shelby was thrown. "Uh, fine. Why?"

"You were pretty loose last night. I thought you might be suffering the consequences like the rest of us mortals."

"Maybe a little," Shelby muttered, walking away as she headed for her work area.

But Zeke followed, then propped his skinny six-foot-three form against her movable wall divider that was supposed to give her a modicum of privacy when she worked. "Someone must have gotten pretty wild, huh?"

"What?" Though she was five-foot-seven, Shelby had to crane her long neck to meet his dark brown eyes.

"The cops," he said, making her tense. "Someone must have gotten pretty rowdy."

"Right. Listen, did you make a list of those supplies we talked about yesterday?"

Zeke backed off, palms toward her, overlarge mouth set in a crooked smile. "I can take a hint. I'll leave you alone until you're feeling a little perkier, chief."

Too bad everyone else didn't choose to leave her alone. But work went on as usual. A supply salesman stopped by to see her. He had a piece of mistletoe pinned to his lapel. She couldn't take her eyes from it—better than seeing Dutch dead. If the guy realized how tense she was, he didn't let on.

The well-developed rumor mill was active. The word quickly leaked out that a homicide detective had arrived on the scene. Who was dead? Shelby was tempted to scream the answer a dozen times, but she didn't. They'd know soon enough, without her giving herself away.

The call came at ten-thirty-six. She was getting good at keeping track of time, Shelby thought wryly. It was Kristen, Randall McNabb's secretary. The regular board meeting originally scheduled for that morning had been canceled. Instead, there'd be a meeting of department managers at eleven o'clock in the boardroom. She was to clear her schedule of any conflicts for the rest of the afternoon.

By the time she stepped into an empty elevator car at five minutes to eleven, everyone knew who'd been murdered in spite of McNabb's attempt to keep the matter low-key. Shelby thought she'd go crazy listening to the piped-in Christmas music as the elevator rose to the executive suite, but she drew herself together and had even curved her lips into a half smile by the time the doors opened.

The smile froze when she stepped out only to realize the paramedics were waiting to use her elevator car. She couldn't take her eyes off the cart they pushed—or the king-size body bag that rested on it. A quick picture of Santa Claus, his eyes staring, his mouth slack behind the beard and mustache, flashed through her mind and made her shake inside. She didn't know how long she stood there staring at elevator doors that had already closed before an angry voice filtered through the haze of her fear.

"Damn it, Jackson! Leave Pippa out of this!"

She turned to see Rand McNabb standing tensed in the open double doors of the executive suite. The faint scar that trailed from McNabb's chiseled cheek to his auburn mustache stood out white against his flushed face. Glowering, he towered over a man who might be small in size compared to the ex-linebacker, but who seemed equally large in dignity.

"I can't leave your sister out of this," Jackson said smoothly, pocketing a small notebook.

A detective. Shelby stopped to look. Beyond a taped-off area, a man who probably was an evidence technician scoured the floor, a plastic bag in his hand. Shelby wondered if he'd found any clues. And a woman was packing up camera equipment. Shelby imagined photos of Dutch as she'd found him....

"It's public knowledge your sister was desperate for a divorce," Jackson said as she passed the men. "Their dirty laundry has been spread across every rag in the area. Maybe this was her way—"

"What about the woman in red?" McNabb demanded.

His startling question almost made Shelby trip. She kept going, eyes focused on the boardroom, pretending she wasn't listening.

"I've made a note of your mysterious dark-haired woman," the detective assured him. "I hope this isn't your way of protecting your sister."

The idea of almost having been caught by Rand McNabb made Shelby's head grow so light that she missed his reply. She steadied herself at the doorway of the boardroom.

Jackson said, "I'm thinking like a cop. It's my job."

Shelby pushed herself into the half-filled room of silent people who must have heard the argument that had ended abruptly. All were department managers other than Althea Westbrook, who sat near the head of the room-long table next to Tucker Powers.

Shelby headed for a seat at the opposite end of the table from the former owner of Westbrook's and the vice president of the legal department. The farther she'd be from McNabb the better, she thought, trying not to panic again. She took comfort in the fact that while she knew who he was, he probably couldn't say the same about her. She'd never met him officially, and since he'd been in and out of town half a dozen times in as many weeks—the six that she'd been working at Westbrook's—they'd never had any reason to speak to each other.

She sat next to Frank Hatcher, manager of data processing. He was a slim man, about her height, with thinning light brown hair. He was checking his watch and clucking to himself. "They tell us eleven, but it's already five after."

"You know why we're here, don't you?" she asked quietly as one person sat on her other side and another across from her.

"Of course I do. Everybody knows. But if you ask me, giving up this whole afternoon is a waste of time. I have a lot of work to do before leaving for vacation at the end of the week. This is going to put me behind schedule."

Shelby stared, shocked at the man's cavalier attitude. She hadn't liked Dutch herself, but to be worried about vacation at a time like this . . .

Rand McNabb chose that moment to sweep into the room, the perfect chief executive officer, no trace of his emotional outburst in his bearing. His square jaw was controlled, his full, sensuous mouth relaxed beneath the thick mustache that was a shade darker than his crisply styled auburn hair. The expensive suit he wore fit him perfectly in spite of his muscular shoulders and taut thighs, remnants of his football career, Shelby thought, remembering seeing him play a dozen times. She'd admired him on the field and off, and had been looking forward to getting to know him better. But not in a situation like this one.

"I'm sure you all know why you're here," McNabb said, taking his place at the helm. He remained standing, looking at each of them individually. Shelby wanted to shrink down in her chair as his amber eyes met hers, but that, of course, would have brought his attention to her directly. "I have the sad duty of telling you that Bertram 'Dutch' Vanleer is dead." Thankfully, he was already looking at the person next to her when he said, "Murdered."

"And the good name of Westbrook's is soiled forever," Althea Westbrook stated shakily, her pale blue eyes threatening tears. Her coiffed silvering blond head was held high, but her pain was evident. The tip of her straight nose was pink, the line of her thin lips pulled tight. She clutched a lace-edged handkerchief as if it could provide support. "The store will never recover from this scandal."

"Shall I get you a glass of water, my dear?" Tucker Powers solicitously asked, his alert gray eyes pinned to her every movement.

The distinguished-looking man with a dusting of silver at his temples was already rising, his thick brows drawn in concern. Though he was in his mid-fifties, a restrained power evident in his stance complemented Althea's seeming fragility. Shelby thought the two close friends. They'd been together for most of the Christmas party.

"Sit down, Tucker," Althea insisted, placing a staying hand on his arm. "You worry too much. I'll be fine, but thank you."

To Shelby, the woman who looked to be a few years older than Tucker seemed a tragic figure somehow, braving this whole thing out when she didn't have to be there. And yet she had her own strength. Westbrook's had been her family's business since her father founded it in 1909. As the surviving youngest daughter, Althea had run the department store for several years until she'd had to sell the controlling interest. Even then she'd held on to enough stock to keep herself on the board.

"I'm hoping you're mistaken about Dutch's death hurting Westbrook's, Althea," McNabb said kindly. "I think it'll take more than a scandal—even murder—to destroy us."

"I can only pray you are correct, Randall."

Tucker patted her on the shoulder and she smiled sweetly at the lawyer.

Then McNabb continued. "We'll have to wait to see how this affects us, but in the meantime, there's a killer to be caught." His eyes were roaming again, skimming from one person to the next. "This afternoon, Lieutenant Isaac

Jackson and some of his men will begin questioning everyone who was at the party last night. He expects it'll take a few days to get around to everyone since more than two hundred people attended." He was looking directly at Shelby when he said, "I expect you and your staffs to cooperate with them fully."

Passing on to the next person, his eyes wavered, then returned to her. Shelby's mouth went dry. Rand McNabb was staring at her oddly, his expression almost calculating, his eyes narrowing.

And she swallowed hard when she imagined she saw a glint of recognition reflected in their amber depths.

## Chapter Two

He hadn't said a word to her, not then, not after the meeting. Whatever Rand McNabb had been thinking, he'd been keeping his game plan close to the chest. Chances were he knew nothing more than she was a woman with dark hair who would have been at the party and therefore was under suspicion. So why did she feel so vulnerable? She could only be tackled if she let down her guard.

Shelby laughed at her football analogy. She had football on the brain. No, she had to admit she had McNabb on the brain. She tried to close her mental door against him, but he intruded, refusing to be vanquished even as she began preliminary work on the Valentine's Day windows the next morning. Though she could leave designing to her staff, Shelby hadn't been a manager long enough to part easily with her favorite component of window-display work. But, even as she drew, she remained distracted: those amber eyes were everywhere, ready to ply her with questions, ready to sack her if they could.

Having gotten used to her vivid imaginings, Shelby was unnerved midmorning when she found the real man standing only a few inches away, looking over her shoulder as she drew.

"Is this what our Valentine's Day windows are going to look like?" he asked, one eyebrow raised.

She looked down at the mess on her drawing board and realized what she'd been doing. One of her hearts looked like two crossed footballs.

"Creative people are prone to experimentation."

The words were the first thing that came to mind. She set the pencil on the drawing board's ledge. Her fingers were stiff as she released the object. Eventually she had to look at McNabb more directly, but for now she was stalling by keeping her eyes on his mustache and the faint scar that trailed into it from his left cheek. As if he knew she was doing it, he parted his lips in a smile that would be perfect if not for the chip in one of his front teeth—a humanizing flaw, she thought.

"I've never formally introduced myself because I've been busy traveling. Now I'll have to take more of an interest in the everyday workings of the store," he said, holding out his hand practically under her nose. She couldn't refuse to take it. "Rand McNabb." His grasp was warm and firm, but not exactly friendly.

"Shelby Corbin, as I'm sure you know, Mr. McNabb," she said, quickly pulling her hand free.

"Rand."

She forced her lips to bow instead of repeating his name, which she had no desire to do. She wanted to ask questions about what he was doing there and why he was studying her so intently. He looked as though he'd like to turn her inside out and give her a good shake—as though all her secrets would fall out on display if he did.

"Speaking of taking more of an interest," he went on, his tone more personal now, "I have to make an appearance at a benefit tonight in Dutch's stead. I was hoping you might be willing to accompany me."

He was standing so close, Shelby almost shuddered. Why couldn't he just leave her alone? There probably weren't many women in Chicago who'd make that request, she admitted while reluctantly recognizing his positive male attributes. A week ago she wouldn't have made it herself. But a week ago, she hadn't found a corpse in a Santa Claus suit. A week ago she wasn't worrying about being accused of a murder she didn't commit.

Her response was sharp. "I can't."

"Can't?"

She thought quickly. "I go to the health club right from work." Actually, it was true, she rationalized, if not of this particular night, then of others.

"But this cocktail party is such a worthy cause—raising money for clothing and presents for deprived kids at one of the inner city's privately funded youth centers. Most of these kids are lucky if they get enough to eat." He was at his persuasive best when he added, "Besides, I'm looking forward to experiencing more of your creative experimentation."

Shelby squirmed under his expectant gaze. If she didn't know better, she'd think he was flirting with her. He was making this benefit thing sound like a real date. She would have given anything to have heard those words under different circumstances. Her next protest was halfhearted. "I don't have anything to wear."

He waited a beat, fixed her with a paralyzing stare, then struck. "Whatever you wore to the Christmas party will do."

Did he expect her to wear the crimson taffeta dress? she immediately wondered. He could get that cagily innocent look off of his face, because she was onto him, Shelby thought. Besides which, he was too late. She'd already destroyed the dress, burned it in her fireplace and, unlike careless killers in the movies, she'd cleaned and vacuumed both the hearth and the rug to make sure there were no telltale bits of the thing left.

"Well, what do you say?" he challenged her. "Will I have the chance to get to know you better tonight?"

A movement caught Shelby's eye, delaying her answer for a moment. Zeke was lurking in the background, waiting to talk to her. If she refused, Rand—McNabb, she reminded herself sternly—would make a fuss. And she didn't need a fuss. Not when there were so many ears around—including Zeke's—who'd heard her telling off Dutch when her employer had made physical advances to her in the office.

She was cornered and she didn't like the feeling, but she knew when to feint. "All right, Rand," she said agreeably. "You have yourself a date."

Seeming satisfied, he nodded. "I'll pick you up at six."

He only stayed a moment longer to get her address. He was all business once he had what he came for, she thought, watching him leave, but then, wasn't that what tonight would be about—nasty business? She'd have to foil him, to charm him into forgetting about the mystery woman. Or at least to forget he'd ever suspected *her*.

But she couldn't forget. The knowledge stayed with her throughout the day, making it increasingly difficult for her to pay attention to her work. How absurd! She was probably worrying about nothing, anyway. McNabb couldn't connect her with Dutch's death.

Once she'd convinced herself of that, her growing irritation competed with her fear of discovery. Being the person she was, Shelby couldn't easily accept someone actually thinking she was a murderer. And she couldn't stand the thought of being forced into going out with any man—not even a gorgeous hunk like Rand McNabb—no matter how altruistic his reasons might be. She was tempted to give him a hard time, but that wouldn't be the smart way to handle him, and Shelby knew that smart was preferable to righteous, in this instance. Besides, she could use the opportunity to find out what *he* knew about the murder.

She only hoped she could handle her after-lunch interview with Lieutenant Jackson with equal aplomb.

"SHELBY CORBIN, manager of window display." Jackson checked her name off a list and scribbled something in his small notebook. "Since you're in management, Miss Corbin, did you work much with Mr. Vanleer?"

"Not really." Shelby hoped neither her voice nor her posture would convey her nervousness. "My direct supervisor is Ben Levin, vice president of display and communications. I deal directly with him and he gets...*got* approvals from Mr. Vanleer. Chain of command, and all that."

The detective perched on the edge of the desk, giving him the advantage of height over her. She looked up into his dark, expressionless face and tried to mirror that seeming disinterest in her own features. "So, you didn't know the victim well?"

"No, not at all."

Shelby knew the kind of man he'd been, however. Dutch hadn't exactly kept his lechery a secret from her, and she had the strong feeling that adultery hadn't been his only vice. She hoped her dislike of her late employer wouldn't be evident when she spoke about him.

As if he knew what she was thinking, Jackson asked, "Do you know anyone who disliked Mr. Vanleer?" and just about looked through her, waiting for her response.

"Everyone has someone who dislikes him, Lieutenant."
She refused to squirm under his intense gaze. "I'll bet even
you have a few enemies."

The detective slid off the desk. He circled the chair,
stopping behind her. Shelby was tempted to bite her tongue
when, his mouth next to her ear, he softly said, "*Enemies*.
An interesting way to phrase it. Did the victim have enemies, Miss Corbin?"

"I told you I didn't know him that well!" Shelby insisted, turning to meet his dark, fathomless eyes. She realized she was letting Jackson get to her, obviously as he'd
planned. He'd be counting on unnerving anyone withholding information. She wondered if he'd learned it as
part of his training in the Chicago Police Department, or
if the method came naturally to him.

He moved away and circled her chair so he was in front
of her once more. He changed tactics. "Let's get to the
night of the party. You were there, weren't you?"

"Yes, of course." Her palms began to feel clammy, but
she didn't dare do anything about it. He'd notice any
physical movement and wiping her hands would give her
away. "I was there along with almost two hundred other
employees."

"For how long?"

"All night."

"What time did you leave?"

She prayed he didn't notice the sudden pulse that leaped
in her throat. "I really don't have any idea."

"You don't keep track of time?"

Only afterward, Shelby thought. "Not really. I was having fun like everyone else. There wasn't any *reason* to keep
track of time."

"Did you socialize with the victim at the party?" Jackson asked without pausing.

"I said hello when I came in. I think I shook his hand. Does that count?"

"Did anyone else socialize with him?"

"I didn't pay any attention." Shelby kept her voice even only with difficulty. "As I've been trying to tell you, it wasn't important to me."

The expression on his dark face friendly, he dropped the bomb she'd been waiting for. "Did any women at the party wear red?"

Shelby forced herself to smile. "Of course. Quite a few. It was a Christmas party, remember."

Jackson nodded. "Thank you, Miss Corbin, though I can't say you've been much of a help."

Shelby was only mildly relieved as she left the office and returned to work. She counted the minutes left in the day, anxious to get away from Westbrook's and its awful memories. And through it all, questions plagued her: What had Detective Jackson thought of his interview with her? Could he possibly guess she knew more than she'd told him?

Later, having hurried home to change, she showered, washed and blow-dried her short black hair and curled the longer right side of the asymmetrical cut. Then she slipped into the black outfit with green and gold beading that matched her eyes. Shelby was satisfied that in spite of her baby face with its dimpled cheeks and snub nose, she looked properly distracting.

Aggravated with herself because the idea of being able to distract Rand McNabb appealed to her—she had to be cool about this or she'd forget that she was supposed to be finding out what the man knew about the murder—she hurriedly grabbed a fake fox jacket from a chair and swept out of her bedroom and into the living room that faced Cleveland Avenue. And not a minute too soon, she realized, as the buzzer shrilled down the long hallway. She'd had no intention of letting him in. She left the first-floor apartment, waving to McNabb through the glass door that separated them before dead-bolting her door.

Though she was amazed that he was wearing a tux with a white pleated shirt beneath a black coat rather than a houndstooth greatcoat and hat like those of Sherlock Holmes, she had to admit they were tailored perfectly for his large, muscular body. He'd be the best-looking man at the benefit. Too bad this date wasn't for real, she thought as she joined him in the small hallway.

"You're certainly prompt," he said.

"I don't believe in keeping people waiting."

He gave her an even better once-over than she had him. "The wait would have been worthwhile."

Shelby was startled by her reaction to his obvious approval. He took the jacket from her fingers suddenly gone numb, all the while holding her prisoner with his gaze. She was going to dream about those eyes and the conflicting feelings they could inspire. Fear, anger and lust—an unnatural combination, she thought wryly before reminding herself that nothing was as she thought it should be these days. Finding a dead body the morning after the company Christmas party wasn't exactly her idea of starting the holidays out right, either.

He was helping her into the jacket when he said, "If you looked this good the other night, I'm even sorrier that I missed the Christmas party."

The words snapped her out of the dreamy state and back into the aggravated one. "You might have been disappointed, since this isn't what I was wearing."

Without giving him an opportunity to ask what she had been wearing, Shelby opened the front door herself and marched down the six steps to the dry sidewalk. A week before Christmas and it hadn't snowed yet. Not so much as a puff. Nothing was going as it should this holiday season.

Sensing McNabb was right behind her, she asked, "I hope you didn't have to park too far from here." She wasn't kidding, either. Lincoln Park West was an automobile owner's nightmare when it came to finding a parking spot.

"I walked from my place."

"Trying to stay in condition?" she asked tartly, knowing that he was as close to being physically perfect as possible. "If we're going to walk to the benefit, I'd better go back in to get my Reeboks." She indicated the three-and-a-half-inch heels she wore. "These won't hold up very far."

But he was already pulling her toward Fullerton Avenue. "You'll only have to walk a block," he said congenially, as though he hadn't noticed her irritated tone. Or maybe he was choosing to ignore it. "We'll pick up a cab over on Clark Street."

Aware of the large, strong hand tucked between her arm and side, Shelby walked without further protest, her steps half the length of his and double in number. She wasn't short—actually, she was considered on the tall side—but the high heels limited her movement. Even wearing them, she was two or three inches shorter than the ex-linebacker.

They didn't have to go as far as Clark Street. McNabb flagged down an empty taxi right on Fullerton. She slid in first—all the way over to the opposite window. He followed, crowding her.

"State and Goethe," he told the driver.

"The Gold Coast, huh?" she muttered, wishing he'd give her some breathing room.

"That's where the money is. You don't have anything against money, do you?"

"Only the fact that I don't have it—not that I'm complaining about my salary."

"Good, because the last thing I want to do on a date is discuss money or business." He snaked an arm around the seat in back of her. "They're both dreary subjects."

That statement surprised her. The businessmen she'd met in the past were enamored of their jobs and the money they made and usually couldn't find other topics they preferred. Of course she had to remember business wasn't McNabb's first choice. "You don't like what you do?"

"Let's just say I'd be happier doing a lot less of it," he said evasively.

"Then why did you retire early?—and why would a football player even think about trying to run a department store without any experience?"

She felt the arm behind her tighten. "I quit football before my knees quit on me. And some of us jocks have enough brains to do mentally challenging jobs as well as physical ones. I'm not a stereotype, Shelby. Don't underestimate me."

He certainly wasn't, and she certainly wouldn't, but she had no intention of telling him any such thing. She had to keep in mind her plan for the evening, trying to find out what he knew about Dutch's murder.

To put him off guard, she leaned close and brushed her hair against his cheek and the edge of his square jaw. He stiffened yet again, though he made no move to inch away. Smiling at his obvious discomfort, Shelby relaxed, pressing herself more intimately into his broad chest and staring out of the window away from him. She might enjoy the evening, after all.

A few silent minutes later the taxi pulled up in front of one of the old State Street mansions. Shelby pulled away from McNabb, realizing she did so reluctantly. That wouldn't do at all, she cautioned herself. He paid the driver and helped her out of the taxi. They approached the brown brick building surrounded by a six-foot black iron-grill fence with her clinging to his arm familiarly. The tiny yard between sidewalk and building was landscaped with brick walkways, a large tree with a black iron bench under its branches on one side, and what looked as if it would be a tiny formal garden in summer on the other.

"This place belongs to Ona Quan."

"The alderwoman who's been trying to fund programs to keep the gangs in check? Is she a friend of yours?"

"An acquaintance."

Shelby questioned that when their elegant Oriental hostess greeted McNabb just inside the front door. Ona stood on her tiptoes, put her hands on his shoulders and kissed him soundly on the cheek. She didn't seem inclined to move away as she said, "It's so good to see you, Rand. It's been too long."

"I've been busy with work, Ona." Circling her small waist with his large hands, he set her away from him.

Their expression almost as inscrutable as Shelby might have expected, Ona's almond-shaped eyes settled on her. "Not too busy, I see."

"Let me introduce Shelby Corbin, manager of window display at Westbrook's."

The women shook hands. "My, you are getting into your work these days." Ona sighed, but Shelby could tell she was more teasing than serious.

"Alderman Quan," Shelby acknowledged her. "I admire your work on the gang problem."

"It's something about which I feel very strongly. I hope my work helps limit crime—thefts, rapes, murders. Well, go right in." Ona was looking toward the front door where a group of four was entering. "The champagne is already flowing."

Shelby glanced quickly at McNabb to see if he'd reacted to the reference to murders, but his expression hadn't changed.

"Don't you want my check first?" he asked.

"I trust you. Besides, there's a large Plexiglas box under guard in the ballroom. The committee didn't want to take any chances that the kids wouldn't get the benefit of this fund-raiser."

They followed the sounds of a musical quartet to a ballroom that looked like something out of a castle with its marble floors, wood paneling with hand-carved trim, and crystal chandeliers. The setting was worthy of being on display to the city, Shelby thought, especially with these elegantly dressed people gracing the mansion. Her fake fox was definitely out of place.

As McNabb helped her remove it, she murmured, "So Alderman Quan is only an acquaintance?"

"She is now. I'm flattered that you're interested."

"I'm not, really," Shelby stated, lying through her teeth. Or rather, she would be interested if it weren't for the impossible situation. "But I like getting my facts straight."

"So do I, Shelby, so do I."

That sounded like a warning. Though she bristled, Shelby didn't challenge him as she would have liked, but allowed him to check their coats. She was innocent and she told herself that that knowledge should be enough to satisfy her. It wasn't, not by a long shot.

Now that she was over the initial shock and panic of finding Dutch, she was angry—with herself for drinking the punch, with the murderer for having the poor foresight to do his dastardly deed with her passed out in the other room, and most of all with Rand McNabb, who probably thought she was guilty of murder and would try to prove it so he could protect his darling sister. She hoped she could get through this charade of a date and get some information out of him. She believed in protecting herself, for who knew what conclusions the police might come to.

McNabb deposited his check in the Plexiglas box, then led her through the crowd, acknowledging someone every few steps. She tried to concentrate on the strangers and to ignore the twinkling lights of the Christmas tree in the corner that caught her eye. It reminded her of the one in the executive suite.

Instead, she paid attention to the people greeting her escort. The voices were well modulated, the laughs polite, the compliments freely given, almost as if the attendees were at a business rather than a social function. They approached everything in moderation except the cigarettes that they all seemed to clutch. The closer she got to the refreshment table, the thicker with smoke the air became.

"You'd think that, with as much attention as these people pay to their health at clubs and spas, they'd give up those things," Shelby said, blinking against the smoke invading her eyes. She waved the air in front of her face. "Nasty habit."

"A drink will make you feel better."

"I didn't know ginger ale had soothing qualities."

His look was questioning, but he got her the soft drink and a beer for himself from the bar, then moved the few feet to the buffet. Picking up a cracker, he scooped some pâté onto it and held it out to her. She shook her head.

"Not hungry?"

"I don't usually eat red meat." She didn't add that she'd been known to indulge in a rare steak when the urge struck her.

"You don't smoke, you don't drink, you don't eat meat." He sounded serious when he asked, "No vices at all?" But she saw the challenge in his eyes and heard her cue to get her plan back on track when he added, "What kind of a fun date are you?" He punctuated the question by putting the cracker and pâté into his own mouth.

Lids lowered, she murmured huskily, "I have my moments."

He swallowed quickly. "Warn me when you feel one coming on, would you?"

"You'll know," she promised. "Words won't be necessary."

He didn't try to hide his flare of interest at her verbal play or at her touch. He set down his beer on a tray and took the empty glass from her hand. "Why don't we dance?"

And be trapped against a hard male body, moving to soft, romantic music? No way—except to execute her plan, she reminded herself. The dance floor would be the perfect place to question him. Subtly, of course.

"I'd love to."

The area set aside as a dance floor was tiny and there were already several couples on it, so their movement would be restricted. Shelby slipped into Rand's arms and tried to ignore the warning signals shooting through her thoughts. But she couldn't vanquish her awareness of the attraction he lit in her, despite her best dousing of common sense.

The other dancing couples, the music, the setting—they all seemed to disappear as she slid her left hand up along his back, not stopping until it came in contact with the delicious warmth of bare skin. Her fingertips caressed his neck to the music's rhythm, striking an immediate response.

He tightened his hold on her so that his breath ruffled the long curls around her forehead and he spun her around so that she found her legs tangled with his at the thigh. When her hair brushed his cheek, she took feminine satisfaction in the purely male groan he couldn't quite suppress. The only problem was that she was having difficulty remembering she was doing this merely to protect herself.

She silently repeated that fact over and over again, but her brain was malfunctioning. It was taking the data and spitting it back out at her. For some reason, she couldn't think how to begin questioning him about Dutch. Rand himself was the only man she wanted to know more about.

He felt so good in her arms, making her adrenaline flow from something other than fear. It had been ages since she'd been with anyone she could get excited about, and Rand McNabb personified excitement in a very physical sense. Brains were more appealing than brawn, she lectured herself, but she was afraid he had those as well. What a potent combination in a man. He'd be difficult to resist if he ever forgot about the woman in red and turned on the charm completely.

"I'll make you a deal," he finally said, startling her out of her thoughts and back to reality. The quartet was now playing a Christmas carol, impossible to dance to.

Suspicious, she pulled back so she could see his face. "What?"

"While I'd love to hold you in my arms all night, I'm liable to drop you from lack of strength if I don't get something nourishing in my stomach. If you sit at one of those little tables over there on the other side of the buffet, I'll get us some hors d'oeuvres." He held up his right hand in a Boy Scout-like pledge. "I swear red meat won't touch your plate."

"Deal."

Shelby was relieved to be set free so she could recoup her composure. Rand was treating her like a real date and she was starting to believe it because she wanted to. She found an empty table and turned her back to the Christmas tree, trying to blot out the unpleasant memory it stood for.

Instead, she remembered the first time she'd seen Rand play ball. He'd been expert, tough, and fast for a man his size and, above all, he'd been known as a player the team could count on. He hadn't gone for personal glory the way Dutch had as the team's replacement quarterback.

It seemed as if that relationship had carried over into their roles as business partners, Shelby realized. Dutch had been the front man, the okay Joe, the guy with the hearty handshake, while Rand had stayed in the background, seeing that things got done.

Suddenly she realized she'd been thinking of her employer as "Rand" rather than "McNabb." She shifted in her seat, knowing she was weakening toward the man. Well, she'd have to get in shape mentally. Toughen up before he got back to the table. Figure out how to find out what he knew about the murder.

"Merry Christmas, pretty lady," came a voice at her ear.

Shelby whipped around and came face-to-face with Santa Claus. Without warning, her heart tripped over a beat. For a second, her vision clouded and she saw staring eyes and a slack mouth; a sprig of mistletoe torn from a crimson-covered chest and fallen to the floor. She shook the memory away. This Santa was alive and looking clearly puzzled that she wasn't taking the mistletoe he was offering her.

"No!" she choked out, backing away from his hand.

The large room began closing in on her. Voices became distorted. The Christmas music sounded off-key and the twinkling lights of the Christmas tree glared at her. Shelby's head began to throb. She imagined Santa Claus was glaring at her malevolently.

"I don't want . . . I'm allergic to mistletoe."

"Well, Merry Christmas anyway," Santa said, backing off.

Wanting nothing more than to run out of the place, she forced herself to stay rational. She couldn't act so idiotically every time she saw some guy dressed as Santa Claus. They were everywhere at this time of the year. But she couldn't help it. A suspicion formed when she looked around and didn't see this particular Santa anywhere. Perhaps Rand had hired the guy to be here purposely to upset her the moment she was alone.

"Here you go—the vegetarian special."

Rand set the loaded plate in front of her. She stared at the blob of ratatouille in the center—vegetable bits swimming in a red sea of tomato sauce—and remembered the clotting blood on Dutch's chest. Swallowing hard, she looked up into Rand's rugged face. His expression was as odd as she was feeling.

"Something wrong with the selection?" he asked. "I can get you something else. There's—"

"I'm not very hungry. Actually, I've got a headache," she added quickly, rising just as Rand sat, his own plate in front of him. "I'd like to go home, if you don't mind."

He frowned up at her. "Try some of this stuff. Maybe the headache's from hunger."

She was already backing away. "Listen, why don't you stay and eat. I'll go over to Division and flag down a taxi."

"Don't be ridiculous." The frown turned into an outright scowl as he rose. "I brought you, so I'll escort you home. Are you sure there's nothing wrong?"

Like what? A guilty conscience? She didn't say anything, merely led the way back toward the entrance and their coats. A few minutes later, they were in a taxi heading north for her place.

Shelby was thankful that Rand neither tried to start a conversation nor made any moves on her. He stared at her thoughtfully from his side of the taxi. The ride calmed her imagination if not the dull throb at the back of her head, and she began to feel foolish. She'd allowed the ordinary to become the extraordinary in her mind when there wasn't the slightest reason to do so. She was sure Rand would be glad to be rid of her, but when they pulled up in front of her building, he handed the driver a large bill.

"Keep the change," he said, opening the door to exit.

"Why don't you just keep the cab?" Ignoring the hand he offered, she helped herself out. "I can see myself in."

"I know you can. But I'd like to walk you to your door."

She didn't argue. As a matter of fact, when she got into the hallway, she felt odd just leaving him there. In spite of the charade of the date, she felt guilty for taking him away from his party and his food.

Unlocking the hall door, she said, "Listen, I've got some cold chicken in the refrigerator if you'd like to come in."

A raised eyebrow indicated his surprise, but all he said was "Cold chicken sounds wonderful."

She unlocked her door and led him into the hallway that ran the length of her apartment. "Give me a few minutes to change into jeans and a sweatshirt. And I've got to look for some aspirin. My brain is beginning to feel too big for my skull. You can wait in the living room," she said, pointing to the right. "Or go down the hall to the kitchen if you want something to drink. There's a couple of bottles gathering dust in the cabinet above the refrigerator if—"

"Go find those aspirin," he said, gently pushing her forward into her bedroom.

Rand turned right into the living room but didn't sit down. While admiring her taste in decoration—the clean, simple lines of pearl-gray seating against pale mauve carpeting and two-tone fireplace mantel, woodwork, gray storage units and smaller tables—he seethed over his dilemma while listening to her movements in the next room. From the sounds of it, she was gathering her change of clothing.

Protective of his sister Pippa and irritated by Lieutenant Jackson's casual attitude toward finding the woman in red, Rand had begun making deductions of his own. When he'd seen Shelby in the meeting the day before, he'd realized she could have been the woman on the fire stairs. Unsure, he'd said nothing to the police. He'd asked her out, thinking he could get a better idea if she'd been the one—and hoping he'd have the chance to search her apartment for the red dress.

He heard a door close. The bathroom? Rand quietly moved to the hallway and looked into her bedroom. Empty. Still, he hesitated.

He hadn't counted on being so damned attracted to Shelby Corbin. Without any encouragement, he could see that mischievous look that darkened her hazel eyes, the twitch of a smile that continuously seemed to pull at her Cupid's-bow mouth, the dimples that popped into her pleasantly rounded cheeks when she let herself smile naturally. He was torn between wanting to take Shelby in his arms and completing his self-appointed task.

Loyalty to his sister won.

Listening intently to the sounds of Shelby moving around in the bathroom, Rand slipped into the bedroom and over to the half-open closet next to the queen-size bed. He tried to ignore the bed, but the head was surrounded by a cloud of white gauze, and there was a lacy negligee thrown across the foot, a splash of intense purple against the pale mauve coverlet. He could almost picture her in the thing....

At the sound of running water in the next room, he tamped his imagination and got to work on the closet.

The first thing he spotted was a pair of red high-heeled sandals discarded on the floor. There must be a dress that went with them. He checked her things hurriedly but thoroughly. No red dress, not even in the zippered bag that held other garments. Maybe she'd hidden it in another closet, Rand decided, half closing the door as he'd found it.

But before he could take more than three steps, the door to the bathroom opened and Shelby stood there, dressed in jeans and sparkly green sweatshirt, staring at him oddly from the other side of the bed. "What do you think you're doing in here?" she asked, a slight frown marring her broad forehead and puckering the delicate arch of her thin eyebrows.

Quickly improvising, Rand said, "I wanted to make sure you were all right."

"Where were you planning to do the checking? In my bed?"

Relieved that she had no idea he'd been searching her closet, Rand went along with her suggestion. He shrugged and gave her a mildly searing glance. "Well, after the way we were so close on the dance floor, I thought—"

"That we could be close in here, too?" she finished smoothly. "Let's not rush things, shall we?"

Shelby's expression was curiously void of either anger or approval, almost as if she'd made her face go blank purposely so he couldn't guess what she was thinking. A black curl fell to the middle of her forehead when she threw her clothes down onto the bed. He wanted to catch the stray hair in his fingers and smooth it away from her face. Instead he said, "Look, I'm sorry if I made a mistake."

"I invited you in so you could have a taste of my chicken, Rand McNabb, not of me."

"Consider me removed from your bedroom," he said, already in the doorway. "Now, why don't we go into the kitchen and—"

"I hope you don't mind, but I'd like to take a rain check on the chicken. This headache is so bad I doubt the aspirin will do more than dull it."

He thought about arguing, but she really did seem to be in pain. For the moment he was defeated in finding the red dress—and in getting closer to her. "All right. Another time, then."

"Thanks."

But Shelby didn't feel thankful when she locked the door behind Rand. Even knowing why he'd asked her out in the first place, she couldn't help wishing things were different, that she could treat him as an attractive man she could possibly get involved with. But thinking about it wouldn't do. She walked into the living room, listening intently to his footsteps in the hall. A door closed.

She turned out the light and glanced out the front-room window, telling herself she *was not* watching for Rand. She merely wanted to pull down the roll-up window covering she'd raised earlier. Still, she didn't reach for the cord.

She could hardly believe the ex-linebacker had gone into a partnership with someone like Dutch Vanleer. If she'd found *him* in her bedroom, the lecher wouldn't have left until he'd got what he wanted. Dutch hadn't been nearly as nice a guy as he put on, Shelby remembered, watching Rand walk down her front steps. She'd discovered the clever deception the first time he'd tried to corner her. Dutch had intimated that her job would be on the line if she weren't "nice" to him.

She'd wondered why her predecessor, Meg Harding, had left the position without notice, right in the middle of the rush to get the store ready for Christmas. Hints dropped here and there by other employees eventually had convinced her Dutch had been after Meg as well. Meg might be a quitter, but *she* wasn't, Shelby thought, as Rand strode toward Fullerton Avenue without so much as a backward glance.

The last time Dutch had challenged her in her own office, she'd opened up all guns on him, loudly declaring that she'd see him in court for sexual harassment on the job if he didn't lay off. That had happened less than a week before, and at least Zeke and Dana had been present to hear the heated exchange.

To anyone who didn't know Shelby, it might seem as if she had a violent temper. And basically, the members of her staff didn't really know her since she'd felt it best to maintain a professional distance as manager of the department. They might decide she was capable of anything after hearing her tell Dutch off. And Shelby knew what they'd think if the incident that occurred on the job she'd had two years ago came to light.

Suddenly realizing that Rand had disappeared out of sight, Shelby was about to pull down the window covering when she spotted a dark figure slide furtively from the shadows of the building on the other side of the street. She would have thought nothing of it except the man turned toward the window where she stood. A broad-brimmed hat hid his face. Even knowing he probably couldn't see her because the room was in darkness, Shelby stepped to the side of the window. Then the stranger hunched down into his trench coat and turned into the alleyway on the other side of the building.

Heart pounding, she stared after him until he disappeared. The man had been watching her. But why? She didn't want to face the obvious, but the thought that it had something to do with Dutch Vanleer's murder wouldn't go away.

## Chapter Three

Shelby was feeling much better and a lot less paranoid after a good night's sleep. She was almost able to forget about Rand and about Dutch's murder while immersing herself in work.

Unfortunately her midmorning meeting with the head of lingerie about one of the special windows for Valentine's Day brought the memories flooding back. Like a small town where everyone knew everyone else's business, Westbrook's was ablaze with speculations about the murder, and Joy Upton was delighted to share every shred of gossip with her whether or not Shelby wanted to hear about it. Joy was even looking forward to Dutch's wake, which would be held that evening. She made Shelby promise to go with her—Shelby was afraid not to go, in case her absence would raise suspicions.

Eager to get back to the quiet of her own office, Shelby escaped the first chance she got. Ears still buzzing from Joy's gossip, she entered the window-display office through the side door near her work area only to hear more of the same.

"Dutch's being in that Santa suit was pretty weird," Zeke was saying to her two designers. "He must have been on something. The police found a Ziploc minibag with traces of a white substance near the body."

Obviously they were so wrapped up in their conversation that none of them had heard her enter.

"And the coroner can't figure out what kind of weapon was used," Harriet added. "Supposedly it left squarish holes."

"I'll bet it was some kind of tool," stated Dana. "If you ask me, Dutch was either murdered by his wife . . ."

"Would you blame her?" Harriet quickly inserted.

"Or by her brother Rand."

"No one did ask you," Shelby said from her position at the door. Joy had made the same speculations on behalf of the rest of the department store, and she had felt that same tightening in her gut when Rand's name was mentioned in connection with the murder. "But I'm asking you to get back to work. Now."

Her staff dispersed. Amazing how fast they could look busy, Shelby thought, going on into her work area. No sooner had she put down her notepad and sketchbook than she heard the main door open. She looked around her divider. It was Rand himself. Had he seen her coming from the meeting and followed her?

Shelby felt a ripple of fear shoot through her. Not of discovery this time, but of speculation. Maybe he *had* murdered his partner and had been around to see her when she stumbled over Dutch. Something kept her from believing it.

Still, her voice was tight when she asked, "What can I do for you?"

Not even a hint of a smile hovered around Rand's lips this morning, and his expression was speculative. "I thought I'd stop by to see how the plans for the new windows are coming."

"I've barely begun working on the Valentine's Day—"

"Not those. The postholiday windows."

"They've already been approved by both Ben," she said, mentioning her direct supervisor, "and Dutch."

"But I'm in charge now," Rand said bluntly. "And I haven't seen them."

Shelby eyed him suspiciously, wondering if this would be his way of getting even with her for asking him to leave the night before. He might look at her and her staff's designs and decide he didn't like anything, thereby making her start over. What a time she'd have then! Her holiday would be nothing but work. Aware of his closeness, feeling trapped within her own work space, she reluctantly pulled out the art boards and set them on her drawing table and desk. Rand looked over them silently, not commenting until he'd checked every detail.

"They're fine," he told her, allowing her to breathe again. "That's really all I wanted—to look over your plans and to let you know that since Dutch isn't around to approve things, you'll be working with me more often."

At the moment Shelby couldn't honestly say she was looking forward to it, so she didn't respond. She wasn't sure whether his words sounded more like an invitation or a threat.

Rand left, waving at the members of her staff, who were surreptitiously keeping an eye on him. From her position at the room divider, Shelby stared openly until the telephone rang, shaking her out of her speculation.

She picked up the receiver. "Window display."

"Shelby, this is Kristen."

"Rand...Mr. McNabb just left," Shelby informed his secretary. "And he didn't say where he was going."

"I'm not looking for him. I'm coordinating things for Lieutenant Jackson. He wants to question the members of your staff in the executive suite tomorrow afternoon."

Just thinking about the detective made Shelby nervous. "They'll be available," she promised.

She tried to get back to work, but thoughts of her staff being questioned by the police intruded. What if Zeke or Dana mentioned the argument she'd had with Dutch the week before? Jackson would be suspicious because she hadn't mentioned it herself. She had to trust in her luck, but it wasn't easy. She couldn't forget her last awful experience with the law, the main reason she'd run from the scene of the crime.

It had happened two jobs ago. She'd been working for a less prestigious Chicago department store as a window dresser then. One of the male supervisors from the business office had been after her to go out with him. Pete Wolenski had been single and she hadn't felt threatened by him as she had by Dutch, yet neither had she been interested in seeing Wolenski on a personal basis.

The trouble had happened at a private party given by another member of the staff. Shelby had gone with a couple of her co-workers, but she'd been alone and slightly tipsy from a glass of wine when Wolenski caught her wandering around the second floor of the large house, looking for the bedroom that held her coat.

Even in his drunken state, Wolenski had been too strong for her to fight off. When he'd thrown her down on the bed and had pinned her under him, Shelby had done the only thing possible—she'd hit him over the head with the half-empty beer bottle he'd set down on the nightstand. Unfortunately, she'd not only discouraged him, she'd sent him to the hospital for stitches.

That's how the police had become involved.

Later, when the arresting officer made out his report, Wolenski's office buddies had stood by him, claiming Shelby had been giving the poor guy a hard time all night and that *she* attacked *him* out of sheer anger. The charges of assault and battery had later been changed to that of disturbing the peace. When her case had gone to court she'd gotten off with a warning from the judge, who'd seemed sympathetic to her side of the story.

Things hadn't been the same at the store. She'd quit her job to avoid further trouble and embarrassment. And knowing she might have difficulty finding another position in Chicago because of the incident, she'd checked out Milwaukee department stores. She'd found an opening at one of them—assistant to the manager of window display—so the move had been to her advantage.

Although Milwaukee was only an hour and a half from Chicago, Shelby hadn't been able to find time to see her family as often as she liked. She'd missed not only her parents but her two sisters with whom she had a close relationship. And the smaller city couldn't compare with Chicago. Frankly, she'd been bored.

So, after gaining two years of experience at that job, she'd put out feelers in Chicago. Any knowledge of her past seemed to have been buried. She'd lucked out—or so she'd thought at the time—when she heard from Westbrook's two weeks after contacting the store.

Now she wished she were back in Milwaukee being bored.

The incident with Pete Wolenski had been a humiliating experience, but murder hadn't been involved. If she were to be arrested this time, Shelby thought, she wouldn't be lucky enough to get off with a warning.

SHELBY, JOY UPTON and Frank Hatcher shared a cab to the funeral parlor directly after work. Shelby let them enter first, then forced her feet to take her over the threshold. She'd always hated funerals, ever since she was a kid. The strong smell of flowers made her light-headed, not because she didn't like the scent, but because of what they stood for.

She glanced at the information board: Bertram "Dutch" Vanleer, Salon C.

"Come on," Joy said in a loud whisper. "Let's see who's here."

"This is a wake, not a party," muttered Frank. "Your enthusiasm is . . . morbid."

Joy ignored the comment and led the way down the hall. Shelby agreed with Frank about Joy's eagerness to attend the function, but then the middle-aged woman was one of the biggest busybodies at Westbrook's. She'd probably enjoy the evening. As for herself, Shelby planned to stay only for five minutes, to allay any suspicions her absence might cause. No, that wasn't altogether true. She had to see Dutch laid out for herself, so that she would know she was dealing with reality, not some nightmare that had followed her from her sleep.

The first person she spotted in front of the wide double doorway of Salon C was Rand McNabb. He had his arm around a young woman whose bright red hair contrasted with her plain black dress and pinched white face.

"There's the grieving widow now," Joy whispered as they drew closer.

So that was Rand's beloved younger sister Pippa. And from the looks of several other auburn- and carrot-topped people, the family had come out in full force to support her. As she drew closer, Shelby noted the haunted expression in the young woman's vivid green eyes as well as a single tear that slid down a perfectly formed cheek.

Without ever taking his eyes off Shelby, Rand introduced each of them to his sister. His expression was unreadable, but definitely not grief-stricken, making her realize he wasn't exactly mourning Dutch's loss.

"My condolences," Frank said, moving on.

"I'm sorry about Dutch's...death," Shelby told Pippa, hoping she sounded natural. She'd almost said murder, and she surely would have choked on the word.

"Thank you for coming." Another tear slipped out, this time down Pippa's other cheek. Shelby noted Rand's fingers squeezing his sister's arm reassuringly. "It means a lot to me that so many people have turned out to pay their respects."

And there seemed to be more than a hundred people, counting those both inside and outside the salon. A handful stood behind them. "You have our sympathy," Shelby said, speaking for herself and Joy, who was staring rudely at Pippa as if the young widow were some kind of a curiosity. Instinctively Shelby prodded the head of the lingerie department to enter the salon before she could say something to embarrass them all.

"Do you think she used soap?" Joy whispered.

"What?" Shelby was looking back at Rand. His expression still veiled, he was staring after her. Realizing Joy was waiting for a response, she asked, "Soap?"

"Right. In her eyes, to make her look like she's been crying?"

"Those tears looked real to me." Shelby frowned at Joy, not that the other woman seemed to notice.

"No way were those real. She was trying to divorce the guy, for Pete's sake. And what an ugly mess!"

"That didn't mean she didn't care about him," Shelby argued as they caught up to Frank who was waiting for them.

"I don't know why she would," he said, obviously having heard them. "Dutch didn't love Pippa. He was only using her like any one of his other possessions."

Though Shelby wondered what he knew about it, she didn't ask. Maybe if she refused to continue the conversation, they would both drop the subject.

Besides, they were approaching the coffin. As she drew closer, the smell of floral bouquets and wreaths smothering her, Shelby felt a little muddled. Her mouth went dry and her feet felt weighted. Suddenly changing her mind about looking at the dead man, she stopped a short distance away. She studied the floral offerings, read the inscriptions—In Memory of Our Beloved Son, For the Good Times, To the Dutchman—anything so she wouldn't have to confront her nightmare.

But she saw it anyway: staring eyes, slack mouth, chest covered with clotting blood.

Horror welled in her mind, making Shelby shake inside. Her head lightened and her stomach threatened her. She squeezed her eyes shut for a moment until the sick feeling receded. When she opened her eyes, the image was gone, replaced by that of a man at peace, his eyes and mouth closed, hands folded across his chest. Shelby took a shuddering breath.

Would she ever forget the horror of her discovery?

"Come on," Joy whispered, pulling Shelby toward a tall, dark-haired woman in a pumpkin-colored dress. "There's Loretta Greenfield, the Midwest rep for André Kuryokhin."

The French-Russian designer was the hottest around. In the Chicago area, Westbrook's had an exclusive with him.

One window was reserved for his latest designs. When Joy introduced her to Loretta, Shelby recognized the sales rep's voice—unlike the last time when she'd hidden in the washroom stall after finding the body. Loretta had been the woman talking to Iris. And she'd been at the Christmas party as well, Shelby realized, having a heated discussion with Dutch in one of the inner offices.

"I'm surprised to see you here, Loretta," Joy said. "I didn't know you and Dutch were *friendly*."

"We weren't. Our relationship was strictly business," Loretta said. "I'm really here to talk to the surviving partner. It's difficult to do business with the dead one."

"Don't you think doing business at a wake is a little out of place?" Shelby asked, surprised that the woman would even consider it.

Loretta raised an eyebrow, her dark brown eyes appraising. "That depends on who died. A crass person like Dutch Vanleer might even be amused if I sealed a deal over his coffin."

Shelby wasn't amused. As a matter of fact she was ready to leave. The place was swarming with people, yet she didn't think there was anyone—except for Pippa and Dutch's parents, perhaps—who gave a damn about the dead man. She was suddenly ashamed that she, herself, had a motive for being at the funeral home. Whatever he'd been in life, Dutch Vanleer was dead now and deserving of a little respect. But before she could excuse herself, her attention was diverted to the vision in the doorway.

Iris Dahl, whose wildly curling blond hair framed a face made up with every item of cosmetics she sold, was wearing a low-cut black cocktail dress. She stared at the coffin, her expression tragic. Like a sleepwalker, she moved down the aisle, never once shifting her blue eyes to anyone else in the room. The steady murmur of voices drifted off as attendees noticed her dramatic entrance. When she got within several feet of the coffin, she burst into tears and threw herself forward, over the corpse. The room went still except for her heartfelt wails.

Shelby's mouth dropped open when Iris sobbed, "Oh, Dutch, you can't be dead. You can't!" And Shelby's feet seemed glued to the spot as she watched the drama unfold.

Rand stood in the salon's doorway, amazed at Iris's display. So she, rather than Shelby, had been Dutch's mistress, he thought. By the time he recovered and stepped forward to get Iris off the body, Edgar Siefert had beat him to it. The security guard, dressed in an ill-fitting blue suit, had his arms around the blonde and was gently pulling her away from Dutch while everyone else stood around in stunned silence.

"No, don't make me leave him," she pleaded.

"Come on, Iris, honey, that's a good girl," Edgar murmured, inching her away from the coffin.

"But I don't want to be alone."

"You won't be. Come on in the other room. We'll get you some coffee."

"I don't want coffee," she moaned brokenheartedly as she stumbled forward, gripping Edgar for support. Her mascara was running down her cheeks in great black rivulets. "He's mine. I want Dutch."

"And Dutch wanted whatever he could get without having to pay for it, no matter who he hurt," Edgar murmured softly as they passed Rand. "You're too nice a girl for that . . . that . . ." He let his voice trail off as though he didn't want to crush Iris's feelings.

So Dutch's infidelities weren't any secret from anyone, Rand noticed, his protective instincts for Pippa rising. Thank God his mother had insisted on taking his sister to get something to eat. How she could still love that creep after the garbage he'd piled on her, Rand didn't understand, but Pippa had been devastated by her unfaithful husband's death. She'd hardly stopped crying since she'd heard the news.

Disturbed by the other implications that someone who didn't know Pippa as well as he did might read into that fact, Rand almost missed Shelby's attempt to get through the crowd to the door. He quickly took a few steps forward and cut her off.

"Leaving so soon?" he asked, unable to keep the challenge out of his tone. Something about this woman made him react in unexpected ways.

The beginning of a glower creased her brow. "I came here to pay my respects. I did that."

"*Did* you respect Dutch?" he asked, wondering if he'd get a reaction out of her. She might not have been his late brother-in-law's mistress, but that didn't mean she hadn't been in the executive suite after the party.

She gave him a sharp look and said, "Mr. Vanleer was my employer."

"That's not an answer." And he knew she wasn't going to give him one—not about Dutch; not now. But he couldn't give up the idea that she'd been the woman in red, so he changed tactics. "You don't still have that headache I gave you, do you?"

Her finely arched brows rose. "Headache? Are you talking about this morning? You were only doing your job by checking the plans for the January windows. I understood that."

"That's not what I meant."

"Oh."

His built-in radar told him she was ready to bolt. From the way her eyes flicked in either direction around him, she seemed to be gauging her chances of getting away from him. "So are you over the headache or not?" he insisted.

"I've forgotten why I had it in the first place."

That was a lie. He saw a flare of wariness in her expression, and her eyes darkened into golden-brown pools that matched her slacks and silk shirt. "If that's true, maybe we can try again. How about having dinner with me tomorrow night," he suggested, pulling her to the side as Althea Westbrook made her way down the aisle. The older woman walked toward the coffin, her back straight, her head high.

"I don't know."

"I promise to make it . . ."

His voice drifted off as he watched Althea. Shelby turned to do the same. The other woman merely looked down into the coffin, her face void of emotion, then turned and walked back to the doorway where Tucker Powers waited for her. The company lawyer didn't step a foot into the room. How curious. When Althea approached him, Tucker put a supporting arm around her and led the former owner of Westbrook's away.

Sensing Shelby was anxious to leave and edging toward the doorway herself, Rand turned his full attention back to her. "I promise that I'll make sure dinner is vegetarian if that's what you're worried about." Realizing he was anxious that she accept, and not only because he thought she was the mystery woman and he was going to try to prove it, Rand raised his left hand. "Scout's honor."

"Wrong hand," she informed him wryly.

She couldn't quite hide the smile tugging at her mouth. Such a tempting mouth, Rand thought, switching hands. How had Dutch managed to keep himself away from her? Rand was more bothered by that question and the image it brought than made him comfortable. He hadn't been able to stand the notion of her being in his late brother-in-law's arms, and knowing that Iris had been Dutch's current mistress had come as a relief. But he couldn't dwell on that. He had to protect Pippa. He had to remember his plan.

"So, what do you say?" he persisted, wondering what he had to do to make her agree. They were drawing the attention of people around them, especially that of the nosy woman from lingerie.

"I thought the funeral was tomorrow."

"In the morning. But I've got an appointment I don't intend to cancel at the store late tomorrow afternoon. And a man's got to eat." Realizing he had Joy's undivided attention, Rand took Shelby by the elbow and steered her through the doorway out into the hall. Her arm tensed under his hand. Aware of other interested ears around them, he kept his voice low. "So will you have dinner with me?"

He could tell she wanted to say no. But the words coming from her sweetly bowed mouth belied the spark of irritation crossing her features. "All right, but be forewarned. If you think I *play around* on the second date," she said, leaving no room for him to misinterpret her meaning, "you'll be very disappointed."

"My game is football," he reminded her, even while wondering what her game was. She'd played hard to get the first time he'd asked her out, then on their date had turned on the charm—all too successfully. Now she was aloof, yet agreeing to see him again. Why? "I play by a whole set of different rules. Why don't you meet me in my office at five-thirty, then?"

"I'll be there," she said, turning away.

Deciding he could use a breath of fresh air himself, Rand followed her to the coatrack. "How are you getting home? Do you want me to flag a taxi for you?"

"No, thanks," she said, slipping into her down coat and heading for the outside door. "I'm walking."

"Your place is almost two miles from here."

"You're not the only one who likes to stay in condition. And by coming here, I missed another session at my health club." He could tell she was trying to hide her rising irritation. "The walk will help me make up for it."

He opened the door for her and followed her out onto the empty street. "But it's dark."

"There's a full moon out tonight—and before you object to that, I've always wanted to meet a werewolf." She pulled on her leather gloves, her sharp movements telling him she was feeling pushed and not liking it. "And don't worry, I won't get lost as long as I follow the North Star. Now I'll see you tomorrow."

Wanting to object, Rand silently watched her head down the street. His protective instincts were acting up again, for her. They were a little out of place, considering what he had in mind for the following night.

SHELBY KEPT UP A BRISK PACE, truly wanting to get the aerobic benefit of her walk home. The down coat provided an oven effect, making her swelter, but she didn't dare remove the garment or she'd get a chill.

The walk gave her plenty of time to think, mostly about Rand.

She'd agreed to have dinner with him to avoid a confrontation, and he'd been set on having one if she hadn't come around. There'd been too many witnesses at the wake, perhaps some who knew about her disagreement with Dutch. So she'd acquiesced. But she hated the feeling of being cornered, even if it was only mentally, and that was what Rand was trying to do to her.

Successfully, she might add.

Oh, he might be attracted to her just as she was to him, Shelby thought, reluctantly admitting it, but that hadn't been his purpose in wanting to see her. He was still trying to psych her out and to protect Pippa. She sensed it.

Not wanting to worry about future problems until she was confronted with them, Shelby shoved thoughts of Rand from her mind and concentrated on the Christmas decorations in the Clark Street storefronts, admiring many of the window displays as did other pedestrians who actually stopped to look. Unfortunately, one featured a Christmas tree with twinkling colored lights, reminding her of the way she'd found Dutch. She turned away from it and stared at the sidewalk in front of her, suddenly depressed.

Christmas Eve was only a week away, and she hadn't even dragged her ornaments and lights out of her basement locker—she who was touted as the undauntable Christmas spirit of the Corbin family. She didn't know if she'd have the heart to decorate this year.

It was going to be a deadly holiday, for sure.

Shelby slowed when she hit Belden, deciding she'd better begin her cool-down. She turned onto the dark side street at a more leisurely pace and felt her heart's immediate response. It slowed accordingly. She couldn't wait until she got home so she could get out of her clothes and into the shower. The heat was becoming unbearable and the sweat was pouring out of her under the down coat.

A moment later she was turning onto Cleveland. She hadn't gone far when she saw him coming toward her from halfway down the block—a man hunched into his winter coat, a broad-brimmed hat pulled low over his face.

She let her pace falter as her heartbeat quickened again. The furtive figure watching her apartment—could this be the same man?

Slowing even more as he drew steadily closer, Shelby couldn't decide if she should go on, go back the way she'd come or cross the street. On, she told herself, tired of being afraid. She wrapped the shoulder strap of her bag around her hand so she could use it as a weapon if necessary. Her adrenaline pushed her boldly forward and she stared defiantly at the dark figure who came right up to her—then passed her without incident. The quick look she got of his face identified the man as someone she'd seen around the neighborhood.

Her extra energy crashed and she almost fell to the sidewalk, laughing like an idiot. Her imagination was really strained. Show her some twinkling colored lights and *bam*! She was off to the races!

Shelby continued on to her apartment, feeling foolish, yet mentally lifted by the incident. Maybe she was imagining too much these days. Maybe she was even wrong about Rand's motivation in asking her out.

She was at the bottom of the steps leading into her building when she looked through the double set of glass doors to the inner hallway and saw something hanging on her apartment door. A Christmas wreath—from Rand?—what a nice surprise! She ran up the steps, telling herself not to get too excited. More than likely her parents had sent it.

It wasn't until she was in the process of unlocking the glass hall door that she wondered how the delivery person had gotten into the inner hallway. She stopped short on the threshold and took a better look at the wreath itself, which oozed a familiar sweet scent.

Her heart accelerated and her mouth went dry. It couldn't be! But it was. The pine branches were laden with flowers. The small banner read To the Dutchman.

Someone had left a wreath from Dutch's wake on her apartment door!

## Chapter Four

Shelby couldn't help looking over her shoulder when she left her apartment building for work the next morning. She practically ran toward the bus stop and nearly lost her bus pass in the process. Flipping to the ground, the card eluded her knit-covered fingers for a few seconds before she was able to grasp it. Rising quickly, she scanned the area to see if anyone was watching her. But, as if daylight could blind her to any lurking sinister forces, she saw nothing more threatening than a teenager huddled against the cold in an apartment-building doorway on the other side of the street.

The number thirty-six pulled up to the corner of Fullerton and Clark. Shelby ran the remaining quarter of a block and climbed in behind several other people. After showing the driver her pass, she took the only empty seat, which happened to be situated in front of a shabbily dressed old man with an unkempt gray beard and mustache.

He rocked back and forth, tuned in to his own world, talking to no one in particular. "Sinners. You're all sinners. But *He* knows your secrets."

Wryly realizing that weirdos on buses didn't have the power to surprise her anymore—there always seemed to be one on this particular route—Shelby ignored the old man and lost herself in thought.

The wreath had disappeared during the night, making her wonder if she'd been imagining things.

A shiver crawled up her spine as she remembered the sweet scent that had threatened to choke her as she'd entered her apartment. That had been very real. And how could she forget the fear that had prompted her to turn on every light and search every closet before she'd been satisfied that she was alone? She'd even checked under her bed....

She still hadn't felt completely safe—not then, and certainly not when she'd opened her front door early that morning with the intention of trashing the spooky offering. The wooden panel had been bare of decoration. The damned funeral wreath had vanished without a trace, as if into thin air.

But Shelby didn't believe in magic.

Thinking about someone creeping outside her apartment door even as she slept made her shudder.

The wreath had been meant as a gruesome warning, but she hadn't done anything. She didn't *know* anything. Was someone merely trying to tell her she'd been seen coming out of the executive suite? Rand? He knew she intended to walk home from the funeral parlor.

No. She couldn't believe it—subtlety wasn't his style. He was the confrontationist type. Who, then?

And why?

"Death and destruction! The wicked will pay."

The old man's feverish muttering jerked Shelby back to the present with an unpleasant rush. Already in a skittish mood, she couldn't tolerate listening to some crazy man's dire predictions, not on this of all mornings. Shifting uneasily, she thought about getting up and standing somewhere in the back of the bus.

"An eye for an eye and a tooth for a tooth," the old man mumbled.

Trying to ignore him, she glanced at the people in the aisle who were concentrating on keeping their footing as the bus lurched around a corner. There wasn't even standing room left. She looked out the window. Westbrook's was a half mile away. Not much longer.

The old man uttered his next words close to her ear. "Bloodshed begets bloodshed."

Startled, Shelby whipped up out of her seat and forced her way through the crowded aisle to the back exit while her pulse took a roller-coaster ride through her body. The mystery surrounding Dutch's death was really getting to her. She remembered he was being buried later that morning. Heart pumping like mad, she got off at the next stop and raced the remaining three blocks to the store. The nine-story red brick building with its boldly projecting roof cornices and terra-cotta frieze was a welcome sight.

Catching her breath, she slowed down as she circled the building and approached the employees' alley entrance. In the process of leaving the store, Edgar Siefert held open the door for her.

"Shelby, you okay?" The fatherly sort, he wore a concerned expression.

"Uh, yes." She passed him and stopped just inside the doorway where she unzipped her down coat and removed it as well as her knit hat and gloves. "Of course I am."

Edgar came back inside, letting the door swing shut behind him. Still filling in for the lone midnight-shift watchman who was on vacation through the weekend, he normally worked late afternoons and evenings. Shelby often stopped to chat with him for a while before catching her bus home. She'd found him to be a nice man—as he'd proved when he'd comforted Iris at the wake the night before.

"You're looking a little peaked," he insisted worriedly.

"It's the cold."

But it wasn't the cold that made her shiver and glance over his shoulder and out the glass door.

"I hope you're not coming down with the flu. That'd spoil your holiday for sure."

"What?" Having seen nothing to worry her, she turned her attention back to Edgar, who seemed to be staring right through her. He'd mentioned the flu.... "No, I'm not getting sick."

"Maybe not, but something's bothering you. If you need someone to talk to—"

"I always enjoy talking to you, Edgar, you know that. But there's nothing wrong." Shelby forced a smile and hoped it looked natural. "Really."

"If you say so. Now that I think about it, you look more nervous than ill. I guess you're letting the murder get to you, same as the rest of us." He shook his balding head. "Not that Dutch didn't deserve it."

Disturbed by that coming from the normally kindhearted man, Shelby said, "I don't think anyone deserves to be murdered."

"That's because you're too nice a lady to know anything about Dutch's type." Edgar scowled, the expression making him look more menacing than kindly. "The scum of the earth, that's what he was. You ask me, Dutch deserved to die and his murderer deserves a medal, not no jail sentence."

Now Edgar was making her nervous. Surprised by the security guard's unexpected fervor, Shelby edged away from him just as one of the secretaries opened the outside door. "I've got to get to my office. I'm a little behind in my work," she explained as the other woman passed her with a nod.

His expression softened and so did his tone. "You take care now, Shelby."

"You, too, Edgar." She headed for the elevators.

Judging by Edgar's attitude, he'd hated his employer. *The scum of the earth.* That sounded as if he was speaking from personal experience, yet Shelby couldn't figure out what kind of connection Dutch could have had with the man. Undoubtedly the security guard had been talking in generalities, yet she couldn't help but wonder if there was more to his animosity. The conversation with Edgar was soon consigned to oblivion, however, when Shelby faced the stack of work on her desk.

Though the holiday season was usually the slowest for window display—Christmas windows stayed up from early November to the beginning of January rather than being changed every two weeks—she was working on a special project. André Kuryokhin himself would appear at the store in March and all the fashion windows would be dedicated to his designs. She had to finish the preliminary paperwork involved. Resignedly she began tackling the least favorite part of her job.

Aware of that fact, her employees gave her a wide berth. Zeke handled the small crises that inevitably cropped up every time she didn't want to be disturbed. Midway through the morning, he poked his head over her divider and, his smile apologetic, interrupted her. "Telephone" was all he said before quickly retreating.

Grumbling to herself, she lifted the receiver. "Shelby Corbin, here."

"Good morning." The masculine voice at the other end was familiar as was the involuntary thrill of anticipation that shot through her. "Keeping busy?" Rand asked.

"Of course." She silently instructed herself not to snap. "That's what you pay me to do."

"I won't keep you long, then." His tone was almost intimate, and yet there was mettle backing it up, as if he'd brook no argument. "I merely wanted to remind you about our dinner appointment."

"Sounds like we're going to talk business," she forced herself to say sweetly.

"I thought I explained that business was one of the two topics I avoid when I'm socializing with a lovely woman."

What *did* he want to talk about? Murder? "I'll keep that in mind."

"Good. What time are you planning to quit today?"

"Five, five-thirty."

"I'll expect you in the executive suite at five-thirty, then."

Though she would rather have avoided getting anywhere near the scene of the crime lest finding the body came back to her in all its vivid details, Shelby couldn't object without raising Rand's suspicions. Besides, she was confident they wouldn't remain in the executive suite long. He probably wanted to get her to a restaurant where he could ply her with before-dinner drinks and questions.

"I'll see you then," she agreed.

Concentration was difficult to recover as anticipation warred with dread over her coming encounter with Rand. If only things could be different. If only he were asking her out because he was attracted to her. If only....

She was distracted for the rest of the morning, and worse, annoyed that she forgot a business-lunch appointment with a mannequin salesman. Her first clue came when he entered her office as she was about to order a sandwich from the deli. She pasted a smile on her face and went with him. Listening politely to his pitch but hearing little of what he said, she barely tasted her food before cutting the meeting short. She returned to Westbrook's at a quarter after one— trudging through snow she hadn't expected when she'd left the house that morning wearing expensive leather shoes.

Entering from the State Street side, she walked through the cosmetics department, stopping halfway to the elevator to stamp the remaining snow off her feet. Iris Dahl was behind her counter as usual, chatting with a customer, no sign of grief marring her face. Maybe all the makeup was acting as camouflage. Odd that Iris would have shown up to work on the day of the funeral, especially after the dramatics she'd displayed at the wake the night before.

As she thought about the blonde's tragic air and grief-filled sobs, Shelby was startled by the touch of a fragile hand, one belonging to Althea Westbrook.

"Shelby, I never had a chance to tell you how much I admired this year's Christmas windows. They're breathtaking. Easily the finest on State Street."

"Thank you, Miss Westbrook." Though she'd been introduced to the former owner of the department store and had exchanged friendly greetings at the Christmas party, Shelby didn't feel comfortable using Althea's first name. Something about her demeanor—the unconscious carriage of someone used to old money, perhaps—kept Shelby at a respectful distance. "You must remember that Meg Harding was still in charge during the planning stage."

"But you executed those plans, and splendidly, I must say."

"I'm happy that you're pleased."

"Spectacular Christmas windows have always been a tradition at Westbrook's, and when I sold the store I was afraid the quality might suffer." Althea smiled, but her eyes were sad. "Am I holding you from your work?"

"Actually, I was on my way upstairs."

"Well, we can share the ride. I'm meeting Tucker for a late lunch," Althea explained, her suddenly youthful smile revealing a personal fondness for the distinguished lawyer.

"Fine." Shelby smiled and led the way to the bank of elevators.

"The windows are a small thing to worry about, really, in comparison to Bertram's death and all, but they're something solid that I can hold on to," Althea went on. "You understand, don't you?"

"I think so."

"Did you know Bertram well?"

Far too well for her own peace of mind, but Shelby wasn't about to say so. She stepped into an empty elevator car. "He was my employer."

Following her and punching a button, Althea nodded. "A difficult man to work with."

The elevator doors closed and the car began its ascent. As she'd been doing for two days, Shelby blocked her mind against the soft Christmas music that filled the small area. Deciding to remain neutral about Dutch's competency as a businessman, she finally said, "I've been with the store for such a short time."

"But some things are so evident," Westbrook's former owner went on. "Poor Randall. He must have had the patience of a saint to put up with that one-sided partnership for as long as he did."

"I really wouldn't know."

"Of course you wouldn't. Don't mind my babbling." Althea sighed. "It's just that I had such hopes for Westbrook's when I sold the major portion of my stock. Randall was everything I expected him to be. Sharp and aggressive. Determined to revitalize the store. If only Bertram had given half of his efforts to Westbrook's."

Shelby urged the old elevator to hurry. She had no desire to discuss the dead man. The coiffed silvery-blond head shook and Althea seemed to be talking to herself.

"Not only did Bertram let his partner do three-fourths of the work, but he turned his marriage into a living hell for poor Pippa, which, of course, had to upset Randall greatly since he's very close to his sister. I know the whole thing is an awful scandal, and it may be unkind of me to say so, but Randall is far better off without his partner."

Shelby barely had time to digest the possible implications of Althea's words before the elevator doors opened, revealing the executive-suite hallway and Tucker Powers, who stood on the other side. His gray eyes flicked over them curiously before he entered the car and kissed Althea's lifted cheek.

"So good to see you, my dear," he murmured. "Shelby, aren't you getting out?"

"No, Mr. Powers. Miss Westbrook and I were so busy chatting we forgot to punch my floor."

Shelby resolved that oversight immediately. The doors shut and the mechanism whined as the car descended to the floor below. Tucker seemed oddly tense, as if he couldn't wait to be alone with Althea.

Always at work, the rumor mill had it the couple was enjoying a long-standing affair, even though Tucker had been married—supposedly happily—for more than thirty years. Come to think of it, Shelby remembered seeing Althea with Tucker at the Christmas party, but not any woman she thought might be his wife. Then again she'd never had the opportunity to meet Mrs. Powers in the short time she'd been with Westbrook's.

The doors slid open, revealing her floor. "Have a good lunch," Shelby said, stepping out.

"We shall," Althea assured her.

Once in her office, Shelby tried to concentrate on her work. But every time she settled down, part of the conversation with Althea replayed itself in her mind. She couldn't forget the former owner's statement about Rand being better off without his partner, and she couldn't help wondering whether Rand felt the same way.

Suddenly it occurred to her that Rand might already know for sure that she was the woman in red. He could have been in the executive suite when she found the body; he could be playing games with her merely to find out exactly how much else she'd seen.

She could be planning to dine with a murderer.

THE THOUGHT WAS A CHILLING ONE, making Shelby wonder if she were crazy for going out with Rand McNabb for any reason, even if it was to determine whether or not her horrid speculations had any basis. She ought to leave it alone, to make her excuses. She went on as planned. Her sense of vulnerability intensified when she found herself alone in the executive suite at five-thirty and realized that while they would have dinner together, Rand wasn't planning on taking her to a restaurant.

Standing in front of the doorway, she inspected the setup before her: a white linen-covered table laden with china and crystal had been placed in the middle of the reception room—directly in front of the Christmas tree; next to it sat a stainless-steel cart bearing cold and hot serving dishes as well as a wine bucket. Rand meant for them to eat right there, mere feet from where she'd stumbled over Dutch's body. Shelby was aghast.

And trapped.

"I'm glad you're as prompt as your word," Rand said, stepping out of his office, stopping her from leaving as she longed to do.

"Being on time for appointments makes good business sense."

Unwilling to move closer to his snare, she warily watched him approach. More casually dressed than usual, he wore a cinnamon-colored blazer that intensified the auburn of his hair. He encased her elbow in a no-nonsense grip and easily propelled her forward toward the table. Her suddenly racing pulse beat her there as she was snared by the Christmas tree's twinkling lights that threatened her with nightmarish images.

"This isn't business, remember?" Part of her mind registered his soft words, enabling her to tear her gaze away as he assured her, "I was hoping for a pleasurable evening."

Shelby hadn't the faintest idea how she was going to get any pleasure out of this dinner. Or any enlightenment, for that matter. Her nerves were stretched taut as Rand seated her and briefly brushed her shoulders with both hands. She tried not to shudder as, his gaze never leaving her, he crossed to the cart and the waiting wine bucket.

If she didn't remain calm, she'd never be able to figure out whether or not he might have murdered his partner.

He pulled the bottle from the ice-filled bucket and showed it to her. "I hope this vintage meets with your approval."

Shelby started. "Sparkling grape juice?"

"I thought it a viable alternative to ginger ale."

A part of her wanted to smile, but her cheeks remained frozen. One auburn eyebrow slashed upward, but Rand didn't say anything more while he opened the bottle and filled their crystal wineglasses. Replacing it in the bucket, he lifted the top from one of the serving dishes that held two small plates with crabmeat-filled avocados.

"I assumed that if you ate chicken," he said, referring to her invitation the other night, "you ate seafood as well."

He set her salad in front of her and took his place on the other side of the small table. He held up his glass. "To a more successful evening than our last together."

Shelby didn't miss the double meaning of his words. She clinked glasses and sipped at the grape juice. He watched her every move.

"Strangely enough," she said, relieved as she felt a detached calm fight her surging emotions, "I had the distinct idea that we'd be going out to a restaurant this evening."

"I wanted to have some privacy, to get to know you better." The slow smile under the thick mustache would have melted her down to her toes if she didn't have so much reason to mistrust it. "Since I don't cook, I did the next best thing. I let Westbrook's restaurant provide the meal."

The real reason he wanted them to be alone didn't elude her. She concentrated on taking a forkful of crabmeat. "I'm flattered."

*And worried.* What if he thought she'd seen the murder and had decided to make sure she wouldn't talk? No one even knew she was there.

Shelby immediately shot that dark thought full of holes. Though no one was around at the moment, someone had delivered the cart and the table and would know that Rand was entertaining a woman. Besides, if he wanted to do her physical harm, he'd had ample opportunity the other night. More than likely he was looking for a way to frame her to protect himself—*if* he was the guilty one, she reminded herself, even while she hoped he wasn't. That's what she needed to settle in her own mind.

To that end, she boldly stated, "Actually, I wasn't objecting to having dinner someplace other than a restaurant. What I meant to say was that I was surprised you'd want to eat in a place where tragedy had struck so recently, especially such a *personal* one.''

Rand's eyes locked in on hers. ''I guess I didn't think of it that way.''

*Like hell!* Determined to break his composure, Shelby attacked. ''You and Dutch must have been pretty close.''

''We had a history together.''

''I'll say.'' Now she was the one watching him intently, he the one camouflaging his own reactions to her directness by concentrating on his plate. ''First you were teammates...then he married your sister...finally, you bought Westbrook's together. You and he must have been best friends.''

Rand swallowed his mouthful of food. ''Not exactly.'' The scar on his cheek was white against his flushed face.

Though she could have guessed at his reaction, Shelby didn't smile in spite of her sense of triumph. She speared a piece of avocado. Let him stew for a few minutes, wondering what offensive she would take next.

''Dutch was all veneer,'' he went on, the admission surprising her. ''Wonderful to look at on the surface, nothing of substance underneath. I wish to God Pippa had never met the bastard.''

Shelby thoughtfully digested the last. ''It sounds as if you blame yourself for their bad marriage.''

''In a way, I do. I introduced them. Dutch was at the peak of his career. Pippa was captivated. They got married shortly before Dutch and I retired. I wasn't thrilled to have him as a brother-in-law at the time, but I didn't object because I hadn't yet seen through to the real man.'' Eyes blazing with contempt, Rand added, ''If I had known then what I know now...''

''You probably couldn't have stopped her.''

"Maybe not, but damn it—" his fist hit the table with a clatter of china "—I could have tried. I could have saved her so much grief."

*He didn't do it.* The thought struck her like a bolt of lightning, but Shelby couldn't deny its truth. If Rand were the murderer he wouldn't openly admit his true feelings for Dutch. He would have gone along with the best-friend ploy. She'd been right in the first place—he was merely trying to protect his sister. She shouldn't have let Althea's innocent statement rile her imagination. Tension and distrust flowed out of her, leaving a sense of satisfaction she couldn't quite define.

Rand didn't know how, but Shelby had managed to turn the tables on him. He'd purposely arranged this dinner at the scene of the crime in hopes of getting a reaction out of her and weakening her defenses. Instead, she'd managed to pull information out of him.

What had he expected?—a confession?

His fork assaulted his plate and he forced himself to eat the last of its spoils. He had to be patient, to remember he was doing this for Pippa. Shelby was bound to trip up, to say something incriminating. She was neither tough nor a great actress. All he had to do was wait her out and strike at the right time.

And yet he couldn't help hating what he was trying to do to her, couldn't help believing she was innocent, couldn't help denying how very much he was attracted to Shelby Corbin.

"What kind of man was he?" she asked suddenly, her hazel eyes fathomless.

He knew she meant Dutch, but until he had the conversation back under control, Rand was not about to discuss his late partner. "Let's talk about something else."

"All right. You'll do for a start."

"Boring topic."

"I disagree. I've seen you play ball. What got you started? A high-school league?"

She sounded sincere, as if she really wanted to know. Rand told himself not to let her get to him. Maybe she was a better actress than he realized. Noticing she'd finished her salad, he rose and transferred both of their plates to the cart. He served up the cheese-filled spinach tortellini and stir-fried vegetables while he reluctantly talked about himself.

"I was playing football long before high school. My father taught me, my three younger brothers and the rest of the boys on the block a street version of the game. He believed in keeping his kids too busy to get into trouble." Rand watched her carefully when he explained, "Dad's a cop."

He thought the statement made Shelby shift in her chair, but he couldn't be sure. He set the entrée in front of her.

"Didn't you ever want to be like him?" she asked after he sat down.

"What, a policeman? No, not really."

At least not until recently, when his sister had come under suspicion for something she couldn't possibly have done. For the past forty-eight hours Rand had fervently wished he'd followed in the old man's footsteps so he'd know how to help Pippa. As it stood, he was fumbling in the dark.

"Tell me more about your father."

"He's a great guy. Actually both of my parents are terrific," Rand stated. "My mother used to take in sewing for extras, like spending money for us, but we were her career. Our family was never very well-off—a policeman's salary doesn't stretch too far with five active kids to feed—but my parents took pride in giving us high moral values and a strong work ethic."

Rand wondered about the odd look Shelby gave him, but all she said was, "They sound a lot like my parents."

"Your dad is a cop, too?"

She shook her head. "A carpenter. He used to help me build sets for the plays and musicals my two sisters and I gave the neighborhood as children. Before that, being the middle daughter, I always got kind of lost in the shuffle."

A stray curl was brushing the right side of her forehead, tempting Rand to reach across the table and touch it. Annoyed with himself, he said, "Managers have to be take-charge kind of people."

"I was never the leader then, yet I wasn't a follower, either. I went in my own direction. Building sets with my dad led to my studying theater set-design."

"You didn't come from a merchandising background?"

"Nope. I fell into visual merchandising because I graduated with a degree that impressed absolutely no one in the overloaded theater community," she said with a wry laugh. "I took a job as a window trimmer, foolishly thinking it was a temporary side-path from my true professional course."

"Are you ever sorry you strayed from your original goals?"

She shrugged her gold-sweatered shoulders. "No, not really. I love what I do for a living."

"Window display isn't as exciting as working in theater."

"And running a department store isn't as exciting as running with a football."

They shared a smile. Rand suddenly realized that, rather than skirting around each other as they'd started out doing, they were talking to each other as if they were having a real dinner date. He liked the feeling. Liked her. No matter how much he wanted to protect Pippa, instinct told him Shelby wasn't capable of murder. Of course, that didn't eliminate her from being the woman in the stairwell. It merely put a different perspective on the fact. If she'd been in the executive suite, why didn't she come forward and admit it? What was she trying to hide?

The importance of the questions faded as Rand got caught up in Shelby's stories of life with her two sisters whom she made sound prettier, smarter and more successful than herself. If everything she said about them was true, he thought, they had to be superwomen. Considering how talented—and clever—Shelby herself was, perhaps her sisters were exceptional.

In what seemed like a few short minutes, they'd finished not only the main course but the white-chocolate mousse with raspberry sauce, as well. Not wanting to end the evening yet, the desire having nothing to do with his private murder investigation, Rand offered her a second cup of coffee. He suggested they retire to the couch where they would be more comfortable. Hesitating only a second, Shelby agreed. He carried their cups and sat with his back to the Christmas tree, which stood a yard away.

"So where do you fit in among five kids?" she asked, fixing her hazel eyes on his face.

"Number one."

"That's why *you*'re a take-charge kind of person."

"I had to learn fast," he admitted. His gaze kept straying to her sweetly bowed mouth. As if to hide it from him, she took a sip of coffee. "My mother was so busy changing diapers, cooking and cleaning house that someone had to help her keep the others in line."

"Even Pippa?"

"Especially Pippa. Being the youngest and the only girl, she was spoiled and headstrong."

Rand didn't know why he was telling her this, especially after the way the evening had begun. He was fully aware that Shelby had agreed to see him under duress, and he suspected her motives had something to do with covering up being in the executive suite. Because he'd coerced her for Pippa's sake, his trying to explain his relationship with his sister was an apology of sorts.

"Pippa was also incredibly lovable and loving in return. And fiercely loyal."

"And your favorite."

He didn't answer the obvious. "She always thought I was some kind of a hero."

"So did a lot of women during all those years you played for the Chicago Bears."

"Were you one of my fans?" he asked, expecting her to deny it hotly.

Her simple "Yes" surprised and pleased him as did her expression, which he interpreted as a cross between fear and longing.

Because of and for him?

Unable to help himself, Rand reached out and brushed back that stray curl from her forehead as he'd been tempted to do for at least a quarter of an hour. When she didn't object, he slid his hand under the edge of her V-necked sweater and around the back of her neck. He leaned in closer, then paused, giving her the opportunity to retreat. Though her eyes widened perceptibly, Shelby didn't move away.

A taut awareness stretched between them, making Rand groan softly as his body reacted with a natural interest.

That he was supposed to be making her reveal what she knew about the murder occurred to him, but only briefly.

The thought slid away as he pulled her head forward, ignoring the slight resistance of her stiffening neck muscles. She wanted this, just as much as he did, no matter that she tried to deny it to herself. He could see the truth of the matter in the flare of her nostrils, could hear it in the quickening of her breath, could feel it in the surging of her pulse.

Senses heightened by the emotions and doubts he'd felt since meeting her, Rand kissed her without restraint. He took Shelby's mouth with a hunger born of denial, with a desire fueled by the forbidden.

Shelby responded to his intensity, opening under his mouth, giving passage to his tongue. She pressed herself against him, taking pleasure from her breasts flattening against his warm chest. Her nipples hardened, making her stomach tighten. Eyes closed, she allowed her head to whirl and fling thoughts of resistance in every direction. She traced the ragged edge of his chipped tooth with the tip of her tongue. Rand's kiss felt so good, so exhilarating, so unlike anything she'd experienced with other men that she didn't want it to stop.

He murmured something low and urgent against her mouth, then trailed quick, moist kisses along her jawline to the tip of her chin. Shuddering, she arched her neck for him while splaying her hands through his hair. His lips nuzzled her long throat, his tongue lathed the smooth skin, his teeth bit the soft flesh under her jaw. And then his mouth slipped lower, brushing the valley between her breasts. With a quick intake of breath, Shelby let her eyes slit open.

Through her lashes, blobs of color danced through darkness. Red. Green. Blue. Familiar shimmers . . . gleams of fuzzy brightness. Widening her eyes, she focused on the elongated silver star topping the Christmas tree. The reflected twinkling lights on its gleaming surface reminded her of similar images she'd seen on the door to the inner office the morning after the party…and consequently, they reminded her of why she was in the executive suite now.

So how had she ended up in Rand McNabb's arms?

Her escalating pulse had nothing to do with the desire that was still fighting to claim her. Horrid images tried to slip past her guard, but she closed her mind to them.

Rand's head rose, changing her view to softened masculine features and mussed auburn hair. She took a deep breath. His lips loomed closer for another kiss. Panic replaced the more beguiling sensations still zipping through her body. She arched her neck farther in a successful attempt to block him. Determinedly, she placed flat palms against his chest and pushed.

He let go of her immediately, withdrew and stared. His expression changed from passion to surprise to confusion to blankness. Nothing. She couldn't tell what he was thinking. She didn't want to know. Somehow, she'd been lulled into pretending she was in a situation that was, in reality, a fantasy. Rand had forced this evening on her because of Pippa.

She told herself she was relieved to be free of his embrace.

"It's late." Her voice came out a hoarse whisper. She waited for him to object since it couldn't be eight o'clock yet. When no denial came, she scrambled off the couch. Straightening her sweater, she imagined she could still feel the imprint of Rand's lips on her neck and in the valley between her breasts. When he started to rise, she quickly held out a staying hand. "I have to get home."

He continued upward. "I'll take you."

"Don't worry. I don't plan on walking. I'll grab a taxi this time."

"We'll grab one together."

His tone brooked no argument. Shelby hated the sound. She preferred the soft murmurs he'd made with her in his arms. Thinking like that would muddle her senses again, she warned herself. She had to stop it . . . and give in gracefully.

"All right. My coat's in my office."

"Go downstairs and get it, but wait for me. I'll take care of things up here and meet you outside your office."

She nodded and did as he asked.

Fifteen minutes later they were out in the dark, snowy night, climbing into a taxi. Another twenty minutes of thoughtful silence interrupted only by instructions to the driver and they were in front of her building.

"You don't have to see me in," she said quickly, opening the taxi door.

Rand grabbed her arm and kept her from getting out. "Are you busy tomorrow?"

"I'm going to the health club in the morning and to my sister's place for dinner," she said truthfully.

"What about the time in-between? Can we do something together?"

She had to agree, of course, or he'd be suspicious. Without hesitating, she said, "You can pick me up in front of my health club at ten. I go to Lake Shore at Fullerton and Southport. If the weather's not too bad, maybe we can do something outside."

"I hope the weather's rotten." A hint of a smile lifted the tips of his mustache and caused her stomach to flutter. "That way, we'll have to stay inside and think of a way to keep ourselves entertained."

When he let go of her, she hurried up the icy steps and into her building. The unaccustomed eagerness in her step had nothing to do with seeing Rand the next day. She'd *had* to agree. Even as she thought it, Shelby knew the excuse to be absurd. She *wanted* to spend more time with Rand.

That kiss had opened other possibilities for her...and hopefully for him as well.

## Chapter Five

Rand took his foot off the gas and let his Saab coast along behind the blue salt truck that literally inched its way west on Fullerton. A minor blizzard had swept Chicago's streets sometime during the night, turning the predicted three to five inches into more than a foot of traffic-stopping snow. Flakes still fell from the overcast skies, but the WLS weatherman was assuring his radio audience that the worst was behind them.

*He* wasn't sitting at the vehicle-jammed six-corner intersection of Fullerton, Lincoln and Halsted listening to the scrape of his windshield wipers, Rand thought impatiently.

Rock music suddenly blared from the car's speakers, its grating sound annoying an already irritated Rand. He slipped a cassette of Tchaikovsky's *Nutcracker* into the player in the dash and tried to relax as the soothing classical ballet music filled the enclosed space. Tension drained from him . . . for the moment.

He knew it would be renewed the second Shelby slid into the bucket seat next to him.

When he'd asked her to spend time with him, he'd convinced himself he did so in the name of his sister's innocence. The instant Shelby had agreed, however, the elation he'd felt had informed him otherwise. Though he'd tried, he couldn't lie to himself. He wanted to see the manager of window display, not for Pippa's sake, but for his own.

Shelby was obviously a woman of strength, capable of taking care of herself; and yet he sensed an underlying vulnerability that she covered with her wiliness. Instinct assured him she was no murderer though he was equally convinced she had something to hide. Certain she was determined to conceal the fact that she'd been the woman in the executive suite, he wasn't sure why she'd agreed to see him. He could only hope she was attracted to him as he was to her.

Once through the intersection and crawling up Fullerton, Rand realized his guilt was increasing in direct proportion to his sense of anticipation as he drew closer to Shelby's club. He should be doing something to help Pippa.

Damned if he knew what.

Late last night, he and his family had talked about hiring a private investigator. Being a policeman, his father had been uncomfortable with the idea. He'd wanted to work from within the system, even if it meant unofficially. The senior McNabb would ask an old police friend of his to run a surreptitious computer check on Dutch's professional contacts both in the store and out, as well as on the dead man's personal acquaintances. Perhaps the results would reveal helpful information in the way of arrest records or credit instability.

Until then, all he could do was wait.

And enjoy being with Shelby.

He spotted her standing in front of the health club, peering down the street for him. Prepared for the weather, she wore bright orange stretch pants and a waist-length zip-up jacket with contrasting gold knit hat, scarf, leg warmers and gloves. She reminded him of a brilliant flame against the murky skies and pollution-tinged slush on the streets. He honked; she waved and stepped off the curb as he pulled up in front of the building.

She slid into the passenger seat and threw a black athletic bag of parachute material into the back. "I was beginning to think you'd changed your mind."

"I don't change my mind easily when I really want something."

Her expression wary, she asked, "What is it you do want, Rand?"

"At the moment, to appreciate your company."

Her responding smile was warm and natural, far more attractive than the one she often forced around him. Dimples popped in both cheeks. "Even if you'll be coerced to enjoy it in this mess?"

"I'm not sure." He raised a querying eyebrow before checking his mirror and pulling the car into traffic. "What did you have in mind?"

"Cross-country skiing through Lincoln Park. The rental concession is open."

"Sounds like hard work. I thought the weather appropriately wretched so I could look forward to spending a restful couple of hours with you indoors."

"We can do that, too. *After* we use up all our energy outdoors."

"Trying to weaken me to keep me out of trouble?" he asked, amazed that he was not only unexpectedly relaxed with Shelby but that he felt like teasing her as well.

"How do you know it's not myself I'm worried about? You have quite a reputation for knowing how to get what you want from a woman."

"Really? Who says?"

"Everyone at Westbrook's." She grinned. "You'd be amazed how well-oiled the rumor mill is."

"Don't tell me you listen to gossip."

"Not usually. But in this particular case, I don't find hearsay too difficult to believe."

Rand laughed. "All right, I give up. Since you're so good for my ego, I'll let you win. *This time.* Lincoln Park, it is."

Turning off Fullerton, he planned to take a maze of side streets. Though they'd be slippery and rutted with snow, the alternative was chancing getting stuck in another traffic jam on one of the main routes.

"Do you mind if I turn off the music?" Shelby asked as if she'd just noticed the strains of *The Nutcracker* filling the interior of the car.

"No, go ahead. If you'd rather listen to less classical Christmas music, I've got another tape—"

"I can listen to music any time," she interrupted. "I'd rather talk."

"Don't tell me you're one of those people who has something against Christmas."

"Not at all. I just get tired of too much of a good thing."

Her voice had an edge to it, telling him there was more to her reason than that, but he didn't want to push and put her in a defensive mood. He wanted to forget unpleasantries for a few hours.

"It all depends on the thing in question," he said softly. "Take you, for example. I'm not sure I would ever tire of your company."

"You don't even know me. I might be the most boring person alive."

He cleared his throat and flashed her a smile. "Rumor has it you're pretty stimulating yourself."

"Touché."

Shelby settled into her seat, content that she would be able to savor the couple of hours she and Rand would spend together. Throughout her early-morning workout, she'd thought about nothing but him. She'd been, by turns, exhilarated and wary of being with Westbrook's owner. She'd convinced herself this truly was a date made because he wanted to be with her, yet she didn't want to be caught off guard in case she was mistaken.

But it appeared that Rand wanted to forget about the murder for a short while even as she did, Shelby decided with satisfaction. He acted far more imperturbable than he'd been the night before, and his sense of humor was showing. Added to his potent attractiveness—chiseled cheeks, strong square jaw, amber eyes and thick auburn hair—his unprecedented good-humored disposition made him just about irresistible.

During the slow mile ride to Lincoln Park they talked about nothing more threatening than the ice show playing at the beautifully renovated Chicago Theater and the Bears' chances of making it to the Super Bowl again. Shelby was almost sorry when they arrived and he found a place to park near the rental concession. The snow was still coming down in fat wet flakes when they left the car.

Rand forked over a deposit and his driver's license in exchange for the equipment. He was adjusting his ski bindings when he said, "I hate to admit it, but I'm not much good at this particular sport. I've only tried it a few times over the past half-dozen years."

"So that's why you were so anxious to stay indoors." Shelby purposefully adopted a challenging tone even though she had limited experience in cross-country skiing herself. "What's the matter, McNabb? Afraid that you won't be able to keep up with me?"

"Just because you spent your morning working out at the health club, Corbin, don't assume that you're in any better condition than I am!" Rand sounded properly indignant. "I don't take aspersions on my endurance lightly.

I may have been out of football for a few years, but that doesn't mean I've let myself go to flab.''

''I've noticed,'' she admitted, appreciatively running her eyes over his muscular physique. His thighs molded themselves to his jeans and his broad shoulders strained against the expensive beige-and-white Icelandic sweater-jacket covering them. ''But we'll see who skis who into the ground.''

Laughing, Shelby took off across the park in a burst of competitive energy, easily adapting herself to the smooth rhythm afforded by the unbroken snow. No slouch himself in spite of his protests, Rand followed close behind.

''Shall we make a bet on who hits the wall first?'' he called, referring to the condition that athletes dreaded— being unable to continue because of sudden and complete exhaustion.

''Why not? Whoever lands in the snow first has to make the hot chocolate afterward,'' she returned over her shoulder.

''Deal.''

Rand caught up with her and, side by side, they traversed the northern length of Lincoln Park proper between the lagoon and the harbor, going as far as Diversey before circling back to their starting point near Fullerton Avenue. Then they headed south, past the zoo, along the canal, and finally up an incline that gave them a view of the city skyline fronted by Lake Michigan.

Desperately needing to catch her breath, Shelby stopped and made a show of looking out over the snow-covered field and past Lake Shore Drive where cars crawled at a snail's pace. She pretended interest in the smooth expanse of frozen lake that stretched beyond as far as the eye could see. Rand stopped next to her, obviously trying to breathe normally—as if he could fool her. He had to be as winded and exhausted as she was. Not only did her lungs feel like they were ready to collapse, but every muscle in her body begged her for mercy.

"Ready to cry uncle?" he asked.

"Not yet," Shelby fibbed. "I was merely enjoying the scenery."

Groaning, Rand shook his head. "This calls for desperate measures, then."

She eyed him suspiciously. "What's that supposed to mean?"

"Ever been tackled on skis?"

"Oh, no!" she cried, backing away from him.

Taking off down the incline was tricky enough for Shelby on the cross-country skis that were longer and clumsier than those she normally used for downhill skiing. But with a madman chasing her. . . .

She shrieked as she felt his arms encircling her waist and herself toppling over from his weight. Shrieking again, she let go of her poles and tried to beat him off. She was as successful as a terrier would have been against a Great Dane—a lot of noisy show with no results.

Seconds later, she found herself wedged in the snow, Rand on top of her, their skis tangled so she couldn't move her legs. But she still could move her hands, she thought slyly, grabbing a handful of snow from behind him so he wouldn't be forewarned.

"Okay, are you ready to cry uncle yet?" he demanded just as she plopped the snow in at the back of his neck.

His expression was so genuinely horrified that she couldn't hold back her giggles. Frantically he swiped at his neck with a leather-covered hand, removing what he could.

"It's going down my back!" he growled.

"Maybe *you*'d better cry uncle," she choked out, tears of mirth streaming from her eyes and freezing on her cheeks.

She wasn't laughing too hard to take advantage of her opening, however, when, concentrating on getting rid of the snow, Rand let go of her. She popped up and away from him, but her left foot was minus a ski. Grabbing it, she stayed out of his reach while trying to put the gear back on, but it wouldn't cooperate. From the corner of her eye, she saw Rand undo his skis and rise, his face set in a vengeful expression.

"Oh, damn!"

She tried again but lost her balance. Her left foot broke through the thin crust of punchy snow and Rand caught her in his arms.

"Trapped, oh wily one."

"What are you going to do?" she asked, sure he planned to dump her in the snow again.

"This."

His mustache swooped down toward her face and landed on her lips with a startling jerk as Rand's feet broke through the crust of snow. His mouth laughed against hers, the soft prickles of his mustache making Shelby grin. She kissed him quickly with a loud smacking sound.

Laughter stilled, he demanded, "Again."

Looking into his suddenly serious eyes, Shelby felt engulfed by the same awareness that had stretched between them the night before. But the middle of the park was neither the time nor the place for intimacies, even if the snow had kept almost everyone else away.

"Forget it," she said softly. "We'll melt the snow into one gigantic puddle."

Rand raised an eyebrow that seemed to say *Who cares?* before brushing some fresh snow from her nose. "Speaking of puddles…there's one sliding down my back, as you very well know.''

"Want me to say I'm sorry?''

"That depends. Would you be telling the truth?''

Shelby grinned. "What do you think?''

"I think it's time we left this sport to those younger and hardier than we are.''

"I'll have you know I'm only thirty-two.''

"Perfect.''

"For what?''

"Me. I'm only three years older.''

"I see what you mean.''

"About what?''

"About leaving cross-country skiing to our youth,'' Shelby said in mock seriousness. "Thirty-five is the beginning of middle age, you know.''

"I'll get you for that one,'' he promised.

"But not here.''

"No, not here.''

Reluctantly, she moved out of his arms. "Maybe I'll be able to get that ski on now.''

"I don't know why in the world you were having so much trouble to begin with.''

Not bothering to answer, Shelby settled for giving him a dirty look that he clearly found amusing. At least this time, the piece of equipment cooperated and she was ready to head back toward the rental concession before he was.

She watched Rand gather his poles—and tried not to think about any possible motives he might have for seeing her other than the one he'd declared earlier. She really wanted to believe he was interested in her and that was that. But, as if they'd been in neutral territory, which had changed everything for a few hours, apprehension plunged back into her consciousness as they prepared to leave the park.

"Ready?" he asked.

Unwilling to give up their playful banter just yet, she said, "I've *been* ready and waiting for you."

"If I had even a tad more energy, I'd race you to the concession."

"Good thing you're as pooped as I am, then." She flashed him a brilliant smile before pushing off.

He stayed directly beside her. "We're going to your place so you can make the hot chocolate. Right?"

"Me?"

"You lost the bet when you hit the snow first."

"Only because you tackled me."

"Sometimes a man has to take his opportunities when he can."

"Substitute 'cheat' for 'man,'" she grumbled.

"I don't remember our making any rules for this game."

"All right, already. I'll make the hot chocolate."

"I knew you'd see it my way."

After returning their equipment, they decided to walk the three blocks to Shelby's place rather than moving the car and taking a chance on not being able to find another spot. Always a problem on the near north side, parking became impossible when the snow routes prohibited parking along certain major thoroughfares and the buildup of snow along the curbs blocked other usable spaces.

Though the sky was still flaking, the worst of the winter storm appeared to be over. But an inner storm was gathering in Shelby as, hand in hand, they approached her building. She couldn't forget the kiss they'd shared the night before, couldn't help wanting to renew the passion, to explore the promise it held. And yet the seeds of distrust intruded, cautioning her to take it slow.

How did she know Rand hadn't been thinking about protecting his sister even as he'd been kissing her?

She couldn't remember when—if ever—she'd been so on edge with a man before.

As if he guessed the cause of her nervousness, Rand winked and took the keys from her hand when she was unable to open the door on the first try.

"Wrong key," he informed her, immediately finding and using the correct one.

The door swung wide. Stomping her boots free of any remaining snow on the hallway mat, she preceded him into the apartment.

"Leave your boots here by the door," she said, pulling off her own. "I'll take your jacket and hang it in the bathroom to dry out."

Rand did as she asked, removing his boots and sticking his gloves into his jacket pocket before handing over the garment. "Need any help in the kitchen?"

"No, but I could use a couple of hands in the living room." Shelby backed away from him down the hallway. "To put some logs in the fireplace," she clarified so he wouldn't purposely get the wrong idea.

Stalking her, Rand evidently had some ideas of his own, anyway. "Sounds like a heartwarming suggestion. So you like fires. That means you're a romantic."

"Or a woman who's cold all the way down to the tips of her toes."

"Let me fix that."

Before she realized what he was up to, Rand had Shelby trapped against the wall, his mouth covering hers. Her heart seemed to beat in her throat. The sensual thrust of his warm tongue made her pulse go haywire. Her fingers opened, releasing the jackets wedged between them, and her arms wound around his neck as if it were the most natural thing in the world for them to do. With a quick adjustment of his hips, Rand let the garments fall to the floor. One large hand at the small of her back snugged their lower bodies together.

Though nearly suffocated by his nearness, Shelby couldn't move, couldn't protest and furthermore, didn't want to. Instead, she acknowledged his unexpected romantic attack with some aggression of her own, nudging and teasing him with her lips and tongue until he groaned and came up for air.

"Are we even now?" she murmured, while her body protested that it wasn't done with him yet. "For my heinous comment about your being middle-aged?"

Still imprisoning Shelby between the wall and him, Rand tilted his forehead against hers. His breath fanned her face sensuously when he murmured, "Not by a long shot. We'll continue this discussion later . . . in front of the fire."

"I'll be looking forward to it."

She was sure he liberated her reluctantly, even more sure this kiss had nothing to do with Pippa. Smiling at the realization, she picked up their wet jackets and carried them to the bathroom; he strolled in the other direction toward the living room. By the time she had hung the clothes up to dry and entered the kitchen, she could hear the faint sound of logs clunking as they settled on the hearth and Rand whistling as he worked. She strained to make out the tune.

A Christmas carol.

The reason for their being together in the first place came back to haunt her as it had done earlier when she'd heard *The Nutcracker* in the car. At least she'd been able to turn off the Christmas ballet music and divert her mind with their conversation. Again Shelby tried to shove aside reality as she filled the kettle with water and positioned it over a flame, but Rand's off-key rendition of "Santa Claus Is Coming to Town" continued to distract her.

Couldn't she forget about Dutch for one afternoon?

Apparently not. Her discovery of the dead man and her subsequent actions played themselves over in her mind as they had done at least a hundred times in the past few days.

Though she couldn't prevent it from happening, she didn't have to like it, Shelby thought, slamming through her cabinets until she found the cocoa. Opening two packages she poured them into a set of designer mugs that she then placed on a matching tray.

She could remember finding Dutch calmly now, and she could see exactly how foolish she'd been to run, to try to hide the fact that she'd found the body. If only she hadn't panicked and covered up her presence at the scene of the crime—thereby incriminating herself—she wouldn't have put herself in this impossible situation. But what choice had she had, considering that incident with Pete Wolenski? If only she had someone she could talk to....

The kettle whistled; she poured the water and stirred the powder and liquid together.

Rand. He was the clear choice. Surely he wouldn't use the disclosure against her, once he understood why she'd panicked. She was mulling over the idea of telling him, wondering how best to broach the subject, when the doorbell rang. She glanced down the hall.

Rand stood in the living-room doorway. "Want me to get it?"

"No. I'm coming."

Picking up the tray, she hurried toward him and hit the buzzer with her elbow as she went. Unfortunately, her building's system was too old to have an intercom, but her door did have a peephole.

"Take this, would you?"

She handed Rand the tray, then peeked into the hallway. What she saw made her heart skip a beat. Lieutenant Isaac Jackson waited.

And there was no escaping his ruining the afternoon since she'd buzzed him in.

Her hands fumbled with the lock and handle. As it swung open, the door hit her in the hip. She clenched her teeth against the sharp pain. Aware of Rand a mere yard away, watching from the living room, she tried to keep her calm when she said, "Lieutenant Jackson, what a surprise," but heard the tremble in her voice.

"May I come in?"

"Of course."

She stepped back to let him pass. It would have been impossible to miss his interest in Rand's presence or in the cozy fire and set of mugs on the coffee table.

He bobbed his ebony head. "Mr. McNabb."

"Lieutenant."

The blazing fire was quickly heating up the room. Shelby didn't ask for the policeman's heavy overcoat, hoping the increasing temperature would make him hurry. Jackson unbuttoned the coat and, without invitation, made himself comfortable on the couch.

"I hope you won't mind answering a few questions."

Of course, she minded. She wanted to scream at him to leave, but she merely smiled as Rand took a chair opposite the homicide detective. Picking up her mug of cocoa, she stationed herself in front of a wall unit near the hearth.

"Objecting would be fruitless," she finally said. "So get on with it."

"How well did you know Dutch Vanleer?"

"You asked me that before, Lieutenant. I told you I didn't know him well." Though she tried to keep her voice light and even, as if she were being very patient with him,

Shelby was sure he could sense the strain this second interview was putting on her. She sipped at her cocoa, scalding her tongue. "He was my employer. Since he's dead and buried that couldn't possibly have changed."

"What you avoided telling me was that Dutch *wanted* to know you better."

Clenching her jaw, Shelby refused to respond.

"My late partner wanted to get to know a lot of attractive women a lot better," Rand broke in, to Shelby's boundless gratitude. "It so happens that not all of them fell under his spell."

"Neither did all of them threaten the deceased with a sexual-harassment suit." Jackson turned to her. "But you did, didn't you, Miss Corbin? Before you answer, let me say two witnesses told me the same story."

"I wasn't going to deny it." So Zeke and Dana had related the incident, just as she'd feared. Her seeing Rand had been for nothing—at least in the way of self-protection. "Yes, I did threaten Vanleer with a suit if he didn't keep his hands and his comments to himself."

Both men were watching her warily when the detective asked, "Then why didn't you tell me about your altercation when I questioned you the other day?"

"I didn't see it as being important," she lied.

"I'll be the judge of what is and what isn't important in this case," Jackson stated. "I'd say you were trying to protect yourself, Miss Corbin, and that makes me wonder why."

Sweat beaded his forehead, but Shelby felt clammy all over. The sweet smell of the cocoa drifted up to her nose, making her stomach clench. "I didn't kill him."

"I didn't say you did."

"Then what are you saying?"

Silence stretched tensely between them. Rand was staring speculatively at her rather than at the detective. Shelby's heart began to pound. Had Jackson found out about Wolenski and her subsequent arrest? Was he planning to arrest her now? She grew nauseous simply thinking about it.

"I'm saying that you should have told me to begin with, Miss Corbin. Withholding evidence—"

"His coming on to me wasn't evidence. It had nothing to do with the case!" she cried, carelessly setting the mug on her wall unit. It tipped over. Cocoa sloshed out over the furniture and onto the mauve rug. "Now see what you've made me do. Look, Lieutenant, if you're finished harassing me, I'd like you to leave so I can clean up this mess."

His dark eyes locked with hers, and for a moment Shelby feared he *was* about to arrest her for murder. She swallowed hard, but her breath was caught in her throat, threatening to choke her.

Then he rose.

"I'd suggest you don't try to leave town in the near future, Miss Corbin. You'll be hearing from me."

"Pardon me if I don't look forward to the experience, Lieutenant."

He got all the way to the door before he stopped to face her. Leisurely buttoning his overcoat, he said, "By the way, you never did tell me what color dress you wore to the Christmas party."

Shelby thought quickly: if anyone had been able to tell him, he would have thrown that information at her, too. "Fuchsia. Fuchsia taffeta. It had a fitted off-the-shoulder bodice and full skirts," she boldly lied, describing a dress in her closet that was similar to the crimson one she'd destroyed.

"Fuchsia. That's red, isn't it?"

"Related—a reddish purple. Would you like to see it?"

"No." He stared at her thoughtfully. "I'll save that pleasure for another time."

With that, he left.

The adrenaline that had kept her going suddenly crashed. Shelby grabbed onto the wall unit to steady herself before realizing Rand was still there, keen amber eyes watching her every move.

"I'd better get something to clean up this mess," she said, aware of the sticky cocoa on her hand.

She tried to hurry by him. He whipped out of the chair. Grabbing her by the wrist, he stopped her from escaping the room and him. He loomed over her, large and threatening.

"Wait a minute. You're white as a ghost. Maybe you ought to sit down and take a few deep breaths." His words weren't at all threatening. He sounded as concerned as his expression.

. "I'm fine," she lied yet once again. "It's the carpeting."

She could tell Rand didn't believe her. When she tugged her arm, he freed her wrist instantly. "Sorry. I didn't mean to hurt you."

"You didn't." She saw the questions lurking in his eyes, was afraid he might voice them. "Listen, I hate to do this to you again, but—"

"You're going to ask me to leave," he finished for her.

"Yes. Please."

"Another headache?"

"No. The carpet . . ."

Rand didn't press her. She was thankful for that.

"I'll get my jacket."

She trailed him down the hall, intending to fetch a bucket and sponge. She really was worried about the carpeting and the stain the cocoa might leave, she told herself. If she concentrated on worrying about it, she wouldn't have to think about the other.

Rand quickly retrieved his jacket from the bathroom and then blocked her way. "If you want to talk—about anything—call me."

He pulled out his wallet and extracted a card with his home phone number. Her fingers were stiff when she took it from him. She had no intention of using it, of course.

"Thanks, but I'm all right. He just made me so nervous. And now I have to clean the carpet." She couldn't stop the words from spilling out. "Then I have to get ready to go to my sister's. That's all."

He didn't believe a word of what she was saying. "Call me anyway."

She nodded. Placing both hands on her shoulders, he kissed her gently before taking his leave. As her apartment door closed behind him, she put her fingers to her mouth. It was too late to confide in Rand as she'd been thinking of doing. Even if he was clearly sympathetic to her, he'd heard her lies; he'd never believe her now.

As for herself, Shelby could wait no longer: she had to find the guilty one before she was somehow framed for murder.

## Chapter Six

Somehow Shelby got through the dinner with her elder sister and family without giving away her fears. Jane had read about Dutch's murder, of course, and asked what seemed like a hundred questions. Shelby calmly answered every one of them while making herself out to be a detached observer rather than one of the suspects. She even managed to leave her sister's house before midnight.

All day Sunday she stewed about her predicament, trying to figure out how, exactly, to proceed with a private murder investigation when she had no experience. She wasn't even a murder-mystery fan. If only she had an ally with whom to concoct plans and share clues.

Rand.

He was the logical answer.

He wanted to clear Pippa just as she wanted to clear herself. He'd even given her his telephone number in case she needed to talk to someone. If only she hadn't been forced to lie in front of him....

Not that she really feared discovery about the color of her dress.

She'd worked overtime the night of the party, and no one had seen her until she'd arrived in the festively darkened executive suite aglow with little more than twinkling colored lights and candles. Indeed, she convinced herself, for all anyone would have been able to tell, her dress might have been plum . . . or coral . . . or fuchsia as she'd claimed. And then, within an hour of arriving, she'd quietly slipped into the inner office to lie down.

No one but Rand had seen her after that.

No one but Rand had gotten a clear look at the true crimson of her dress, and there was no way he could prove she'd been the woman wearing it. Hiding the fact had been one thing, lying about it another. The idea of furthering their relationship with that lie between them made her uneasy; Shelby felt as if she'd irreparably breached the affinity she'd felt with him for a few special hours.

Though she stared at the number on his card a dozen different times on Sunday, she couldn't convince herself to pick up the telephone to call him.

Instead, she plotted alone.

Since Iris Dahl had been Dutch's mistress, the blonde might know something of importance. Shelby remembered seeing her at the store on Friday, only hours after her lover had been buried. She hadn't acted as though she was a woman in mourning. Shelby wondered what it would take to find out exactly how in love with Dutch Iris had been. . . and whether or not the blonde had had a motive for murder.

Shelby decided to give Iris her condolences first thing in the morning and find out.

IRIS DAHL was dressed in peacock splendor. Literally. The silk dress that a cosmetics saleswoman couldn't possibly afford on her salary alone was an original André Kuryokhin. And Iris was wearing it. The bulk of the purple, teal, burgundy, copper and gold peacock was displayed in the swinging skirts, but part of the plumage rose to accent one full breast.

Not exactly mourning garb, Shelby thought, approaching the counter shortly before the store opened.

"Good morning, Iris. That dress is quite striking."

"Thanks." Suspicion lurked in the blue eyes that were highlighted with matching peacock colors—every one of them. Even her thickened eyelashes were covered with teal and tipped with gold and copper. "What's up? You need to use my line for a window display?"

"No, actually, I wanted to talk to you."

"Why?"

"It's about Dutch." Watching Iris's brilliantly hued eyes narrow, Shelby used her most sympathetic tone. "I never realized how close the two of you were until the wake. I wanted to give you my condolences."

Iris glanced over her shoulder at the woman behind the next cosmetics counter as if she wanted to make sure the redhead there wasn't listening. Then, in a low voice, she said, "Don't make me gag, Miss Goody-Two-Shoes Corbin."

Startled by Iris's hostility, Shelby fought to keep her jaw from dropping. "I beg your pardon?"

"You *ought* to beg...for my forgiveness," Iris hissed softly.

"I don't understand."

"Don't play innocent." Before Shelby's eyes, Iris became the grieving girlfriend. The suffering martyr. Her face took on a pinched expression and her lower lip trembled. "You tried to steal my Dutch away from me."

"Where in the world did you get an idea like that?"

"Look, let's be frank with each other, huh? I know your type, honey. At least I'm honest. If I want a man—married or not—I don't sneak around hiding the fact." Iris paused and widened her eyes as if to make sure Shelby noted the tears welling in them. "But you—you pretend to be too good to give a guy a tumble, and all the time you're slithering around behind my back, trying to steal away my man."

Shelby was tempted to let the accusation pass; it was too ludicrous to be dignified with an answer. But she'd started this conversation to see what she could find out. She didn't have to like what she heard.

"That's ridiculous."

"Yeah, I thought so, too. Well, it didn't work, did it? Dutch loved only *me*, right up to the end," Iris declared melodramatically.

A single tear slipped down the blonde's cheek almost as though she could control it...as though she didn't want to have to reapply eye makeup ruined by actual crying.

Rather than argue about her own possible involvement with the dead man, Shelby calmly turned the tables on the other woman. "It was too bad Dutch never proved his love for you by giving Pippa the divorce she wanted."

"Pippa!" Stepping out of character, Iris spat the word like a curse. "That bimbo was the only thing standing in the way of my happiness."

"That 'bimbo,' as you call her, happened to be the man's wife."

"Wife! Hah! She never had the vision for Dutch's future as I did." Iris's eyes flashed with hatred and her voice rose. "Westbrook's was small potatoes and once Dutch had what he wanted out of it, he would have gotten rid of it and Pippa. He was only staying married to keep McNabb in line."

"For what reason?" Shelby asked, realizing they now had the attention of not only the redhead, but a gray-haired saleswoman on the other side of the aisle as well.

Blinking her multi-colored lashes, Iris backed up and took a deep breath, which in turn set her lower lip to quivering. "I don't want to talk about this anymore or I'll be too upset to work."

*Like hell!* It was an act, Shelby realized. Iris's grief was about as real as her made-up face. She hadn't loved Dutch, but she was making sure everyone thought she had. Why?

To divert suspicion?

Did Iris have reason to fear she might be accused of murder?

"I think you have an overactive imagination, Iris," Shelby said, continuing to probe for information. "First, you think I'm after Dutch. Now you think he was trying to keep his partner in line for some vague purpose. I don't mean to be unkind, but you really ought to face the truth: your lover didn't want to let his wife go."

The ploy didn't work, proving that Iris was more clever than she looked or acted. She didn't blurt out the reason Dutch had been manipulating Rand, as Shelby had hoped she would. Instead, the blonde raised her head high with a tragic air. Admirable acting, if wasted on the wrong person.

"Well, I'd better get to work myself, Iris. See you later."

"Don't go out of your way to do me any favors."

Shelby gave the blonde one last, penetrating look, but she couldn't break through the other woman's composure. Nodding, she headed for the elevators, satisfied that she'd gotten something, no matter how nebulous, out of the conversation. She really couldn't have continued baiting the woman for information anyway. Westbrook's was about to open its doors to Monday-morning customers.

Nevertheless, Shelby couldn't stop thinking about the exchange. The comment about Dutch's keeping Rand in line until he got what he wanted out of Westbrook's might have been fuzzy, but the implications had been unsettling. Whatever Dutch had been up to might affect Rand directly even though his partner was dead. She had to warn him. Calling his office, she learned that he would be tied up until after lunch. She asked Kristen to have him call her when he could.

In the meantime, she had work to do. Shelby attacked it, only part of her continuing to speculate whether or not Iris held the key to the identity of the murderer.

WAITING FOR SHELBY to get to his office halfway through the afternoon, Rand again wondered if she'd lied about the fuchsia dress. His protective instincts rose as they had when the homicide detective had tried to back her into a corner. Under fire, she'd acted nervous and afraid, certainly, but that didn't make her guilty of murder. Perhaps she'd feared Jackson would use her private altercation with Dutch to railroad her into a formal charge.

When the lieutenant had mentioned the sexual-harassment suit, Rand had, for a moment, wondered if Shelby might not have killed his partner, after all. He'd discarded the idea almost instantly—not that he would put it past Dutch to attack her. But his instincts wouldn't allow him to believe Shelby was capable of killing anyone, not even in self-defense.

He'd tried reaching out to her, but she hadn't been buying—not then. Neither had she used the card he'd left with her. He wondered what had changed her mind; why the urgency to see him as soon as possible. He was certain she didn't want to talk about business.

The intercom shrilled and Kristen's disembodied voice informed him, "Miss Corbin to see you, Mr. McNabb."

"Send her in."

Her sweater dress a field of magenta flowers on a brilliant green background, Shelby swept into his office like a breath of spring. Her too-tight smile, convincing him that she was anxious about something, did little to spoil the effect. She stopped on the other side of his desk, both hands gripping the back of a chair.

"I'm not taking you away from anything important, am I?"

"Not at all." He indicated the seat she was practically mauling for support. "Sit down."

"I'd rather stand."

"Suit yourself." He waited for a moment, but when she clenched her jaw rather than saying anything, he prompted her. "So, what's on your mind?"

"I don't know how to start."

"The beginning would do."

"I'd rather tell you about this morning and my conversation with Iris Dahl," she said in a rush.

Whatever he'd been expecting, it hadn't been a revelation about his late partner's mistress. He had no idea why she'd think he'd want to hear about Iris, but his curiosity was aroused. "Go on."

"At the wake, she made it pretty clear that Dutch was...important to her."

"Don't be delicate on my account."

Shelby nodded. She also let go of her death grip on the chair and began pacing in front of his desk, talking more to herself than to him.

"I found it difficult to believe that a woman in love could be so complacent the next day, only hours after the funeral. Iris was at her station in the cosmetics department, going on with business as usual, hardly the picture of a grieving woman who'd just lost her lover. The more I thought about it, the more the fact disturbed me. I decided to give her my condolences this morning to see what she'd say.''

"And?"

She whipped around to face him. "*And* she accused me of being after Dutch. She made a big deal of how much Dutch loved her and how she'd been open about wanting him. It was an amazing performance, almost as good as the one she gave at the wake. She had total control of herself, even forced out a tear—only one—until . . ."

"Until?"

"I mentioned Pippa and her refusal to divorce Dutch." Shelby set her hands on the edge of his desk and leaned toward him. "That's when she got really heated and said something she shouldn't have. How did she put it?" Her forehead puckered into a frown. "That Westbrook's was small potatoes, and once Dutch had what he wanted out of it, he would have gotten rid of the store and his wife. She said he was staying married to Pippa to keep *you* in line."

"That doesn't make sense."

"It didn't make sense to me, either, but I knew she wasn't lying, because when I asked her to explain, she clammed up on me and went back into her tragic-but-brave act."

"I think you may have stumbled onto something, Shelby." Rand's mind was already at work, wondering about the "small potatoes" comment. What kind of plans had his late partner been concocting behind his back? "Stumbled—what am I saying? Instigated. Why?"

"You know why. Jackson. I think he wants me to be guilty. But I didn't do it." She slammed her right palm down on his desk so hard that his papers went flying. "I didn't kill Dutch. You've got to believe me."

"I do believe you."

He really did, now more than ever. Rand gently took the abused hand in his own; an immediate response tempered the anger and frustration darkening her eyes. He recognized the desperation in her tone, wanted to take her into his arms to comfort her. Unfortunately, he didn't think she'd appreciate the gesture; he had the idea that even now she was restraining herself from pulling her hand out of his.

He freed her before asking, "Shelby, are you telling me you made a conscious decision to investigate Dutch's murder on your own?"

Nodding slowly, she sank into the chair behind her. "I had to do something."

"You could have started by calling me yesterday."

"I thought about it."

"But you decided not to."

He wanted to ask why, but he was afraid he might not like the answer.

"I'm talking to you now," she stated quietly.

And Rand knew that she'd said as much as she was going to without his encouraging her further. He sensed she wanted his help but wouldn't ask, even though she'd exposed her own vulnerability to warn him. In doing so, she'd earned his complete trust.

"I'd like to make a proposition," he stated, rising and circling his desk. He balanced himself on the edge, his leg within nudging distance of hers. "Since we both have a personal interest in this case—I don't want Pippa railroaded into a murder charge, either—why don't we work together to see what we can find out?"

Taking a deep breath, she closed her eyes. When she opened them again, their hazel depths seemed less troubled. "I was hoping you'd suggest that. Where do we begin?"

"If Westbrook's was small potatoes to Dutch, we'd better find out his idea of prime rib."

"You mean talk to Iris again?"

"I doubt that would be a smart move just now. If she has anything to hide, she'll be on her guard." Rand thought aloud: "Pippa and Dutch hadn't been close for a long time before his death, but it wouldn't hurt to find out what my sister knows. He refused to move out of the house, and being both spoiled and stubborn, she refused as well. Pippa may have heard or seen something that could help us."

"You'll talk to her then?"

"We'll talk to her together, after work. Unless you have any objections."

"No objections." The start of a smile dimpled her cheeks. "Just an overwhelming sense of relief that I don't have to do this alone."

"Allies," he said, holding out a hand that she immediately took for a businesslike shake as she stood. "You can talk to me anytime, Shelby. Remember that."

"Thanks."

"Meet me at the employee entrance at a quarter to five."

"I'll be there."

Rand knew her dimpled smile would haunt him for the rest of the afternoon. He only hoped he could live up to her obvious expectations so that she would still have reason to thank him by the time any arrests were made.

SHELBY LEFT Rand's office with mixed feelings—not about their working together to solve the crime, but about getting involved further with the man himself. She was sure his personal interest in her was as great a factor in his agreeing to collaborate as was his wanting to protect Pippa. At least she didn't feel as bad as she might have. Though a lie still stood between them, her having told him about the conversation with Iris made up for it to some extent.

Kind of a trade-off.

Besides, she rationalized, she hadn't lied to him directly. She'd lied to Lieutenant Jackson, and Rand just happened to overhear the description of the dress. She ignored the small voice in her head whispering that she wouldn't tell Rand the truth about finding Dutch dead in the executive suite, even if he did ask.

After spending the next hour going over figures for refurbishing the windows completely in preparation for the Kuryokhin display, Shelby closed her notebook at exactly four-thirty. No overtime tonight. She freshened up quickly, then headed for her rendezvous with Rand. If only this night's work would produce results.

The store was open late every evening that week, so it was packed with last-minute holiday shoppers. It took some effort to get through the crowd. An elderly woman whose arms were overloaded with purchases ran into her a dozen yards away from the employee entrance.

"Oh, Lord, I'm so clumsy," the gray-haired lady apologized as two small bags went flying. "Excuse me."

"Don't worry about it." Shelby caught the one that bounced off a man's back and handed it to the woman. "Let me get the other one for you, too."

"Bless you, child."

Shelby retrieved the second package from behind the counter. "Maybe you ought to get a shopping bag."

"Good idea," the wizened woman said, taking her purchase. "I'll just do that right away. You have yourself a Merry Christmas, darlin'."

"Merry Christmas."

For the first time since the party, Shelby felt like getting into the spirit of the holiday. She was thinking about the reason why—or rather who—when she spotted Edgar. Back on his normal four-to-midnight shift, the security guard was listening to an obviously distraught Iris Dahl. His expression troubled yet sympathetic, Edgar nodded his balding head as the blonde spoke.

What were they talking about? Dutch?

When Iris glanced Shelby's way and saw her, what looked like a sharp oath passed her lips. She patted Edgar on the arm and abruptly strode out to the alley where a dark-haired woman waited for her. Shelby couldn't be sure from the quick impression she got, but the woman might have been Loretta Greenfield, the Kuryokhin sales rep.

What an odd pair to be friends.

Thinking she'd talk to Edgar while waiting for Rand, Shelby crossed to the security guard. "Hi, Edgar, how does it feel to be off the graveyard shift?"

Rather than greeting her with his usual smile and good-humored retort, he gruffly muttered, "Okay, I suppose." He clutched his belt and jerked at his pants. "I gotta get on my rounds now. Gotta check on a couple of rookies we hired."

Without another word he stalked off, leaving her staring and wondering if Iris had been talking about *her*. It seemed as if Edgar was reflecting the blonde's hostility.

Before she could figure out why, a familiar masculine voice close behind said, "There's my date now."

"Rand." Turning, Shelby saw him approach her, a well-tailored camel overcoat flapping around his legs. He wasn't alone. Tucker Powers walked next to him, a silvery brow lifted in surprise at seeing her. "Hello, Mr. Powers." She slipped into her down coat.

The distinguished-looking lawyer inclined his head as the men stopped at her side. "Shelby."

"Well, we'd better be running along if we don't want to be late." Rand took Shelby's arm and gave her a clandestine signal. "See you tomorrow, Tucker."

"Can't I give you two a lift? My limo should be waiting for me at the curb."

"I have my car, but thanks anyway."

"Yes, of course," Tucker muttered, looking confused.

Rand led Shelby out the door and down the alley. She zipped up her coat against the chill and turned to wave to the lawyer who followed them out of the store.

"The old boy's getting a bit vague," Rand said in a low voice. "He asked me about the ride home in the elevator. I told him I had my car parked in loading dock."

Shelby glanced over her shoulder and saw Tucker approaching a black limousine. A chauffeur hopped out and opened the back door.

"You must pay him a fortune if he can afford one of those. I think I may ask for a raise, after all."

"Don't get the wrong impression. He couldn't afford his life-style on his salary. Tucker's from an old, moneyed family. His grandfather Tyler was Aldous Westbrook's best friend when the old man founded the store. Tyler also happened to be the store's first lawyer and one of the minor shareholders. Apparently he invested his profits wisely."

They reached the end of the alley and the loading dock where the Saab was parked. Rand opened the passenger door and Shelby slid in. A moment later they were crawling east through rush-hour Loop traffic toward Lake Shore Drive.

"So Tucker followed in his grandfather's footsteps at Westbrook's," Shelby said, still thinking about it. "How unusual."

"Not really. His father did the same. It's been a family tradition. A Powers has always been head of the legal department. Unfortunately the inheritance of that position ends with Tucker since his children never took an interest in the law.''

''What a shame. I'll bet that makes him kind of sad.''

''Some days I'm not even sure he realizes how close he is to the end of his road at the store.''

''But he's only in his early sixties.''

''Fifty-nine, actually. But from what I've been able to tell, he's slipping already, especially during the past few months.''

''I hope you're wrong. Maybe he has personal problems,'' Shelby said, thinking about his rumored love affair with Althea. ''You know, a middle-age crisis.''

''I hope you're right. I really like the old guy. He's part of the tradition I always associated with Westbrook's when I was growing up.''

Once on Lake Shore Drive they moved along a little faster, but not much.

''Where does Pippa live?''

''A half block from the lake on Hawthorn,'' he said, mentioning a street that was a mile and a half farther north than Fullerton.

''Is she expecting us?''

''I called and told her I was stopping by with a friend. I didn't want to say too much in case anyone could hear. I think we'd better keep our investigation low-key. That's why I told Tucker I was meeting my date. I hope you don't mind.''

''Not at all.''

Actually, Shelby was a little disappointed that he put it so clinically. She wouldn't mind being his date. An inner voice reminded her of the lie, but she snugged it away in a dark recess of her mind.

''Made any exciting plans for the holidays?'' he asked.

"My parents always have a big family get-together on Christmas Day."

"You don't sound too enthusiastic. Are you sure you aren't related to the grinch?"

"It's not that. I love Christmas. Actually, it's my favorite holiday. But under the circumstances..."

"I know what you mean. Two of my brothers will be flying in for the second time this month."

Shelby knew the oblique reference was to their having to fly in for the wake and funeral. She stared out at the frozen lake on her right. They both lapsed into silence that lasted the rest of the drive to the old frame house on Hawthorn. The ecru-painted building was more a mansion, really, situated on a double lot on prime property one half-block west of Lake Shore Drive high rises. Taxes on the place had to be more than Shelby paid for a year's rent—and she lived in a high-rent district.

Rand pulled the Saab into the old carriage drive. They approached the house from the front of the steps since the side didn't come quite to the ground but ended at a high cement block where people would have alighted from their carriages when the house was built. Shelby followed Rand to the door where he rang the bell. Through the broad expanse of front windows, she saw glass doors in the living room, a side exit onto the porch that swept halfway around the house.

When Pippa opened the front door, her appearance shocked Shelby. Her bright red hair was frizzed and uncombed. Dark circles under her eyes made them look like huge green pools in her delicate face, and the tender skin around her nose was raw, as if she'd been spending a lot of time crying. Shelby couldn't imagine Pippa being so overwrought about Dutch's death when she'd been so determined to divorce him.

"How are you doing, Brat?" Rand asked, hugging his sister.

"Better."

"This is Shelby Corbin."

"We've met, haven't we?"

"At your... Mr. Vanleer's wake," Shelby admitted uncomfortably.

A cloud passed over Pippa's features. She retreated into the hallway. "Come in. Can I get you something? Coffee?"

"This isn't a social visit, Pippā. We need to talk to you about Dutch," Rand said gently. "We're trying to do what the police haven't."

"Playing private detective?" Her expression blank, Pippa looked from Rand to Shelby. "Let's go into the parlor."

The place reflected money, but not ostentatiously. The small, cozy parlor off the living room held a couple of chintz-covered couches and end tables. Sheers covered the windows, and plants gave the room a homey touch.

They'd barely removed their coats when Pippa asked, "Why are you interested in my late husband, Miss Corbin?"

Shelby looked at Rand. How was she supposed to tell the wife of a dead man that he'd been after her body? She might not have been able to, but that's exactly what Rand did.

"Dutch was too interested in Shelby, Pippa. He threatened her job, so she threatened him with a sexual-harassment suit. The police found out about it. She's right up there with you as having a reason to want Dutch dead."

"I'm sorry." Pippa's eyes welled with tears and she bit her lower lip.

"Please, don't apologize," Shelby said, oddly disturbed by the other woman's reaction. After all, Dutch's widow didn't have anything to do with what happened to her.

Taking a shaky breath, Pippa composed herself. "What can I tell you that will help?"

Rand repeated Iris's comment, ending with, "Do you know of any deals—slightly shady or otherwise—that Dutch might have been involved in?"

"He never told me anything. Lack of communication was the most minor of our problems, as you know. We weren't even talking the last couple of months."

"Think hard," Rand urged. "Maybe you overheard or saw something that can help us figure it out."

"Not really. Only..." Pippa rubbed her forehead thoughtfully. "There was that nervous little man with the leather briefcase who showed up here a few weeks ago. Dutch and I had been having one of our famous arguments, so when he whipped the man into his study, I figured it was to get away from me. Maybe I wasn't supposed to see him."

"Who was this man?"

"He works at the store. Slim, five-seven or -eight, thinning light brown hair. He kept checking his watch like he was short on time."

"Frank Hatcher?" Shelby asked.

"Yes. Yes, I'm sure I heard Dutch call him Francis."

"I sat next to Frank at the meeting you called about Dutch," Shelby told Rand. "He was looking at his watch then, mumbling about your being late and something about leaving for vacation. He was very callous about the murder."

Rand was already on his feet. "Let's check the study. Maybe we can find some clue as to why Frank was here."

They spent more than an hour going through the room—desk, filing cabinets, shelves—carefully checking and sorting every scrap of paper. They found no clue to any deal Dutch might have been involved in.

"Anyplace else we might look?" Rand raked his hand through his hair in frustration. "Another room, perhaps?"

Pippa shook her head. "This was his sacred inner sanctum. He'd disappear in here for hours at a time." She looked around and her gaze stopped at a sheet of paneling next to the fireplace. "The wall safe!" She turned a carved piece of wood in the mantel and the paneling popped open. Inside the cavity stood a five-foot safe with a large tumbler. "I haven't seen it since we moved in, so I almost forgot it existed. Now the only problem is finding the combination."

"You mean he never let you have it?"

"Brother, dear, you knew Dutch almost as well as I. What do you think?"

"That he wouldn't trust you with it. He must have written the combination down somewhere," Rand said. "He had a rotten memory. Our search isn't over yet."

Though they examined every drawer and crevice in the room during the next quarter of an hour, they found nothing resembling a combination.

"My younger sister Brenda has a really bad memory," Shelby volunteered when they were forced to give up. "She always uses her birth date on her license plates so she can remember the number."

"That might be it," Pippa agreed. "We've got nothing to lose."

She supplied the numbers and Rand tried various combinations on Dutch's birth date, license plates, social security number, address and telephone numbers, both work and home. Still no luck. The safe stood impenetrable.

"We can't give up." Shelby was so frustrated she wanted to rip every paper in the room to shreds.

Pippa threw herself on a leather couch. "There's nothing left to try."

"No, there is one more thing," Rand argued, giving Shelby renewed hope. "Dutch's famous play. Remember when he took over as quarterback the last time we opposed Green Bay? He bragged about that play for months until hearing about it drove me nuts. Damned if I can remember the numbers."

"You don't have to." Pippa scooted off the couch and went directly to one of the shelves behind the desk. Pulling out a scrapbook, she threw it on the desk and flipped it open to a series of articles proclaiming Dutch the hero of the day for Bears fans. She scanned one of the pages. "Here it is. Red forty-five, three-thirty-two."

Rand copied down the number and split it into several variations. "Red starts with *r* like right," he mumbled as he tested the first combination. It didn't work, but on his third try, the ancient safe rewarded him with a loud clunk. "That's it." He turned the handle. "We did it!"

Shelby couldn't hide her sense of elation. "What a team we make. Lieutenant Jackson, watch out!"

Even Pippa smiled at that, but her expression soon turned to awe as did Shelby's when Rand opened the door. Stacks of money crowded a shelf inside. She could see they were hundred-dollar bills.

"There must be thousands of dollars here," Pippa said.

"More like hundreds of thousands." From a lower shelf, Rand picked up a small stack of folders and opened the one on top. "And more important, we found what we were looking for."

## Chapter Seven

With Shelby and Pippa crowding him on either side to see, Rand carefully checked the papers first in the top folder, then in the others, hardly able to believe his eyes.

"The bastard bought out three of the seven minor shareholders behind my back. He'd been the senior partner holding forty-one percent of the company to my twenty-six for more than two weeks before his death. Frank Hatcher witnessed the transactions."

Arms crossed over her chest, Shelby backed up against the safe's door. "Do you think Dutch was planning a takeover?"

"Sure as hell looks like it."

"But that doesn't make sense." She frowned. "Iris said Westbrook's was small potatoes and once he got what he wanted out of it… That sounds like he was planning to sell and use his profits to get into something a lot bigger."

"Like what?" Pippa asked.

"Frank Hatcher would be the man to tell us," Rand suggested, "but he's on vacation until next Monday. What foul luck. We get onto something big and the holidays stop us cold. Damn it all!" He slapped the folder against his hand. "Pippa, if you don't mind, I'll take these transactions with me. Maybe I can figure out a way to use them to get more information.''

"What about the money?'' Pippa said, indicating the piles of hundreds.

"We could use it to leave the country.'' Shelby's dimpled smile faded even as Rand glared at her. "Oh, for heaven's sake, I was joking.'' With a glower, she shot away from the safe—and him.

He closed the heavy door and spun the tumbler. "I'd suggest you leave the money in here until we find out more about what's been going on. It wouldn't do to draw suspicion to yourself by coming into newfound wealth.''

"I have no intention of touching that money,'' Pippa assured him. "I don't know where it came from…and I'm not sure I want to. I'm afraid it didn't even belong to Dutch.''

"We'll worry about that later.'' He turned toward Shelby with an apologetic expression. He wanted to share her sense of triumph…and frustration. Then he glanced at the mess they'd created. Drawers were open, books had been unevenly piled back on shelves, and papers covered every available surface. "Before we go, Pippa, maybe we'd better help you clean up.''

"No. Leave it. I have to go through everything in here anyway,'' his sister murmured softly, the helplessness in her voice diverting his attention. "And don't worry, I won't try to do it all tonight.''

Rand took her in his arms. He knew what his sister was going through, and until she was able to deal with the unresolved love-hate relationship she'd had with her husband, he'd be there for her. "It'll be okay, Brat,'' he promised, using the nickname he'd given her as a kid.

"I know. It's just that sometimes I think I'll never make it through this mess.''

"You will. Want me to call Mom to come over and spend the night?"

Pippa shook her head. "I'm fine."

"Then we'll get going. Shelby?"

"I'm ready."

"Listen, I'm sorry about taking you seriously before."

"It's all right."

They retrieved their coats from the parlor and left. Rand was so wrapped up in his thoughts about Dutch's double-dealing all the way home that he practically forgot about the woman beside him. Rather than looking for a hard-to-find spot, he double-parked in front of her doorway and saw her inside. It was only then he realized how he'd been neglecting her for most of the evening. He'd been so concerned about his sister's fragile emotional state that he hadn't been as attentive to Shelby as he would have been otherwise—maybe because she seemed so self-sufficient compared to Pippa.

Wanting to make up for the oversight, he asked, "Are you feeling better now that we found our first clue?"

She backed off from the door and leaned against the hallway wall, a trace of a smile playing over her lips as she lowered the zipper on her coat. "Tremendously."

"Maybe we should get together tomorrow night, too."

He stepped forward and placed a palm on the wall next to her head. She stirred slightly but didn't try to move away.

"For more detective work?"

Her eyes were smiling at him and he couldn't remember a more beautiful sight.

"If that's what it takes to convince you to see me. Sure."

"What else did you have in mind?"

"Christmas shopping?" he asked, half expecting her to refuse. Her apartment didn't have a single decoration on display and it was only three days before Christmas Eve.

"Sounds like fun."

Pleasantly surprised, he said, "I'll take a taxi to work, then. Bring your walking boots. We can shop our way home." With that he backed off, afraid that if he kissed her he wouldn't want to leave—and he had a lot of thinking to do. "I'd better get going before someone tows my car away."

Round cheeks flushed, she seemed disappointed. He leaned forward, kissed the tip of her snub nose, then left her apartment. Five minutes later he was a half mile away, pulling the Saab into the lot in back of his town house.

As he entered the open living area on the first floor, his thoughts were split into two camps, half of him wanting to concentrate on the mystery, the other half wanting to think about Shelby.

He'd enjoyed the thwarted dinner in the executive suite in spite of himself. And the few hours he'd spent with her on Saturday had been special. She'd made him forget everything else, especially unpleasantries. Anything might have happened if Lieutenant Jackson hadn't shown up on her doorstep. Remembering the way the homicide detective had managed to raise his protective hackles made Rand think of Dutch.

The sleaze.

He was beginning to think his late partner had been born corrupt. Not that buying out other stockholders was illegal. Immoral, maybe. But Dutch had proved himself to be immoral in so many ways.

Whenever he thought about the way the slime had turned his sister from an outgoing, positive person into an insecure emotional wreck, Rand was sickened by his own stupidity in not grasping Dutch's true nature sooner. He would have done something to protect Pippa. Well, someone else had recognized Dutch for what he really was and had done something about it. More and more, Rand was beginning to believe that whoever had killed Dutch had been justified.

He was only slightly bothered by the fact that the thought made him sound like he condoned murder.

Before going to bed, Rand went over the papers he took from the safe. If only he could use them to forward his own investigation.... It looked as if he'd have to put the clue on hold—and hope the police wouldn't do anything foolish, such as arrest the wrong person in the meantime. He put the folders aside. The documents seemed authentic enough, but it might be a good idea to let a lawyer take a look at them.

That's why, early the next morning, he found himself sequestered with Tucker Powers in the lawyer's office. Though the room was large, it was filled with monstrous mahogany furniture, outdated and slightly musty, a little like the lawyer himself.

"So, what do you think?" Rand asked as Tucker hemmed and hawed over the documents. "Do they look legal?"

"Mmm. I'd say so." Tucker closed the folder. "Can't find a fault."

Rand looked at him closely when he said, "You don't seem surprised."

"That these three sold out?" He shook his silver-dusted head. "They inherited the stock, never had any loyalty to the company."

"Then you didn't know about these sales?"

"Wheeling and dealing is common when stock is involved."

"Had you heard anything about Dutch planning a takeover of some kind?" Rand thought it a logical question since Tucker was one of the minor shareholders himself.

"Dutch was always trying something tricky. But now you won't have to worry about his game plan, will you?" Handing him the folders, Tucker gave Rand a piercing glance. "I mean, with Dutch dead and buried, he's no longer a threat to you or the store. Is he?"

Rand left, wondering if Tucker didn't suspect *him* of murdering his partner.

Entering his own office, decorated in Eurostyle black, white and chrome with blue accents, he also wondered if the police were making any headway with the case. One way to find out—*if* Lieutenant Jackson would tell him anything. He looked through his desk calendar for the page where he'd jotted down the Lieutenant's number. Finding it, he called the station and patiently waited to be put through.

"Jackson here."

"Lieutenant Jackson, this is Rand McNabb."

"Well, well, Mr. McNabb," Jackson said smoothly, sounding not a bit surprised. "What can I do for you?"

"Tell me you're making headway on the case. I'm concerned about my sister."

"And Miss Corbin."

A muscle twitched in Rand's cheek and he found it difficult to respond without letting hostility color his voice. "And Miss Corbin," he echoed. "Do you have any leads?"

"Nothing substantial. But we're working on it."

"What about the murder weapon?"

"Not a clue, I'm afraid."

"The Ziploc bag found near the body—what was in it?"

"At the moment, I really couldn't say."

"What *can* you tell me?" Rand asked, trying to tamp his irritation.

"That approximately one-third of all the women at the party wore red. About half of them had dark brown or black hair."

"That narrows it down to only fifteen or twenty women."

"We're trying, Mr. McNabb. We're trying."

"Let me know if you come to any conclusive guesses about anything, will you, Jackson?" Rand suggested caustically.

"I'll be sure to do that, McNabb."

Rand replaced the receiver and leaned back in his leather chair. Jackson hadn't been any more helpful than Tucker in providing new information. He wondered if the detective was incompetent—or merely holding out on him. He didn't have long to think about it before his secretary buzzed him.

He pressed a tab on the intercom. "Yes, Kristen."

"Miss Loretta Greenfield—the rep for Kuryokhin—is here to see you."

"I know who she is. Do we have an appointment?"

"No, sir, but she said you'd want to see her."

"Send her in."

Rand stood as his secretary opened the door for the sales rep whose cherry-red designer suit set off her bobbed dark hair and hugged her slender yet voluptuous figure. He took her hand, which she allowed to linger in his longer than necessary.

"Miss Greenfield."

"Loretta. And I intend to call you Rand. I like dealing with people on a first-name basis, don't you?"

She sat in the chair opposite him, crossing her legs so that the slit in her skirt parted, revealing a shiny cherry-tinted length of thigh.

Rand raised a brow at the purposeful display. "What can I do for you . . . Loretta?"

"I think we can do things for each other, now that Dutch is gone. I tried to talk to you at the wake, but you were too involved with your family, among others."

Had she been planning on conducting business at the wake? Nothing should surprise him anymore. Her dark eyes settled on him, their intense perusal making him uncomfortable. She was sizing him up, but for what?

"I'm here because I'd like to continue our relationship without an awkward break."

"Relationship? I didn't know we had one."

Her lips stretched into a smile that was at once wry and flirtatious. "We can discuss personal affairs after we take care of business."

The way she said it made him think she might have had an affair with Dutch. Hard to believe, but other beautiful, intelligent women had fallen under the bastard's spell; Pippa was a perfect example. Loretta opened her leather bag and pulled out a cigarette case, which she unlatched easily in spite of her long red nails.

"You don't mind if I smoke, do you?" she asked, the cigarette already out of the case.

"Go right ahead." Instincts on edge, Rand handed her an ashtray from the credenza behind him. "You're being so mysterious and I'm simply confused. Why don't you enlighten me."

"Then Dutch did keep our understanding to himself?"

Rand nodded and Loretta took the time to light her cigarette. She inhaled deeply, arching her long throat to let the smoke back out.

"I would like to continue the understanding with you."

"Go on."

"As I'm sure you know, your store has a Chicago-area exclusive with Kuryokhin. A very lucrative situation for everyone concerned. From time to time André gets restless, talks about getting more exposure—even if contracting with several stores would mean holding down prices because of the increased competition.''

''But you don't want him to do that,'' Rand guessed.

''It wouldn't be in everyone's best interests.'' She studied the ash she flicked into the tray. ''So far, I've made sure he's kept the status quo.''

''Exactly how have you managed that?''

Loretta took another drag on her cigarette and gave him a searing look that told him he was a fool if he couldn't figure it out. ''I have my ways.'' She exhaled and flashed him another smile.

He'd just bet she did, Rand thought. Now they were coming to the interesting part of the conversation. Knowing Dutch, he already had the deal figured out. Even so, he realized he was expected to prompt her.

''And what do you get out of this exclusive?''

''Ten percent of your profits on all André Kuryokhin designs.''

How the hell had Dutch hidden that kind of a loss from him? Rand wondered grimly. And why would he have been willing to let go of that kind of money in the first place?

''A kickback.''

Loretta's smile didn't even falter. ''I like to think of it as a finder's fee.''

''I'll bet you do.'' He leaned forward, elbows on his desk and spoke clearly so that she couldn't possibly misunderstand. ''Sorry, Loretta. No deal.''

Her lips stiffened. ''I can take our business elsewhere.''

''I'm nothing like Dutch. I don't make deals under the table. I won't be involved in anything unethical. Is that clear enough for you, Loretta?'' He could tell she was getting angrier with each word that left his lips. Her dark eyes were blazing daggers at him. ''So you feel free to take your business to whomever you wish...after our contract runs out, which doesn't happen until we get next fall's collection. In the meantime, I think Kuryokhin might be very interested to learn of our conversation. What do you think?"

"That you wouldn't dare."

"Don't press me, because if you force my hand, I certainly would."

With a vicious jab, Loretta smashed her cigarette against the glass ashtray. Clearly furious, she was practically going up in smoke herself. Rising, she banged the ashtray on the edge of the desk. He was surprised she didn't dump the contents in his lap.

"You'll be sorry," she stated through clenched teeth.

"I don't think so."

With a toss of her bobbed dark hair, she swung toward the exit and continued out of the room. As the door closed on her, the quick glimpse Rand got of her from behind reminded him of the morning he'd found Dutch. Loretta was slender, with dark hair, and it was obvious she wore red to good effect.

What if *she*'d been the woman he'd seen on the fire stairs rather than Shelby? Loretta had been dealing under the table with Dutch, a man who couldn't be trusted in any kind of partnership. Perhaps he'd agreed to get her into bed, and once he was tired of her he wasn't willing to pay out anymore. If he'd threatened to back out on their deal, or worse, go to André Kuryokhin himself....

Loretta Greenfield might have been furious and desperate enough to commit murder.

SHELBY'S MORNING, busy with meetings, settled into a fairly boring, paperwork afternoon, so that when the mail was delivered she viewed opening it as a welcome break from tedium. She sorted outside mail—the usual bills, solicitations and professional magazines—from the interoffice mail. Opening the latter first, she found a memo from the public-relations office on procedures for touring guests and an invitation to a New Year's Eve party from Joy Upton.

The third and last interoffice envelope aroused her curiosity. Rather than writing or printing her name on the envelope as was customary, someone had taken the time to type a label. And that someone had sealed the envelope rather than using the attached clips to secure it. She slit one end open with a mat knife, then pulled out a sheet of perforated computer paper. Unfolding it, she gasped as a single sentence printed on the page jumped out at her. "Keep your speculations about Dutch Vanleer's murder to yourself . . . or else."

No signature.

Her breath caught in her throat, and the warning dropped from her suddenly nerveless fingers. The murderer must have sent her the missive. Sucking in a breath of air, she looked behind her, as though the killer might be standing there to make sure she understood his intent.

No one.

Picking up the paper, she stared at the words as though they could give her a clue to the perpetrator's identity. She couldn't deny that this had been sent by someone who had access to the interoffice mail, and the dot-matrix lettering and ordinary computer paper could be found throughout Westbrook's offices. That the murderer knew who she was and had access to her on a daily basis was chilling.

And it was a detail she couldn't share with her ally in the investigation unless she wanted to tell Rand *everything*.

Covering up finding the body had been a mistake. If she'd called the police then, they could have protected her.

Instead, she'd made herself a target. Going to the police now would only serve to implicate her, especially considering she'd lied to Jackson about the dress.

Confused, unable to make sense of the warning—for she was sure that she had no clues to the killer's identity, had picked up nothing, had seen nothing—Shelby felt the same sense of terror at the unspoken threat as she had when she'd seen the wreath on her apartment door. That had been five nights before. Something must have happened since to make the killer nervous again.

But what?

Who knew she was working with Rand to track down the killer, other than the two of them?

And Pippa?

Even as she thought about it, Shelby denied the possibility. Pippa was barely able to take care of herself. She certainly was in no shape to harm anyone, especially not an ex-football player like her late husband.

Shelby ripped the note to shreds as though she could rid herself of the words inside. But they remained, indelibly burned into her memory.

ANOTHER SECRET BETWEEN THEM, Shelby thought, waiting for Rand to settle the score with the taxi driver. After walking through the North Dearborn and Rush Street areas with boutiques too pricey for her budget if not for his, they'd decided to take a cab to Clark Street. More reasonable shops dotted their neighborhood. Fortunately, she'd done most of her shopping before the Westbrook's Christmas party, so she only had a couple of items left to purchase—something for her sister Brenda and for her nephew Charlie.

"Let's go," Rand said, stuffing his single package into his coat pocket and wrapping an arm around her back. "Where should we start?"

"ARTifacts always has interesting things to look at."

"What about to buy?" he asked as they negotiated the slushy curb. "You're empty-handed."

"But I'm having fun looking. The company's exceptional."

"You should be in public relations."

"Does that mean you're willing to promote me?" she asked, stopping in front of the shop.

Rand raised a brow as he held open the door for her. "I didn't think you were the kind of girl who'd resort to consorting with the boss to further her career."

Wondering if he might actually be serious, Shelby stopped cold in the doorway. "Rand, I hope you don't believe that."

"Take that frown off your pretty face. I was only teasing." The tips of his mustache curled as he smiled at her.

Warmed all the way down to her toes, Shelby entered the store that was an outlet for local artists and headed for the jewelry counter. "My favorite display," she explained, looking over earrings designed by Anna. The artist used precious metals, usually a combination of hand-carved silver and fired copper. "Aren't these beautiful?" she asked, pointing to layered triangles with small semipolished crystals attached to their centers.

"For Brenda?"

"No, for me," Shelby whispered. "When they go on sale, after Christmas." She simply couldn't afford them at the moment. "Brenda would never wear something so creative. She's the tiny-pearl type. *Very* conservative. I don't understand how we can be related."

"Amazing," he agreed, shaking his head in mock seriousness.

Ignoring his goading, Shelby next headed for a glass display where a beautiful blue-and-green art deco vase caught her eye. The price was right and so was the item. Brenda would love it. About to announce her find, she caught sight of a glass Christmas ornament she couldn't resist—two white doves inside a red heart. She picked up both items.

"For Brenda?" Rand asked.

"The vase is for Brenda, the ornament for me. It's a tradition I started when I moved out on my own," she explained. "When I'm old and gray, I want to have wonderful memories when I decorate my Christmas tree, so I buy one special addition each year."

He feigned surprise. "The grinch is going to have a tree?"

"Stop that. I told you Christmas is my favorite holiday. I just haven't gotten around to buying a tree yet."

Actually, she hadn't decided that she was going to for sure until that moment. She'd been too caught up by depression and fear to give Christmas a whole lot of thought. Thank goodness for Rand. He'd restored some of her holiday spirit. To think that less than a week ago, he'd been pursuing her for a very different reason than he was now....

"How about tomorrow night?" he asked. "I'll help you pick out a tree and cart it home."

"An offer I can't refuse. Especially since I don't have a car."

He looked offended. "I thought it was the company you couldn't resist."

"That, too."

"Good." His expression softened. "So we'll buy the tree tomorrow night. Then we'll decorate on Christmas Eve.

You have to give the branches a chance to thaw out and spread,'' he said in justification.

That he wanted to spend three evenings in a row with her was not lost on Shelby. She smiled warmly. "Let me pay for these. Then we can discuss the tree."

But when they left the shop, heading for a nearby toy store, Rand unexpectedly turned their conversation to a more serious topic.

"I had Tucker check over the documents we found yesterday. According to him, they're all nice and legal."

Shelby's good cheer ran right out of her when she couldn't prevent herself from picturing the warning she'd received. "Was he surprised?"

"Hard to tell. Tucker was his usual vague self, kind of talking around the issue."

"So he didn't have anything significant to add."

"I'm afraid not. But I did have an interesting visit with Loretta Greenfield later this morning. It seems she and Dutch had an under-the-table deal that I didn't know about."

The statement pricked Shelby to attention. She stopped short and pulled Rand toward a display window, out of the way of other pedestrians. "What kind of deal?"

"She was getting a kickback for giving us an exclusive with André Kuryokhin. She mistakenly thought I would continue the deal she had with Dutch. I had the distinct feeling their understanding was personal in addition to monetary."

Incidents from the past several days linked together, forming a hazy clue that Shelby couldn't quite put her finger on. "This might be important." She lowered her voice. "It might have something to do with the reason for Dutch's murder."

Though he asked "How?" Shelby was pretty sure he'd had similar thoughts and merely wanted to hear her reasoning.

"I don't know, Rand. But yesterday, before you picked me up, I saw Iris leave the store. A woman was waiting for her in the alley. I could have sworn it was Loretta."

"I don't understand the connection."

"Don't you think they're unlikely friends—especially if they were both sleeping with Dutch? He may not have been the love of Iris's life as she tried to pretend, but she clearly was possessive of him. Also, Iris was wearing a Kuryokhin design that she couldn't have afforded on her salary. I figured Dutch must have bought it for her. But now that I think of it, I overheard Loretta and Iris talking about the new swim-wear line. Iris told her to save one of everything *as usual*."

"Where did you hear this?"

Hoping he wouldn't want her to be specific about *when* she heard the exchange, she admitted, "In the ladies' room. I was in one of the stalls when they came in together."

Rand laughed. "Great detective work. Spying on your fellow employees in the ladies' room. Did you get up on the seat so they couldn't see your feet?"

"Ho, ho, ho," she muttered, not seeing the humor in her admission. She'd been terrified at the time. But then, Rand couldn't know that, and she wasn't about to explain.

"Don't get angry," he pleaded. "I'm taking this seriously, I promise. I only wish I could figure out how it all ties together."

They stood thoughtfully for a moment before Shelby heard a bell and a male voice issuing Christmas greetings. Her pulse picked up and she looked around intently, half expecting to see a threatening-looking Santa Claus glowering at her. She sagged in relief when she spotted the black-garbed Salvation Army officer standing next to his red metal pot and collecting donations in front of the grocery store across the street.

"Is something wrong?"

"No. I, ah, was thinking that maybe I'd get my nephew's present tomorrow at lunchtime. Our conversation has kind of drained the Christmas spirit out of me."

"All right. We'll go to my place for a drink."

Unable to think of a reason to protest, Shelby let him take the lead. She wasn't sure her apartment was the safest place to take refuge, anyway. They made a pact to forget about the mystery for the remainder of the evening, and to concentrate on enjoying themselves. Rand managed to soothe her worries, at least for the moment, and while she couldn't forget about the warning totally, at least it receded to the dark corners of her mind. His town house was barely a ten-minute walk away.

Shelby hadn't thought about what Rand's place might look like, but she never would have expected decor so at odds with his office. The entryway floor was covered in bold brown-and-blue Mexican tiles, which were duplicated around the fireplace and in the kitchen. Two area rugs that might have been gigantic knit scarves—cream-and-beige wool peppered with darker tans and browns—decorated the wooden floor in the living room and dining nook. Desert colors predominant in the modern couches combined with the pale oak living-area wall units, kitchen cabinets and dining furniture to give the place a light, airy feel.

After taking her coat, Rand tried to talk Shelby into a glass of wine, but still wary of what had happened to her after consuming a single cup of punch, she insisted tea would do. He invited her to make herself comfortable, put her feet up and relax. Shelby didn't argue. She let herself be mesmerized by the lights of his Christmas tree. She was almost asleep by the time Rand readied the refreshments. The clink of pottery made her sit straight up with a start. She blinked, adjusting her eyes to the lowered light. He was carrying a tray holding a blue ceramic pot, two mugs and a bottle of cognac. An embarrassing and unhidable yawn escaped her lips.

"I thought you were in such good shape," Rand said, placing the tray on the coffee table. He sat next to her. "What's wrong? Can't take a little Christmas shopping?"

"I guess I'm pooped." He'd changed out of his regulation suit jacket, white shirt and tie to a rust-colored sweater with a V-neck that revealed silky-looking auburn chest hair. Realizing she was staring in fascination—and that he was amused—she said, "You have two mugs there. I thought you were going to have a glass of wine."

"Tea sounded good." He poured and handed a mug to her. "I hope you don't mind if I spike mine with brandy."

"Go ahead. I have nothing against brandy other than my own low tolerance to alcohol in general." She took a sip of the hot liquid as he prepared his mug. Warmth wound its way down into her stomach and she admitted, "I get giddy from a glass of wine." Another long sip and she placed the mug on the tray.

"What happens if you have two?" he asked with open interest. "Do you lose all your inhibitions?"

"Who said I was inhibited?"

"I suppose I could blame the rumor mill."

"Hmm. Good scapegoat," she said as he tasted his spiked drink, "but I'll bet you made that up. I would also bet you were never inhibited about anything. You probably came into the world with both fists flying." She'd show him just how inhibited she was, she thought, mischievously moving closer. "Did you get this fighting...or playing football?"

With a fingertip, Shelby lightly traced the faint scar that disappeared into his mustache. His involuntary shudder fed her self-satisfaction. He caught her wrist with his free hand and held it to his face, lightly brushing his mustache back and forth against her palm, making her shiver in return.

His eyes trapped hers so she couldn't look away. In their amber depths she read amusement, desire and something less definable. She closed her eyes against the last as he moved in to kiss her. The lingering taste of brandy on his tongue made her wonder if she could get drunk vicariously. Her head was floating, her heart beating at an irregular pace, her fingertips and toes were tingling. And her breasts went taut, her nipples hardening without being stroked.

He deepened the kiss and her senses reeled. Heat crept along her nerves, readying her for more intense exploration. He didn't touch her anywhere—except her hand and mouth—and yet she couldn't be more turned on if she were lying naked under him. Or could she? Deciding she might be uninhibited enough to want to find out, she was disappointed when he pulled back, keeping only her wrist comfortably trapped.

"Pippa."

"What?" she asked hazily.

"The scar."

Through the haze, she focused on his face. "Your sister scarred you?"

"Indirectly. When we were kids, there was an old abandoned building on our corner that cried to be explored. Our parents told us never to go there—and were very specific about the punishment we'd receive if we disobeyed. One of my brothers told me Pippa had taken a friend's dare to investigate the building by herself. She was only six at the time, and I was twelve. Of course I went after her. She got out just fine by herself, while I had an altercation with a rotting stairway. Dad really gave it to me after I got stitched up.''

''Didn't you tell him why you went into the building in the first place?''

''No, of course not. We kids had our own code of ethics.'' He set down the spiked tea. ''One of the tenets was that we did not snitch on one another.''

''But Pippa was in the wrong.''

''So was I for going to get her instead of telling my parents.''

Clearheaded now, Shelby wondered how far Rand would go to protect his sister. Cover up for murder? As quickly as the thought popped into her head, she shoved it away. He wasn't a criminal. He was merely a loving, concerned brother. It was one of the things she liked about him. His dynamic personality also appealed to her, not to mention the way he teased her when he was relaxed. And he wasn't bad to look at, either. The scar was a dashing, heroic-looking addition to an already handsome face.

''Want to touch it again?'' he murmured with a sensuous smile that made her stomach dance.

Shelby realized that she'd been staring again. ''What if I do?''

''I give you permission to explore all you want.''

Before she had the opportunity to take him up on his generous offer, the doorbell rang, making her jump and him let go of her wrist.

''Damn!'' he swore softly. ''Who could that be? Never mind, I won't answer it.''

But the bell shrilled over and over until she pushed him out of the couch. The romantic mood was broken, anyway.

Grumbling about unwanted interruptions, Rand made his way to the front entrance while Shelby smoothed back her hair and straightened her sweater. The sound of the door opening was followed by Rand's surprised "Althea!"

Shelby turned to look. Westbrook's former owner stood in the doorway, elegant as always, wrapped in a full-length mink the exact shade of her silvering blond hair. She was also outwardly distressed at having disturbed them. Her forehead creased as she looked from Rand to Shelby to Rand.

"I am so sorry, Randall, to have chosen such an awkward moment to disturb you."

He didn't deny it. "Now that you're here, come in." He held out his hands. "And let me take your coat."

Though she stepped across the threshold, Althea said, "That shan't be necessary. I shall only be a moment. I have a taxi waiting at the curb." She swept past the couch and perched at the edge of a chair opposite it. "Hello, Shelby."

"Miss Westbrook. You look lovely tonight. Out on the town celebrating the holidays?"

"I had an earlier dinner engagement."

A date? Shelby wondered. With Tucker Powers? Is that why the woman was eyeing her uneasily?

Rand reclaimed his seat next to Shelby. "What can I do for you, Althea?"

With a sigh, Althea turned her complete attention on him. "I've come on a delicate matter, Randall." She edged forward, her fingers fidgeting with a lace-edged handkerchief. "I know that I don't have the rights that I used to in the matter...but I was wondering...if it's no secret...what do you intend to do about Westbrook's?"

"Do? What do you mean?"

"Well, now that Bertram is deceased," she began, clearly reluctant to put voice to her fears, "I thought you might have changed your plans for the store."

"I don't want you to worry, Althea," Rand told her, his tone sincere. "I don't foresee any major changes in the near future. You know I'm committed to seeing Westbrook's regain every bit of prominence it once enjoyed. I won't let you down."

"I see." She digested the information without looking completely appeased, as if she didn't quite believe him. "I can't help worrying about all our futures. I'm sure you mean what you say now, but you may change your mind. Whatever happens, don't get greedy, Randall." She seemed to turn inward. Her brow creased and her voice lowered to a whisper. "I would hate to think that there might be more blood spilled because of something to do with Westbrook's."

"Blood..." Shelby echoed, horrified at the idea.

"Althea, do you know something you're not telling us?"

She blinked. "N-no, of course not." Pale blue eyes wide, still clutching her handkerchief, Althea rose and backed toward the door. "I was merely speaking in generalities. Some decisions can have far-reaching effects that we cannot even imagine. And because I think you are a fine young man, Randall, I would hope that you will choose wisely." She turned away from them. "I—I must go now."

"Althea, wait a minute!"

Rand's words fell on deaf ears. She whisked herself out the door. The wooden panel banged but didn't shut properly. He followed her to secure it, then watched out the window after her.

"What was that all about?" Shelby asked, trying to ignore the vision of Dutch that was determined to haunt her to ruin what was left of the night.

Rand wandered back to the couch but didn't sit. "You know as much as I do."

"It sounded like she was trying to warn you that if you're not careful you might end up..."

Shelby's voice trailed off as she and Rand stared at each other. She sensed he was as appalled as she by the implication: someone might be willing to kill again to get what he wanted.

## Chapter Eight

Althea's unexpected visit served not only to put a crimp in the evening but in Shelby's productivity at work the next day. Even while attending the ritual meetings, giving her staff instructions about cleaning out the prop storage area and delving into the mound of paperwork that inevitably replenished itself, she couldn't stop thinking about the danger in which Rand might have unwittingly placed himself by probing into his late partner's dirty laundry.

Perhaps it was the common element of danger they currently shared that brought her closer to Rand, that freed her tightly guarded emotions. No matter if she'd enjoyed being with him during the past week, Shelby faced the fact that she'd unconsciously put her deeper instincts on hold. She'd been too aware of her own secret and her own fears to let herself admit anything more than a basic attraction to the man. But her fears were for him now, as well as for herself, making her realize that she was starting to care for Rand—probably far more than was wise.

Anticipation at their going shopping for her Christmas tree increased with each hour that passed. She tried focusing on those plans—on being with Rand—rather than on some unknown menace that lurked in Westbrook's shadows. She had to take happiness while she could, for once

Rand learned that directly or not, she'd been lying to him, he'd probably want nothing more to do with her. She tried to justify not telling him everything by convincing herself it wouldn't matter; the revelation would introduce nothing new to help solve the crime.

Guilt lingered anyway, setting her on edge.

All morning, she mentally reviewed Althea's visit—wondering if the woman had warned Rand to be careful out of knowledge or instinct—and went over anything and everything she herself knew that might have some connection with the murder. She considered facing Iris again, if only she could figure out how to make the blonde talk about Dutch's plans.

No brilliant ideas.

Except....

She could talk to Edgar. He might know something. He'd been very concerned about Iris both at the wake and afterward. Iris might have confided in him. Shelby remembered the way he'd avoided talking to her the other night, however. She hoped Iris hadn't made Edgar distrust her for some reason. If so, he wouldn't be willing to give her the time of day.

Only one way to find out.

After purposely waiting until late afternoon before dropping by lingerie to show Joy Upton some preliminary sketches for the Valentine's windows, Shelby then took the opportunity to pass by the security-guard station after four o'clock. With the younger guards at their various posts around the store, Edgar sat alone, scanning the wall of video screens that revealed activity in every department.

Almost expecting him to rebuff her as he had the last time, she pasted a smile on her face, then wedged a shoulder against the doorjamb for support. "Hi, Edgar, all set for the holidays?"

To Shelby's surprise, he seemed pleased to see her. "Not bad, but you know how it is. Always gotta do some things last minute."

Her tense smile deepened into one more genuine. "I know what you mean. I don't even have my Christmas tree yet. Rand and I are getting it tonight."

His disapproval apparent in his suddenly narrowed gaze, he asked, "You going out with the boss?"

"Well, we've seen each other a few times."

"You be careful, Shelby. McNabb seems like an okay guy, but you never can tell. Them football players have game plans all mapped out when it comes to women. They sack you without worrying about the fouls they make."

It was the closest she'd ever heard the security guard come to being crude, yet his intentions were good. She was touched by his concern, although she was no Iris and Rand was no Dutch.

"Don't worry, Rand isn't anything like..." Edgar's open scowl made her leave the statement unfinished and gave Shelby the opportunity to lead the discussion in the right direction. "Look, I realize you're fond of Iris, but she's a big girl. She knew what she was getting into when she made the decision to see a married man."

"But my Cassie didn't," he said, throwing her off balance.

Responding to the combination of anger and helplessness she'd heard in his voice, she softly echoed, "Cassie?" When Edgar didn't reply, merely sat there glowering, his hands balled into fists, Shelby stepped into the small room, quietly closing the door behind her, the plan to get information about Iris forgotten. "Listen, I'll mind my own business if you want, but it sounds as if you could use someone to talk to."

He glowered. "I don't burden no one with my problems."

"I'm not 'no one.' I was hoping we were friends."

His balding head bobbed. "Sure we are. Don't mind me. Ever since my missus died last year... Well, I used to talk to Myra."

Shelby swallowed hard at the pain of loss and something else in his voice. "Tell me about Cassie."

"She's eighteen years old and the sweetest, most beautiful daughter God ever gave a man." He pulled out his wallet and opened it eagerly to show her a picture of a wide-eyed delicate beauty with long, tawny hair. "Am I telling the truth, or what?"

"She is very beautiful."

"And trusting. Too trusting. That son of a bitch ruined her."

Shelby's "Dutch" was a statement rather than a question.

"It started last September. Cassie's still in high school, for God's sake. She always came around to see her old man when she was out shopping with her friends. You know how high-school girls are—impressed by clothes and makeup." Edgar touched the picture of his daughter lovingly. "Dutch spotted her when she came to see me and decided he had to have her, I guess."

"But he was twice her age."

"Part of the appeal for a slime like that. Dutch turned Cassie's head by telling her she could be a model. He was going to introduce her to the right people. She knew I wanted her to go to college, so she didn't tell me nothing. He told her he was getting a divorce, too, so she saw him in secret."

Poor, misguided kid, Shelby thought. "Young women are often too romantic for their own good."

"Gullible, you mean. Dutch convinced Cassie she'd be perfect to represent some new cosmetics line he had an in on. What she was perfect for was something else entirely. She was an innocent, for God's sake. When he got bored with her, he abandoned her without so much as a 'See you around.' To think my Cassie's heart was broken over scum like that." He folded the wallet and replaced it in his pocket.

"I'm surprised she told you about it after all those months of secrecy."

"It's kind of hard to avoid your only parent forever when you're eighteen and three months pregnant," he said bitterly. "Otherwise I might never have known nothing."

*Pregnant.* The silence that followed was deafening. From his expression, the security guard regretted revealing his daughter's condition. Worse, a horrid realization crept along her nerves.

Edgar Siefert had a motive for murder.

"I hope my daughter's...condition...won't go any further than this room."

"No, of course not," Shelby said, as troubled by the promise as she had been by the bizarre thought. How could she keep this information from Rand?

"His unmarried daughter getting pregnant is not something a father is proud of. But I'll stand by my little girl. I'll see her through this."

"Cassie's lucky to have you."

"Yeah, but everything is changed now," he said sadly. "All my dreams for her... She had such a bright future, on the honor roll and everything. Now she'll have to quit high school her last semester. She won't graduate."

"She can finish school once the baby's born."

"I know. I tell her she can go to night school. She says she has to think of the baby, to get a job." His eyes swam with unshed tears. "She doesn't want to be a burden on me—as if my Cassie or any baby of hers could be a burden." He rubbed the bald spot on his head. "If only her mother were still alive, she'd know what to do."

Refusing to believe this tender-hearted man could have committed such a heinous crime as murder—not even to avenge his daughter's honor—Shelby knew question time was over. She didn't have the heart to probe him about anything that had to do with Dutch.

She patted Edgar's shoulder. "It'll be all right. Cassie's scared now, but she'll have plenty of time to think things through."

Her words were nothing but platitudes. She knew they both knew it, but he pretended to accept them as the truth. "Thanks, Shelby. You're a good listener. Maybe you can talk to Cassie sometime. Tell her how important an education is. I don't want her stuck in no dead-end job like I've had for twenty-five years. She could be something, you know?"

"Sure, I could talk to her," Shelby said, not believing for a minute that it would ever happen. Even if Edgar did mention her to his daughter, Cassie wouldn't welcome the interference of a stranger. "In the meantime, if you need a sympathetic ear, you know where I work."

"Yeah. Speaking of work, I gotta get back to mine."

"Me, too. I guess I'll be staying late to finish up the report I started." Shelby opened the door. "See you later."

"Shelby...thanks."

Already feeling guilty, she nodded. He wouldn't thank her if he knew she was going straight to Rand's office to report their conversation.

Of course, she told herself, she didn't have to repeat *everything*.

WONDERING WHERE THE STORY was leading, Rand continued listening in silence as Shelby recounted her conversation with Edgar.

"So Dutch promised Cassie he'd get her into modeling for some cosmetics line." She paced in front of his desk where he was perched on the edge. "The poor kid fell for it, hook, line and sinker. He seduced her and—"

"Abandoned her when he had his fill."

Shelby nodded and stopped in front of him. "I didn't tell you this so you'd think Edgar was the murderer. I mean, it crossed my mind, but I can't believe that man could harm anyone. I just figured I'd better tell you about it in case I'm reading the guy wrong. I don't want to be responsible for making a mistake that could mean more blood spilled."

Knowing she'd taken Althea's warning seriously—and that she was worried about *him*—Rand was warmed by her concern. "I can't see Edgar going in for violence, either," he admitted. "If every angry father decided to seek revenge because his eighteen-year-old daughter lost her virginity, we'd have a lot more murders than our police department could ever handle." He noticed she was fidgeting with the twisted leather on her belt. "That's all he told you, right?"

"Right," she said a little too quickly.

So why did he get the feeling there was more to the story? He sensed something was wrong, like the time Jackson asked Shelby about the color of her dress.

"Let's go back a minute to this modeling thing. Kind of odd Dutch would pick cosmetics, unless he said the first thing that came into his head because he was thinking of how furious Iris would be if she caught him cheating. Did Edgar mention the name of the line?"

"No. He said it was new. Do you think it's important? I figured Dutch was lying."

"Maybe. Maybe not. It just struck me that he wanted this kid, so he used a new cosmetics line as a lure. Iris, who sells cosmetics, intimated Dutch was ready to get out of Westbrook's and into something bigger. Could cosmetics be the link?"

"There's a tremendous amount of money spent on the industry," Shelby admitted. "I don't know, Rand. Are you sure you're not reaching?"

"Probably. I'd rather reach for something more satisfying." He pulled her into his arms and cradled her loosely against him. "Looking forward to this evening?"

"Maybe." Her twitching lips told him she was teasing. "Probably." They curved into a full Cupid's bow. "Yes."

"Good." He kissed those lips lightly while imagining how much more he could enjoy them later at her place. He'd make her smile so he could explore her dimples with the tip of his tongue as he'd been wanting to do for days. "I'm looking forward to being together, too."

"There's only one problem. There's this report I have to finish. It has to be turned in first thing in the morning."

"It's after four-thirty," he protested.

"My boss is a slave driver."

"He ought to be whipped."

"Later, using pine branches," she promised, laughing when he winced at the idea. "In the meantime, it'll only take me another half hour to finish that report. Then we can search the town for the perfect Christmas tree."

And tomorrow he would have to remember to buy her the perfect ornament to go on it, Rand thought, one that would remind her of him every time she saw it. He wanted her to think of him often.

"I suppose I could use that half hour to search Dutch's study again, to see if I can find the cosmetics connection," Rand said. "Tell you what. Pippa is here now, packing up the personal things in his office. I think she'd be ready to go anytime I said the word. I can drive with her. I'll give you the keys to my car, and when you finish your report, you can pick me up at her place."

"You trust me with your Saab?"

"It's only a car."

In spite of the doubts that had thrown them together in the first place, Rand thought he might trust her with anything, even with his heart.

"But you never asked me if I had a license."

"Do you?"

"Too late now." Hazel eyes full of mischief, she held out her hand. "Keys, please."

Rand rummaged through his pocket and pulled out keys and the time card for the garage. He placed them in her palm and reached for his wallet. "It's parked on the lower level of Grant Park Garage North. I wrote down the location on the ticket. This should cover the freight," he said, extracting a bill from his wallet and handing it to her. "And this should hold me until later."

Though he kissed her more fully than he had before, Rand held himself in check. He didn't want to be too distracted when he rummaged through Dutch's things. Even so, when he released her his pulse was beating a little quicker than before.

"I'll rush through that report," she promised. "See you soon."

Following her into the reception area where they parted, Rand headed for the office in the corner opposite his, passing Tucker as he went. Pippa sat behind Dutch's desk and the two boxes she'd filled with her late husband's personal effects. She was staring at a framed photograph of Dutch and herself taken on their honeymoon.

"Hi, Brat, ready to call it a day?"

She blinked and started. "As a matter of fact I was about to leave. I didn't get everything."

"I know how difficult this is. I told you I would do it for you."

Pippa stood and added the picture to one of the boxes. "As much as you would like to, big brother, you can't protect me from life."

"Can I hitch a ride to your place instead?"

"Sure. What's up?"

"I'll tell you in the car," he said. "Shelby has the keys to mine. She'll pick me up later."

Pippa nodded in understanding. She slipped into her coat, and each carrying one of the boxes, they headed down to her car. They were on Lake Shore Drive before she asked him to explain what was going on.

Not wanting to tell his sister about another of her husband's infidelities, Rand merely said, "I have reason to believe Dutch was thinking of investing in a new cosmetics line."

Pippa's hands tightened on the wheel, making him figure she was probably thinking about Iris.

"You want to take another look at his papers?"

"Right."

Her voice strained, she said, "I don't remember seeing anything about cosmetics."

"Neither do I, but it won't hurt to look again."

But once they arrived, they spent the better part of a quarter of an hour going through the files and desk to no avail. All they'd managed to do was make more of a mess. Rand was willing to admit defeat. He really had been reaching.

"If you're done with these," Pippa said, picking up a stack of folders from the desk, "I'll put them away."

"Let me take those."

"I can manage."

But Rand already had his hands on them. Several slid off the top of the stack and went flying onto the desk, knocking over a cylindrical holder containing pens and pencils.

"Big help you are," she complained.

"What in the world is that?"

"What?"

A tiny plastic bag with a Ziploc lay on top of the pencils. She picked it up and turned it over in her hand, then started to stick it back into the pencil holder.

"Wait a minute. Let me see that." Rand set down the folders and took the bag from her. "It's like the one they found near Dutch's body, only this one's not empty."

"Drugs?"

"Maybe. Or chemicals—a secret ingredient for a new cosmetics line."

"Brother, what an imagination." Pippa reached to take the packet from him. "Too bad we'll never know."

Rand held it away from her. "Who says? I'll get this tested and let the chemist tell us. Who knows what kind of information this might give us."

"Who knows," Pippa echoed.


SHELBY CURSED the slow-responding elevator and pressed the call button for the third time. This delay was ridiculous. She'd been waiting for what must have been five minutes, and she'd started out late to begin with. Completing the report had taken her longer than she'd expected and she was the last employee to leave the floor. She was anxious to join Rand, as much to learn if he'd found anything new as to be with him. The sooner the murderer was caught, the sooner she'd start sleeping normally at night.

Just as she'd made up her mind to use the fire stairs, a loud *ding* and the whoosh of doors signaled the elevator's arrival. She got into the empty car and pressed the button for the main floor, but someone on seven, the other employee floor, had called it as well. The elevator stopped on seven with its usual light bounce.

When the doors opened, Shelby's eyes widened in alarm at the sight of Santa Claus in full regalia, his padded girth blocking the opening. Her pulse speeded up and she was filled with an urgent desire to rush him and start screaming for help. Instead, she stood frozen to the spot, unable to move her legs. Too late. Eyes downcast, Santa nodded to her, stepped into the car and immediately faced forward as the doors swished closed.

Something familiar about the man behind the beard and mustache nagged at her, but Shelby wasn't about to ask him to turn around so she could get a better look. Instead, she huddled against the wall at the back of the car and filled her lungs with air in case she had to scream. The pressure in her chest and the buzzing in her ears alarmed her. She would not hyperventilate, nor would she faint! She gripped the handles of her shopping bag with her nephew Charlie's present like a weapon.

Descending took an eternity, and all kinds of wild thoughts distorted her sense of reality. The scenario of finding Dutch with a hole in his chest had never been quite so vivid in her mind. The elevator stopped at the main floor without incident. She was sweaty and weak-kneed before the doors opened and Santa ambled out of the car. Shoppers surged between them and by the time she forced her legs to take her forward, there was no sign of jolly old St. Nick.

Cautiously heading for the employee entrance, she noticed the abandoned cosmetics-promotion display that called for ''Santa'' to give away free samples of an expensive new perfume. The adrenaline swooped right out of her. She'd never felt so idiotic in her life.

No wonder the guy had looked familiar. He'd been working at the store since Monday.

Shelby wondered what the poor man would have done if she had pushed by him and started screaming as instinct had bade her do. She might have given him a heart attack, and he would never have returned to his station from what probably had been an innocent coffee break.

Grimacing at her own foolishness, Shelby took a deep breath and continued on toward the exit. When she passed the security office, she was surprised to see one of the young guards rather than Edgar sitting at the bank of monitors. He was probably on a coffee break as well. She waved to the guard and left the store, her spirits restored.

She had to stop letting her imagination run away with her. At this time of year, Santas were everywhere. Each major store on State Street had at least one in its toy department, if not another for promotions. Mannequin Santas decorated display windows and live Santas stood on street corners, collecting for the poor. She acknowledged one at the corner across from Westbrook's by dropping a couple of dollars into his bucket. The donation wasn't large, but it would help feed some homeless soul during the holidays.

"Merry Christmas, ma'am," the bearded wonder in red said heartily.

She smiled and winked. "Merry Christmas, Santa."

Cheerfully heading north down State Street, Shelby steered her thoughts to Rand. Rather than dwelling on what he might have found, she thought about him and the time they were already planning on spending together that evening and next. She also wondered what kind of gift would be appropriate to give to a man whom she wanted to get to know better. She couldn't imagine sharing Christmas Eve with Rand decorating her tree without giving him something.

When she stopped to admire a window display that caught her eye and saw the reflection of Santa Claus a few yards behind, she told herself to keep a lid on her suspicions. Still, using the glass, she watched him wander to the curbside bus stop and check the sign.

Shaking her head at her own silliness, Shelby went on.

But so did Santa.

Without thinking about it, Shelby impulsively turned the corner and headed east a block sooner than she would have. She glanced back over her shoulder every few seconds.

Less than a half a minute later, Santa turned the corner as well.

Heart speeding up along with her feet, she crossed the slush-laden alleyway, still trying to convince herself this was a coincidence. Santa was not following her. She turned north on Wabash, hoping he would go straight.

Only he didn't.

Now she fought panic. Santa was gaining on her. Squinting, she tried to make out the features behind the disguise, an impossible feat at this distance with only the street and store lights reflecting off his blur of a white face.

She clutched her shoulder bag and package and began to jog, jaywalking under the elevated train structure, dodging cars, one of which screeched to a halt, horn blaring. The angry driver rolled down his window and screamed something after her. Sure his words were a curse, she couldn't make them out. All she could hear was the thundering train on the tracks overhead whose raucous noise was nearly obliterated by the rushing sound of fear inside her head.

Shelby whipped around the corner at Randolph and jogged toward the underground garage entrance on Michigan Avenue. Fortunately she'd slipped the keys, ticket and money into her coat pocket. She sped down the stairs while pulling out the items and praying she wouldn't have to wait in line. Luck was with her. Though rush hour wasn't quite over, the workers who'd planned on going straight home must have done so. The rest must be shopping.

Handing the man behind the glass her ticket and money, Shelby checked the outside doors. She heard the footsteps before seeing the red-and-white suit turning the corner. She grabbed her receipt with the hand holding the keys and ran for the stairs.

"Hey, wait a minute, lady! You forgot your change!"

Shelby couldn't care less about losing a few bucks as she rushed down to the lower level, only then realizing she'd forgotten to check the ticket for the Saab's location. *Think!* she ordered herself. She'd seen the number. All she had to do was visualize it.

Boot heels clicking hollowly along the stairwell propelled her forward and scattered her concentration. Twenty-something. She remembered that much if she couldn't remember the section. She'd have to scour the garage's length, approximately one block to the north, three to the south. For once glad that the interior was dimly lit, she ran east on tiptoe to the car entrance-exit aisle where she could hide behind pillars while trying to spot the Saab.

She arrived at the aisle not a second too soon, whipping behind a post as the sound of hurrying feet echoed along the low ceiling . . . and stopped.

Trying to pant in silence, for all the breath seemed to have been sucked from her lungs, Shelby prayed he wouldn't come her way. Her heart fluttered as the footsteps began anew, but they headed directly south. Thank heavens! She'd search the block to the north, then.

Oh, so quietly, she moved from her safe place, confident that the cement wall separating two bays of cars would hide her while she searched. Ears attuned to every sound, she was constantly aware of the fading footsteps as she crept from post to post, scanning the area around her. No gray Saab. Damn! It didn't take long for her to realize she was looking in the wrong location.

And the footsteps were clearer now. Santa was heading this way, coming down the aisle she'd just taken!

Frantically looking for a place to hide, Shelby chose an area currently under construction where reinforcement pillars were being replaced. She moved in a crouch, using parked cars to shield her. The echo of his boots told her he was getting closer.

She dropped to her knees and crawled under one of the wooden horses blocking the construction area, briefly panicking when the package caught. If she left it as she was tempted to do, he'd surely find it—and her. She stopped and carefully backed out a few inches so she could pull the package through. Then she was past the barrier and heading into an unlit cul-de-sac of construction materials and barriers, an area fraught with danger.

If she misstepped, he'd hear her.

If he found her, she'd have no escape.

She silently crept into the dark, placing each foot carefully to make sure she was on solid ground before shifting her weight. Twice her caution helped her avoid kicking loose debris. Finally swallowed by darkness, she stopped and, crouching, hugged a wall of cement bags. Aching with the strain of waiting, she listened to the footsteps moving in one direction, stopping, then coming closer. Stunned and dry-eyed, she waited to meet her fate.

Who was he and what did he want? To kill her?

She'd never known such fear.

A nudging at her ankle followed by a scurrying sound almost broke her composure completely. As it was, she dropped her keys. They landed with a soft clunk. More scurrying sounds. A rat, and a big one! Her stomach began to quake. She'd always hated rats. Feared them. She'd almost rather face Santa Claus.

Almost.

The footsteps stopped, this time mere yards away. From where she crouched, she could see only his legs—dull red pants ending in shiny black boots. The legs turned, the toes pointing toward her hiding place. Then, with a flurry of movement that made her scream inside her head, a large rat streaked out of the darkness and scurried between her pursuer's feet, making them do a strange, almost laughable tap dance.

A soft, sexless curse echoed through her dungeon, but Shelby couldn't recognize the sound.

Another curse, even softer, and the legs began moving again, out of sight. Heat washed through Shelby and she felt as if she would suffocate if she didn't get out of there.

She forced herself to wait.

The footsteps receded and finally disappeared.

Hand shaking, she reached down for her keys, praying she wouldn't encounter another rat. If there were other rodents lurking nearby, they apparently had no more desire to socialize with her than she did with them. They didn't make themselves known. She found her keys.

She waited some more, until she was sure.

Cautiously, she crept from her hiding place, gripping her package and shoulder bag as though to let go of them would mean she herself would fall apart. Free of the construction area, she decided to request escort service to her car. No matter that she still didn't know where the thing was . . . maybe they could find the ticket with the location printed on it.

Her mind was dragging behind her feet as she passed into the next bay and headed for the stairwell. She was barely a yard from the doorway when out popped a red-suited Santa Claus.

Shelby screamed and swung her package.

"Hey, lady, what's your problem?" Santa asked, raising dark-skinned hands to protect his face. "Don't you like Christmas or is it me?"

Black. This Santa was black; the one chasing her had been white. She remembered the whiteness of his face under the streetlights. She started laughing. The Santa backed away, staring at her as if she were crazy.

"I'm sorry," she said. "Please, I didn't mean to..." She laughed through the flood of tears that burst through the dam she'd built inside herself while huddling in the dark. "I thought you were someone else."

His dark eyes narrowed in concern. "Are you all right? You want me to call for help?"

"Someone was following me," she gasped out in the midst of her laughter and tears. "I was so frightened." She tried to stop—she really did—but she couldn't. "I couldn't find my car."

Though he was looking at her as if she were some kind of a strange creature, he slowly said, "It's okay now, right? Do you want me to help you find your car?"

Finally feeling the momentary hysterics drain out of her, she said "Yes," followed by a hiccup. The laughter stilled and she wiped at the tears still flooding her face. "Thank you. I'm sorry. It was such an awful experience."

"Maybe we'd better report this . . ."

Reports meant police involvement. "No. I'll do that later. My car. Please. You said you'd help me find it."

"Where is it?"

She shrugged helplessly and waved her hand. "Back there somewhere."

Shaking his head, he said, "Well, let's get started."

The search didn't take long. Ironically, the car was in the next bay south, mere yards from where she'd first hidden from her stalker. Shelby felt like throwing herself on the hood and hugging the vehicle, but she figured the man didn't need proof that she was crazy, so she restrained herself.

"Are you sure you'll be all right?" he asked when she got behind the wheel.

How could she be all right when someone was after her because she'd found a dead body in an incident she couldn't report? "I can drive."

Nodding, he backed off, refusing her offer of a reward for his deed. In the end it was a good thing he hadn't taken her money; she'd lost her receipt and had to pay for parking a second time—the maximum rate.

All the way to Pippa's, Shelby kept herself calm, kept her attention on the road. The other could wait until later, when she was alone with Rand. She had to tell him about this new horror. She knew that, even if she hadn't the faintest idea how she was going to explain it.

But when she arrived at the house on Hawthorn, neither he nor his sister was there. A nervous Pippa arrived almost immediately, saying Rand had to run out on an errand and would return any minute. Shelby smiled and covered her churning emotions as she followed the redhead into the house.

She thought she'd go out of her mind, sitting and waiting and thinking...and saying nothing about what she'd bottled up inside herself. Her off mood somehow spread to Pippa. They sat in silence staring at each other while "any minute" turned out to be almost ten.

"Where were you?" Shelby demanded when Rand entered Pippa's living room.

Her sharp question made brother and sister look at her oddly as though they didn't recognize her.

"Sorry I wasn't here," he apologized. "But don't worry. We still have plenty of time to get your Christmas tree."

"I just want to go home," she said, already putting on her coat. She glanced in the mirror as she zipped it up. She was as white as the trim on Santa's costume. "Forget the tree."

"I don't understand." Rand gave her a concerned look. "Never mind. We'll talk about it in the car."

"Goodbye, Pippa," she mumbled. "Sorry I was such rotten company."

Shelby swept out of the house and down the steps, anxiety level immediately increasing when she heard the soft murmur of voices behind her. What in the world were they discussing now? Couldn't Rand see she had to get home? She climbed into the passenger seat and counted the seconds until he slid behind the wheel.

He waited until they were on their way before saying, "All right. What's wrong? If you're angry because I kept you waiting, I apologize. But I promise—"

"He knows."

Shelby was staring straight ahead, trying to breathe normally, but she was aware of Rand glancing her way when he asked, "Who knows what?"

"The murderer knows I'm looking for him," she said softly. "That's got to be it. He followed me tonight, from the store to the garage, dressed in a Santa Claus suit. I thought he was going to kill me."

"What?" Rand stomped on the brakes and with a screech of tires pulled the car to the curb. "Shelby, tell me everything from the beginning."

Calmly, she recounted the terror-filled hide-and-seek chase as clearly as she remembered it. Part of her was afraid Rand wouldn't believe her without the connection—without her revealing that she was the one who'd found Dutch's body in the crimson-covered Santa Claus suit. Though she pretended the murderer was after her because of their current activities, she knew better: the murderer was after *her* because of what he thought *she* knew. Sympathetic to her every word, Rand drew her into his arms and comforted her.

"You're safe now."

"But for how long?" she whispered. "We can't tell the police or they'll know we're interfering. They already suspect me."

"And me," he added bitterly. "Well, not me directly, but Pippa. They think I'm covering up for her. Look, Shelby, I think whoever was in the Santa suit was trying to scare you, not kill you. Otherwise, why use such theatrics instead of just getting the job done efficiently?"

She moaned. Rand tightened his embrace, making her feel protected. Too bad she couldn't stay in his arms forever.

"Maybe we ought to cool it for a while," Rand continued. "Put off our investigation until next week. Frank Hatcher will be back by then. Hopefully he'll provide the information we need as far as the stock deal is concerned. If we're really lucky, it'll be enough to go to the police."

"And until then, what do we do?" she asked.

"Be very, very careful."

Though Shelby nodded her agreement, deep down she knew that wouldn't be nearly enough to keep herself alive if the murderer seriously thought she knew who he was.

## Chapter Nine

The next morning found Shelby calmer, if not in a holiday mood. She hadn't slept much or well. Rand had volunteered to stay with her, to sleep on the couch, but she'd refused to let him, so he'd insisted on remaining until she fell asleep. She'd agreed to that and had given him a spare set of keys so he could dead-bolt the door on his way out. She wondered when he'd finally left. Sometime in the early-morning hours, no doubt.

Wandering into her living room, she stared at the wall lined with boxes of decorations she'd finally brought up from her basement locker the morning before. How could she have forgotten what day it was?

Christmas Eve. Cause for joy and celebration. Would it always be a crimson holiday to her, fraught with reminders of death and fear? She hoped not. She used to like Christmas. Maybe she would again someday.

Until then, she could pretend....

Rand had insisted they not change their plans for that evening. At least finding and decorating a tree would give her something to do, and being with Rand something pleasurable to look forward to.

Shelby dressed quickly, not stopping to admire the new outfit she'd bought for the holiday season—a thigh-length holly-green shirt of butter-soft suede with matching knee-high boots and tight knit pants. Hardly in a festive mood, she didn't bother with jewelry.

When she left the apartment building a short while later, her eyes roamed in every direction for anything out of the ordinary. But if danger lurked nearby, it cleverly hid itself from her. All she saw were people, most of them rushing to work like herself, a few with no place to go.

Sheltered from the cold wind, a bag lady sat on a stoop warming herself with a cup of coffee—a sight all too common in this particular high-rent district because of its proximity to Lincoln Park, where many of the city's homeless spent their nights. The woman was wearing layers of fairly clean, almost new clothing. The rest of her possessions were neatly stacked in a shopping cart. A bag lady of some affluence, Shelby thought wryly.

Still, no one should have to huddle in a doorway on Christmas Eve, or beg or pick through garbage cans for a holiday dinner. As she approached the woman, Shelby pulled out her wallet and removed the forty dollars she would have used to buy her Christmas tree.

"Find yourself a warm place to stay tonight." She held out the money. "And treat yourself to a real meal."

Tears filled the blue eyes that looked up at her in disbelief as the woman hesitantly took the two bills from her. "Merry Christmas, and bless you, child."

*Child.* The saddest thing was that the woman wasn't all that much older than she, Shelby realized. Poverty had a way of aging the spirit as well as the body.

"Merry Christmas," she mumbled, sprinting for her bus that was pulling up to the corner.

She climbed aboard, feeling better than she had when she'd left home until she realized that decorating the tree was to have been the center of her and Rand's evening.

Though she wasn't looking forward to spending Christmas Eve alone, she might as well cancel the date.

Merry Christmas, indeed.

Totally dispirited by the time she got off the bus, Shelby entered Westbrook's a half hour late, her head in a fog, trying to ignore the aura of holiday excitement around her. Even though the salespeople had to work a full day that would be more harried than usual, they were in good humor.

"Where's your holiday spirit?" demanded Joy, who'd beat her into the store by a few seconds.

"I didn't buy any this year."

The manager of lingerie slowed down so they could walk together to the elevators. "Maybe Santa will bring you some tonight," Joy said with a wink.

If Santa brought her anything, it would be more trouble, Shelby thought, frowning at her fellow employee. About to say she had a headache so Joy would leave her alone, she clenched her teeth against the lie when she noted the clerks and office workers entering the elevators. Many of them carried small wrapped presents or boxes of treats—cookies, fruitcake, candy. Joy immediately let Shelby off the hook by trading recipes with one of the other women.

The elevator couldn't get to eight fast enough as far as Shelby was concerned. Thank God she wasn't alone in the car as she had been the night before....

To her surprise, as she exited with the remaining employees, most of whom headed for the locker room, she spotted Rand coming from her office. His worried expression eased immediately upon seeing her. His stride lengthened and he pulled her to one side of the hall.

"I was beginning to wonder if I should have stayed the night, after all," he said in a low voice.

"So you could be my alarm clock?"

Ignoring her attempt at humor, he studied her face with an intensity that unnerved her. "I'm relieved you're all right. You are, aren't you?"

She nodded and kept her voice down in case someone should pass them. "As good as can be expected, considering the circumstances. Listen, Rand, about tonight..."

His expression softened. "I'm looking forward to it."

"I won't be able to buy that tree, after all."

"Those tree places stay open late in hopes of making last-minute sales."

"No, that's not it." Uncomfortable at having to explain, she merely said, "The tree kind of got shot off my budget."

"Sounds like a grinch trick to me."

"Come on. You know how it is at holiday time—loads of unexpected expenses."

His expression was disbelieving. "What did you do between last night and this morning? Give your money away?" Disbelief changed to amazement when, unable to deny it, she shifted uncomfortably. "You did, didn't you?"

"It's not a big deal," she said defensively.

"Yes, it is."

"Except that since I won't have a tree, there's no sense in your coming over."

"Wait a minute. Let me get this straight. The real problem is that you don't want to see me, right?"

"No, that's not true."

"Then our date is on. We'll find something to decorate," he continued smoothly, giving her no chance to object. "I remember seeing a couple of plants around the place. And don't you have one of those coat trees somewhere?"

"Afraid not," she said, laughing.

"So we'll improvise. You once told me creative people like to experiment," he reminded her. "Besides, the most important thing is that we'll be together."

How could she argue with that?—not that she wanted to. Her pulse thudded through her, bringing her back to life. Maybe the holiday wouldn't be a total disaster, after all. "I'm convinced. What time?"

"We could leave here together at four."

"I don't know. If my boss finds out I not only came in late but left early..."

"Let's chance it."

Smiling, Shelby nodded. Rand took a quick look around at the empty hall, then kissed her lightly. "See you later."

"Pick me up at my place," she said, indicating her office.

For the first time since she'd started at Westbrook's, she was last into her department. Not that her staff was working—Dana was turning up Christmas music on a portable cassette player, while Zeke was begging Harriet for another Christmas cookie. They looked like a bunch of happy kids and Shelby didn't have the heart to ruin their day and have them think of her as a grinch.

Her "Merry Christmas" commanded their immediate attention.

Dana and Harriet looked at each other uncertainly, but Zeke merely stuffed the cookie into his mouth. "Merry Christmas, chief."

"Wait a minute," Shelby protested, unable to pass up the opportunity to tease him. "Christmas isn't your holiday."

"Aw, now you went and ruined it. These two didn't know I was Jewish. Maybe they would have given me a present."

"Right." Harriet poked him in the ribs with her elbow and held out the tin of homemade cookies to Shelby. "Have some."

"Thanks, Harriet." Shelby took two. "Listen, if I've been grouchy this past week . . ."

"You don't have to explain," Dana murmured. "We understand."

They didn't, not really—how could they without having to go through the horror of it all themselves?—but Shelby merely continued smiling and bit into one of the cookies. "Mmm, this is wonderful."

"I made them last night," Harriet said. "They have candied cherries, dates, pecans, almonds, walnuts, chocolate chips—"

"And almost no calories, right?"

They all laughed at that. The mood pervaded the office throughout the morning, with workers and executives alike stopping by with good wishes. Even Althea Westbrook popped in for a minute. Thankful for the invention of plastic money, Shelby left at lunchtime to shop armed with her credit cards. She might not have the cash for a tree, but she could afford to charge a few things. Feeling the need to be free of her workplace and the bad vibes of the past week, she left Westbrook's to brave the hordes of by now desperate last-minute shoppers, uncaring that she managed to take a two-hour lunch.

After finding a present for Rand, she'd stopped in a neighboring department store that had a gourmet deli where she'd bought a selection of mouthwatering treats they could share that evening. Her final purchase had been a box of imported chocolates with real liqueur centers. Let the members of her staff get tipsy on them that afternoon if they wanted to. Christmas Eve came only once a year.

But her designers and assistant were nowhere to be seen when, gift of chocolates in hand, she reentered her department humming the same Christmas carol that was blaring from Dana's portable cassette player. Disappointed, she set the candy down on a table that they all used for sorting accessories when changing the windows. She checked the wall clock. Two-thirty. Her staff must have been invited to share coffee and homemade goodies with another department. Undoubtedly they'd be back any minute.

Still humming, Shelby shrugged out of her coat, picked up her shopping bag and entered her own work area. Who felt like working on Christmas Eve—especially when there was a beautifully gift-wrapped package sitting in the middle of her desk?

"What in the world...?"

She set her bag down and hung her coat on a peg, her gaze never leaving the red foil package held together with silver-edged green ribbon. No card to announce the gift giver. If this was an unexpected present from the members of her staff, she was certainly glad she'd gotten them the box of candy. She eyed the sprig of mistletoe tied to the bow, a romantic touch. If the gift was from Rand, he should have waited to give it to her until that evening.

She could set it aside until later.

Then again...

Despising her lack of willpower, Shelby slid into her seat and rolled the chair up to her desk. She began turning the present in her hands, wondering if she could guess what was inside. Though the package was approximately the size of a shoe box, its contents seemed to weigh more than an ordinary pair of women's shoes. She shook the gift carefully, but that gave her no clues. Nothing slipped around inside. Nothing rattled. What could it be?

The only way to find out would be to open the thing, she told herself logically.

Without hesitating a second more, she carefully freed the mistletoe and set the greenery aside, then loosened and removed the ribbon without using scissors. That left only the foil. She carefully pried the pretty covering loose, drawing out the pleasure of the task, savoring the moment. Free of the wrapping, the white box with green script announced its origins—Westbrook's major competitor on State Street.

Laughter practically bubbling from her lips, she lifted the lid, tapping her foot to "Santa Claus Is Coming to Town."

White tissue was held together by a distinctive gold seal with the store's monogram, next to which lay a small white envelope that she picked up. The greeting on the card inside gave her no clue as to the sender. In an unfamiliar hand were three printed words: "Get the message?"

Message? About what? Now really curious, she tore the seal away, unfolded the paper and removed the wad pressing against the item beneath.

"Aah!"

The strangled sound escaping her lips was accompanied by a frantic movement that sent her sprawling away from her desk and onto the floor with a crash. Heart pounding, Shelby untangled her legs from the chair and gripped its frame to lift herself. Its wheels were still spinning as fast as her stomach.

A foot-long rat in a plastic bag now spilled from the box onto her desk.

She closed her eyes momentarily against the grotesque sight, then opened them with new determination.

"He sees you when you're sleeping," the cassette player blared. "He knows when you're awake...."

"I get the message," she whispered, righting her chair with a determined clatter. Then louder, "I get the message!"

If she ratted on the murderer, she'd end up like the creature in plastic.

Dead.

And the song warned her that she should be good for goodness' sake!

Something in her snapped.

"But I don't know anything!" she shouted, her strained voice competing with the Christmas music blaring from the other side of the divider.

Every person had her limits and she'd just been pushed to the edge of hers. Anger growing in strength against fear, she rose and turned in place, as if to face the culprit. Her hands drew into tight fists at her sides.

"Do you hear me, whoever you are, you son of a bitch? I don't know anything!"

But she would, Shelby vowed, she would. If she hadn't been determined before, she was now. She was already in the corner with no escape. The only thing left to her was to come out fighting.

Gritting her teeth, she picked up the plastic bag and shoved it back into the box. The paper she'd removed so carefully only a minute ago was next. She wadded it into a ball and shoved it and the ribbon and the damned mistletoe on top of the dead rat. After turning off the cursed music, she marched down the hall to trash the grisly offering in one of the janitors' barrels that always seemed to be sitting around. She didn't care if anyone found the rat. Let them make of it what they would.

By the time she returned to the office, Shelby had smothered her seething emotions with a manufactured calm. Good thing, too. Zeke and Dana and Harriet had returned and were sampling the chocolates. They didn't deserve to have their holiday ruined.

Neither did she.

"Hey, chief, these are great!" Zeke enthused.

Forcefully tucking away the incident in a remote part of her conscious mind, Shelby smiled. "I'm glad you like them."

"Aren't you going to have one?" Dana asked, picking up her box of audiocassettes and browsing through them.

"I'm saving my appetite for later." She was looking forward to her evening with Rand, Shelby thought. No one and nothing was going to ruin that! "Speaking of appetites, where did the three of you go? To sample more cookies?"

Harriet nodded. "Among other things. We were all invited at the last minute. Didn't you find the note I left, asking you to join us?"

"No," Shelby said calmly. Someone had removed the note. Undoubtedly the same person who had left the package. But she wasn't going to think about that now. She was going to enjoy the holiday. "Invited where?"

"To interior display," Dana explained, mentioning the other group of designers responsible for the various displays inside the store. She popped open the cassette player.

Zeke licked melted chocolate off his fingers. "They might have something left if you want to go over there."

"After you demolished the place?" Shelby asked, laughing. "I doubt I'd find a crumb."

"Hey, whose cassette?" Her expression questioning, Dana was staring at the one she'd just taken from the player.

"Not mine," Zeke said.

"Nor mine," Harriet added.

Remembering the tune that had been playing when she'd opened her package earlier, Shelby smiled tightly. "Maybe Santa Claus left it for you."

RAND WALKED THROUGH the empty reception area of the executive suite, smiling when he heard the music and laughter coming from the conference room. Anyone who hadn't taken the day off was probably in there loading up on calories.

He entered his office. Everything was set for that evening, he thought with satisfaction, spying the wicker picnic basket sitting on his desk. He'd had the restaurant prepare a gourmet feast for two. Having just returned from completing the task that had taken him most of the afternoon, he'd come in to pick up the food and Shelby. He checked his watch. Five to four. Perfect timing. Grabbing the basket, he headed into the reception area and stopped cold when he spotted the Christmas tree.

The ornament!

He'd meant to buy one for Shelby's tree. Of all the things to forget.... Damn! If he went down to the store's trim shop now, he'd be late. And who knew what might be left in stock, anyway.

Staring at the company Christmas tree, Rand made up his mind quickly. He set the picnic basket down on the reception desk, then removed the silver starburst from the top of the tree. He found a green napkin in the basket, wrapped the star in the linen and set it in among the foodstuffs. Terrible at dealing with embarrassment, he hoped Shelby wouldn't recognize the tree topper.

It was the thought that counted, he reminded himself, and he'd been having some very nice thoughts, indeed, about Shelby Corbin.

Before leaving the floor, he stuck his head in the conference room and asked Kristen to call all the offices and let everyone go home. Of course he couldn't close the store, but the extra bonuses the sales staff would find in their holiday checks should make up for it.

When his elevator stopped at eight, Shelby was waiting for him so he didn't have to get out.

"You're certainly prompt," he said as she entered. The doors swished closed behind her and the elevator started its descent.

"I couldn't wait to start my holiday. Someone," she said looking at him pointedly, "has effectively corrupted me."

Her smile seemed a bit too bright—or was it his imagination? Rand's gaze dropped to her shopping bag. "What's in there? I thought you finished buying your Christmas presents yesterday."

"But it's been a week since I went for groceries and we had to eat something tonight." Her hazel eyes widened as they focused on the picnic basket hooked over his arm. "Oh, no."

"Oh, yes."

"Well, we won't be bored even if we don't have a tree to trim," she said philosophically. "We can spend all night eating and cursing the calories."

That's what she thought…and Rand wasn't about to tell her differently.

The traffic to her place was miserable, but Shelby came forth with a stream of chatter about past holiday disasters that kept him amused. And disturbed. He could swear that her gaiety was forced, that she was trying a bit too hard to be charming. He guessed the scare she'd had the night before hadn't really worn off. He could understand, considering how worried he'd been that morning when she'd been a mere half hour late for work.

Rand instructed himself to put the murder on hold. He wouldn't let it intrude on their holiday. There was nothing they could do until after the long weekend, anyway. Hatcher would be back from vacation then, his own father should finally get the computer rundown his police buddy in the downtown office had promised to deliver, and Rand himself should obtain the results of the workup he'd ordered on the substance from the Ziploc bag. He'd sent half of the contents to a lab, but as it was doing to everything else, the Christmas holiday was bringing work to a halt there, too. He might as well go with the flow or be prepared to be frustrated.

Amazingly enough, a parking spot awaited them directly in front of Shelby's building. They grabbed their respective collections of food and headed in. Wanting Shelby to go first, Rand hung back when she opened the door. She hesitated just inside the hallway where she set down her shopping bag.

"What's that smell?" Shelby sniffed. "Pine!"

She rushed into the living room and stopped dead facing the eight-foot tree Rand had purchased and set up earlier that afternoon. He locked the front door and, entering the living room, set the picnic basket down next to the couch.

"How in the world . . . ?" She whirled around. Her expression serious, she pointed a finger and accusingly said, "You! You did this. You used my extra set of keys to get in here today."

Rand was afraid she was angry that he'd taken the liberty of doing so until a smile dimpled her cheeks—the first natural expression he'd seen her wear since she'd joined him in the elevator. "It's no big deal," he said, echoing her words of that morning.

"Yes, it is." She came straight to him and planted a soft kiss on his mouth. "It's wonderful." She kissed him again, the moist touch of her lips more lingering this time. "But you didn't have to do it."

Restraining himself from taking advantage of her tempting mouth right then, Rand told her, "My mother taught me one good turn deserves another."

"I think I like your mother."

He smiled down at her. "She'll like you, too."

Shelby backed away from him and shrugged out of her coat. "Since we have a tree to be decorated in addition to all this food to be eaten, we have a very full evening ahead of us. Let's get comfortable and figure out what we want to sample first."

Rand had no doubts about what he'd prefer, but he figured she meant the food. "Sounds okay to me."

He stripped off his jacket and allowed her to take it from him.

"I'll just throw these on the bed." Taking her shopping bag with her, she disappeared into her bedroom. "Anything need to be refrigerated?" she called out.

Quickly removing the linen-covered star and a blue-foil-wrapped gift from the basket, Rand hid both under the couch. "A few things, including the bottle of champagne. Before you object," he added as she came out of the bedroom, "I'm not going to force you to drink any—though it would be a nice way to toast at midnight."

"I wasn't planning on objecting. I might even try a sip or two."

Raising an eyebrow, he followed her down the hall and into the kitchen where they spread out everything on the counter. He'd brought vegetarian delights—Brie cheese and French bread, Caesar salad, chicken with walnuts and raspberry sauce. Amusingly enough, she'd purchased items sure to please his palate—shrimp wrapped in bacon, pasta salad with pepperoni and a precooked beef Wellington for two.

When he gave the meat dish an inquiring stare, her expression turned defensive. "Everybody eats stuff they're not supposed to at Christmas, even some of us vegetarians."

Rand laughed. "You won't hear me complaining."

"Good."

Shelby popped the bacon-wrapped shrimp into the microwave and handed Rand a corkscrew and a bottle of wine she'd bought.

"I hope you don't expect me to drink this whole bottle by myself," he said.

"My tasting it won't hurt anything," she agreed, to his surprise. She set the Brie on a plate and found the bread knife. "But if there's any left, we can just cork it and put it back in the refrigerator for next time."

*Next time.* Rand liked the positive sound of that.

A few minutes later they were settled in her living room, soft Christmas music coming from her stereo, appetizers and wine set out on the coffee table. He volunteered to build a fire—one they would enjoy this time, he assured himself. Even Lieutenant Isaac Jackson wouldn't dare ruin their Christmas Eve celebration.

"You do that like a professional," Shelby pointed out when he had the logs blazing in minutes. "I never quite got the knack of building a fire properly. I'm always surprised when it eventually works."

He wiped his hands on a rag, then joined her on the couch where she was curled up like a cat. An exotic green cat, he amended in silent amusement. "I give lessons."

"In log building?"

"Among other things."

"Maybe later. Right now we have a tree to decorate," she said, handing him a full glass of wine.

He noticed she'd only poured herself a half glass and as yet hadn't touched it. "I thought we were eating these first." He indicated the food.

She bit into a piece of Brie-smeared bread. "We are, but that doesn't mean we can't discuss strategy."

"Decorating a tree takes strategy?" He speared a shrimp on a toothpick. "Why can't we just dig in and do it?"

"Because not everyone decorates a tree in the same way. I, for example, start with lights. Next, I add strings of stars and moons and hearts. Then I add ornaments, hanging the special ones very carefully so I can see them."

"What about the tinsel?"

"Last, of course, and one strand at a time."

"But that takes forever," he said, giving her a mock-horrified look.

She returned with a forced-sounding sigh. "That's the problem with some men. They just don't have the patience to see a good thing through."

"All right. I get the picture. We start with lights and end with spending half of our evening hanging tinsel." He lifted his glass and leaned in closer to her. Her light floral scent mingled with the pine was enticing. "But before we begin, we really should make a toast."

"Anything special in mind?"

"You."

Her round cheeks flushed with color as she clinked her glass against his, and Rand realized what was different about her tonight. Her face was free of artfully applied makeup, allowing her to look younger than her years. And more vulnerable. He always had been a sucker for vulnerable, but the only thing Shelby would need to protect herself from that night would be him.

If she wanted to, Rand qualified, heat rushing through him as he watched her lips grazing the glass and sipping the wine.

He knew Shelby had admired him as a football player, but it had taken some effort to interest her in him as a man. That was all right with him. He'd never been easily impressed by groupies as Dutch had been; he'd always had the feeling those ladies were more hormones than substance. And while he was certainly interested in Shelby's hormones, she had a lot more going for her, starting with brains and talent.

Much of her resistance had something to do with the murder, Rand knew. But, believing her innocent, he only wished she would confide in him. He still feared that whatever she wasn't saying would hold her back and that his pushing too far too fast would chance losing the yards he'd advanced with her.

Realizing he was thinking about succeeding in a relationship with her in terms of scoring in a football game, Rand chuckled.

"Something funny?" she asked.

"I always laugh when I'm happy."

Her lips bowed, tempting him yet again. "Why don't we start with those lights," he suggested.

They spent the next hour checking lights, eating, stringing lights and eating some more. Rand let Shelby make all the creative decisions, finding himself gently amused by the way her expression turned intent when she was trying to decide if there were perhaps too many lights in one section and not enough in another. Patiently he followed her directions to correct the ghastly blunder.

She was equally particular about her iridescent strings of beads and even about her more ordinary ornaments. But when it came to the special ones—the treasured souvenirs of Christmases past—the decisions became painstaking.

"This one has to go in the middle where it won't be hidden," she said, pulling out a three-inch-high brass heart from its felt covering. The front was etched with designs surrounding a large 1982. "That was the year I moved out on my own." She pushed at a catch and the heart sprang open to reveal ovals holding pictures. "My parents," she said, indicating the handsome couple on the left. "And my sisters."

Rand caught her hand before she could hang it. He studied the two young women a moment. "They're almost as attractive as their middle sister."

Shelby laughed. "That must be the secret to your success with women. You know how to make them feel exceptional."

"It's not hard when there's so much noteworthy material to compliment."

She was blushing again and avoiding his eyes. He freed her hand so she could hang the ornament. Dressed in green except for her bare feet, she reminded him of a Christmas elf. Her hair—usually gelled in the latest sophisticated style—was brushed back softly from her face except for a curl that had stubbornly strayed to her forehead. He found himself wanting to touch it. To touch her.

Before he could follow his instincts, Shelby reached down into her treasure chest of a box, exclaiming when she pulled the next prize out. "You'll love this one," she promised. From its attached ribbon, she dangled a porcelain horse decorated in Christmas finery.

"A draft horse?"

"A Clydesdale. I lived in Milwaukee last year, remember. These guys used to pull the beer wagons."

"You're right. I love it." *And you.* The involuntary thought startled Rand. "Uh, maybe I should pour us some more wine."

"None for me, thanks. I'll wait for that champagne."

She hadn't even finished the half glass she'd poured for herself, and he was on his third. Maybe he'd better slow down. He took one more sip anyway. A long one. Things were going a little fast for him. Love? Was it possible? He hadn't thought himself in love since his senior year of high school when he'd taken the cheerleader captain to the prom. It hadn't taken long to realize infatuation and love weren't the same thing. But he wasn't a kid anymore. He should know his own feelings; he merely chose not to examine them too closely at the moment.

The next ornament she lovingly placed was a crystal oval with a sleigh etched in its center, an art piece crafted by a personal friend. Then there was the stuffed, brilliant red Christmas tree with the heads of a dog and cat painted on them; she'd bought that to support an animal shelter. Finally she pulled out the ornament she'd purchased with him the other night. Wondering how she would explain the glass heart with lovebirds in years to come, he hoped she might say he had inspired it.

When Shelby began unwrapping some intricately patterned snowflakes that sparkled in the light, Rand asked, "What are those commemorative of?"

"Abject poverty of the student variety." She began hanging them, placing them in strategic positions to catch the light. "I made these my last Christmas in school."

"They're beautiful."

*Like you,* he wanted to say, though he knew she'd make a joke of it, or at best, blush again. And perhaps she wasn't beautiful in the classical sense, but she had a unique loveliness of her own that had captured his heart. Having put the last snowflake in place, she stepped back next to him.

"We can do the tinsel after our salad course," she said. "But so far, what do you think?"

"Perfect."

She poked him with her elbow. "You're not looking at the tree."

"Oh-h, the tree. Hmm." He made a big show of studying it, moving around the room to get a view from different angles. "Something's missing."

"Really?" Frowning, she marched over to him, tilted her head and intently considered his words. "Missing? What?"

"The top is bare."

"Oh, that. I keep promising myself to buy a topper next, but so far I haven't found one I really like."

"Good. Until you do," he said moving to the couch, bending over and pulling out the linen covered starburst, "you can use this one."

"I don't believe you." She took it from him and slowly undid the folds of the napkin. "The tree was more than enough, but thank you."

Nervously he watched her face, which revealed nothing but pleasure. She didn't recognize it, then. "Will it do?"

"It's perfect." She held it out to him. "Will you put it on top for me so I don't have to stand on a chair?"

"Sure, short stuff," he said, making her snicker. He set the star in place.

"You were right. That's exactly what it needed."

"You know what I need right now?"

"Food."

She started toward the kitchen but he caught her by the wrist. "Wrong. What I need is you."

## Chapter Ten

Startled, Shelby looked up into Rand's intent expression. "How literally should I take that?"

He hesitated only a second before saying, "As literally as you want to."

She considered the possibilities for a moment. Heat spread up the inside of her arm from her wrist where he was holding on to it, and yet... "Would a kiss do for now?"

"Would a man dying of thirst refuse a sip of water merely because he wasn't offered a whole bucket?"

Shelby moved into Rand, and, stretching up on bare toes, wrapped her arms around his neck. She stroked the soft velour of his amber pullover with the tips of her fingers. "An awfully melodramatic comparison, wouldn't you say?"

"Guilty as charged, but you can't blame a guy for trying."

She wasn't blaming him at all; she was thinking about how much she owed him. Not for the monetary worth of the tree, but for the release of tension it had brought her. His sweet gesture had given her back the holiday, had negated the negative... at least for the night.

His lips nuzzled hers enticingly. She opened to him and was surprised that he kept the kiss relaxed. Almost chaste.

The tip of her tongue had barely found his chipped tooth when he lifted his head.

"A lovely appetizer leaving me wanting more." His long fingers circling her waist, he set her from him. "I'll be looking forward to the next course."

Shelby slipped her hand into his as they walked toward the kitchen. "The living room is pretty informal for dinner. If you prefer, we could eat in the dining room."

"But the dining room doesn't have a Christmas tree," he protested. "Or a fireplace. Or a cozy coffee table."

Warmed by the romantic side of Westbrook's slick CEO, Shelby aimed a slanted look at him. Rand seemed so different away from the store, and it wasn't just the change of clothing she was considering, but the total man. The air of command was gone—not that he lacked strength, she silently added. But when she was with him away from Westbrook's, she felt as if they were truly on an equal plane.

Just as it should be if they were to become lovers.

Would they?

Shelby couldn't rid herself of the notion as they prepared not only the salad course, but the remainder of the meal as well. Was she ready to make that kind of commitment to a man she hardly knew? Maybe she was being pushed into a deeper relationship too quickly by the extraordinary circumstances; maybe she was being reckless for once in her emotional life. She wasn't sure of anything anymore—not even of her own feelings.

All she knew was that she, too, *needed*, and Rand was the man who could fill that void for her.

When they retired to the living room, she let him arrange the food while she lit candles on the table as well as others on the wall unit and fireplace mantel. Then she turned off the lamps and lowered all the window coverings except the one in front of the Christmas tree.

Rand was sitting on the floor. He'd created a cozy nook by rearranging the pillows to support their backs against the couch. Taking his cue from her, he'd slipped out of his shoes and socks and had stretched his long legs under the coffee table. There was something oddly erotic about seeing one's boss's naked feet, Shelby decided, suppressing a giggle.

She slid down to the floor next to him and looked over their Christmas Eve feast. "Mmm, this all looks so good, but let's not forget about the tinsel."

"Heaven forbid! No tree would be complete without it."

She squinched her eyes at him. "Are you making fun of me?"

"What if I am? Will you throw me out?"

"Probably not. I just want to know."

He kissed the tip of her nose. "Then I probably am."

She couldn't resist the infectious grin that made his mustache quiver. "I take my tree too seriously, huh?"

"Seriously enough that you've made my evening one I won't forget," he said, saluting her with a forkful of Caesar salad.

How could she be offended by a compliment, even if the words were a little on the dubious side?

While they ate, they talked about the ordinary parts of their lives, about their philosophies, and even about their politics. They avoided only one topic.

Dutch.

That subject, so fraught with emotional as well as physical danger, lingered at the back of Shelby's consciousness, waiting to be acknowledged as it had since she'd entered the elevator with Rand. But she'd vowed that nothing more would spoil her holiday—certainly not her own thoughts—so she relegated Santa Claus and his bag of nasty tricks to the North Pole of her mind.

She was relieved when Rand took the opportunity to share his past Christmas disasters with her. His humorous anecdotes gave her the opportunity to laugh—and opened new insights to the man.

"As a kid, I could never stand to wait until Christmas to know what my parents bought me. When they were out of the house, I'd take the opportunity to go on a gift hunt. I'd find whatever it was they bought me and then act surprised on Christmas morning."

"But with five kids in the family, how could you be sure which present was going to be yours?"

"Intuition. And of course there was the name tag." He grinned and stabbed a piece of beef Wellington. "My mother never left anything lying around unwrapped in case one of us was tempted to peek. So I would cleverly open the package without damaging the ribbon or paper, and then I would put it all back together again." He popped the pastry-wrapped meat into his mouth.

"What a rapscallion. You must have been the bane of your parents' existence at times."

"Actually, I wasn't so clever," Rand admitted grudgingly. "A couple of Christmases ago, my mother admitted she'd known exactly what I'd been up to as a kid. She said she never confronted me because she didn't want to spoil my fun."

"Clever mother."

"She's a smart lady, all right. I can't wait for you to meet her."

That was the second time Rand had mentioned his mother in a "meet" kind of context. He made it sound as if he wanted her in his life. The thought warmed her. Taking a last bite of chicken with raspberry sauce, she glanced toward the tree he'd bought and couldn't help but see what was happening beyond.

"Oh, look, Rand. It's snowing."

He tilted his head toward hers until they were touching. "A pretty normal phenomenon for this time of year."

"Don't be so didactic. Snow on Christmas Eve is—" she turned toward him and realized her face was mere inches from his "—is very romantic."

"You don't have to get out there and shovel."

"That's the practical part of you talking. What happened to the romance in your soul?"

"Want to go out back and build a snowman in your courtyard?"

"Not necessarily."

"Then why don't we...listen to the fire crackle, watch the tree lights twinkle and the snow spatter on the window."

"Much better. Let's clear up this mess first."

"I'll uncork the champagne."

"But it's not midnight yet."

"A true romantic would pretend that it was."

She got the message. They cleared the coffee table and stacked the dishes in the kitchen sink. While Rand took care of the champagne, Shelby ran back to her room to get his present. She sneaked it under the Christmas tree and by the time he arrived in the living room, she was moving the coffee table to the side and the cushions in front of the fire so they could stretch out. Rand set the ice bucket on an end table and poured champagne into two fluted glasses.

Handing her one, he settled back against the cushions. "To Christmas elves and midnight wishes."

A whisper of a sigh escaped her as they clinked glasses and Shelby took a sip. The champagne was wonderful, but she warned herself that half a glass should be her limit. She didn't want to take any chances on saying something she'd regret, "under the influence."

"Come here." His expression openly seductive, Rand held out his free arm.

Shelby gladly snuggled into him. "That tree is beautiful."

"Even without the tinsel."

"Tinsel! I almost forgot!" She pretended to rise, but he pulled her back down. "Right. Later. I can appreciate it even now. Twinkling lights. Snow gently falling in the background. Beautifully wrapped present under its branches." Dramatically she repeated, "Present? Why, where did that come from?"

"A Christmas elf would be my guess." Rand's voice was filled with amusement as he allowed her to scramble forward. When she turned back, she held the present out as he pulled his hand from under the couch.

They said "For you" in unison and, laughing, exchanged gifts.

Without ceremony, Shelby ripped the blue foil off hers, saying, "You shouldn't have, not after the tree...." She stared at the copper-and-silver earrings she'd planned on buying on sale after Christmas. "Oh, Rand, you *really* shouldn't have."

"I won't know if you're right until you try them on." By then he had his package open also. He pulled out the green sweater, its design a uniformed player catching a football. "Hey, this is great."

"Try it on," she suggested, releasing the first earring.

"Here?"

Shelby didn't answer. His eyes narrowing, Rand began to tug at his velour pullover. Her hands stilled as she fixed the second earring to her lobe. He moved slowly, as if giving her time to object. She wordlessly watched him pull the shirt up to reveal a broad chest rippling with muscle and a face tensing with need. He lay back on the cushions.

"Come here," he said softly, his gift ignored.

"You want to see the earrings up close?" she asked playfully, straddling one of his thighs to lean over him.

"Closer." Threading his fingers through her short hair, he cupped her head gently and inexorably brought it toward his. "No mistake." But he wasn't looking at the earrings; he was staring into her eyes. "Perfect."

Knowing what was about to happen, that they were on the brink of making love, she resisted for only a fraction of a second before letting Rand pull her to him. This might be crazy, but she didn't care. His kiss plunged her into a maelstrom of heady emotion—a welcome whirlpool of positive and tender feelings—so how could it be wrong? After thoroughly exploring every crevice of her mouth, he ended the kiss, his hands still fixed in her hair.

"Close enough?" she whispered, breathing heavily.

"Almost." His hands slid to her shoulders. "We could get closer if you'd get rid of this." His fingers slipped down the suede and rested lightly on her breasts. Her nipples chafed for more intimacy. When he began undoing the garment button by button, desire curled through her. She lifted herself from his thigh so he could pull the long shirt up, over her head. "You cheated."

Shelby looked down at her deep green camisole edged with wide cream lace. "You don't like this? It's what all the fashionable elves are wearing these days."

His eyebrows didn't even twitch. "It's in the way," he growled, rectifying the situation by ridding her of it as well.

When the camisole was three-fourths of the way off and her arms were tangled in the silky material, he wrapped his hands around her back and tugged her forward. She fell over him, gasping as he planted tiny kisses on her breast. She freed her hands and put them to good use, touching his neck and shoulders, absorbing the very feel of his flesh.

Instinctively she knew that for this night, at least, Rand would give her respite from the dreams that tormented her.

As if to persecute her, the reflection of twinkling lights danced over the fireplace mantel, making her shift her focus elsewhere. She stared into the fire, allowed herself to be slowly mesmerized by the tongues of flame dancing along the logs. Without warning, she saw crimson taffeta burning—yards and yards of the material blackening into ash. She shut her eyes against the memory, but her mind was not any safer in darkness. Santa waited for her there....

Panicking, Shelby determined to drive the unwelcome visions away. She absorbed herself in Rand, watched him intently as he used his mustache in creative ways on her breasts. A bolt of excitement lit her, making her skin shiver. Then suddenly she was under him and, with her help, he was removing the rest of their clothing.

"Perfect," he murmured again, filling her with pleasure.

"You're the one who's perfect."

As they explored each other with eager hands, she concentrated on Rand's changing expressions, on his sensuous face. The firelight warmed his skin, burnished his mustache, made his amber eyes glow. With a fingertip she traced the scar that fascinated her. She loved the way he appeared right now, magnificent and primitively male.

Maybe she even loved him.

Her heartbeat quickened at the thought; she had no desire to deny it.

Under the spell of Rand's holiday magic, she didn't have to face her darker thoughts. Her life had become so confused, so unreal. The only sanity seemed to be the escape she could find in his arms, and she embraced the flight from that other reality for all she was worth.

She embraced Rand, arched to him and made him welcome, wrapped her legs around his back so he could fill her more completely. Bracing her hands against his lifted shoulders, she studied his magnificent male body as it moved with hers until she could watch no longer, think no longer. Feeling became the center of her existence, passion her impetus, satisfaction her motivation.

As he lowered himself over her, his body touching hers at every possible place, twinkling lights filled her vision . . . the Christmas tree behind him. This time the dancing colors portended no evil, but kept pace with their movements, until, in a magnificent explosion of melting snowflakes, they fused and went out.

Her eyes were closed. Rand had stilled. Their breaths mingled as did the perspiration slicking over their naked bodies.

Shifting to his side but leaving a possessive leg straddling hers, Rand murmured huskily, "We're perfect together."

Shelby opened her eyes and smiled up at him despite the twinge of remorse she felt. She touched Rand's face tenderly and hoped he wouldn't think differently if he ever found out about the lie she'd allowed to stand between them even in this, the most intimate of moments.

AFTER SPENDING half the night making love, they overslept the next morning and had to hurry off to their respective celebrations with murmured regrets at parting. As much as Shelby wanted to share the day with Rand, both families had planned midafternoon dinners that would continue on till the small hours of the morning.

Actually, almost every minute of the weekend had been filled with extended-family gatherings, one after another. They made a couple of concessions: Rand accompanied

Shelby to a cocktail party given by her sister Brenda late Saturday afternoon; on Sunday, Shelby finally got to meet *his* mother as well as the rest of the extensive McNabb brood over dessert at an aunt's house.

Still, spending time alone was impossible to arrange without slighting family members who'd come into town for the holiday or Chicagoans who'd made prior arrangements to entertain. Shelby contented herself with the few hours she and Rand managed to squeeze in together.

The flurry of activity helped to relegate the events of the past couple of weeks to the back of her mind. Neither she nor Rand broached any subject connected with the murder. Monday morning and their joint planned chat with Frank Hatcher would come soon enough.

MONDAY MORNING DID COME, but without the manager of data processing. Rand called Shelby just before ten to cancel the meeting. Hatcher wasn't in his department. No one had heard from him. No one answered his home phone.

Rand didn't know what to make of it. The man's absence put him off kilter. Had Hatcher conveniently disappeared because he knew too much? Had he literally run from the scene of the murder? Tempted to call Lieutenant Jackson with his speculations, Rand stopped himself. He didn't want the detective to know he was pursuing his own investigation. He might make trouble for his dad with the force.

Rand decided to follow up his other leads with phone calls. His father's downtown buddy promised to have the computer printouts late the following evening. The lab had not yet come through with an analysis of the powder from Dutch's study. Tomorrow, maybe the next day. No promises. Rand hadn't thought everything would be resolved neatly in one day, but he had hoped for a breakthrough.

Would he never be able to get his life back on track? Now that he'd found someone he wanted to share it with, the idea took on new meaning. As startling as the discovery was, he had to admit he'd fallen in love with a woman he'd known for less than two weeks.

*One more day,* Rand assured himself with as much conviction as he could muster. *One more day, and the pieces will begin to fall into place.*

By early afternoon, he was preparing to leave for the reading of Dutch's will. He knew what his share of the estate would be, but he'd promised Pippa he'd be there for her. His sister was on his mind when he answered his secretary's buzz.

"Yes, Kristen."

"It's Frank Hatcher, Mr. McNabb. He came up to offer his apologies about missing this morning's meeting and I thought you'd want to see him."

Rand thought quickly. He had to get to the lawyer's office, so he couldn't wait to track down Shelby. "Send him right in." He'd tell Shelby the details later.

Rand was almost disappointed: Frank Hatcher hadn't run from the scene of the crime, after all. But when the manager of data processing entered the office, he looked as though he'd been a victim. The right side of his forehead was bandaged with a large white gauze patch that mussed the line of his thinning hair.

Standing in front of the closed door, Hatcher said, "Mr. McNabb, I, uh, heard you scheduled a meeting for this morning and then had to cancel it because I wasn't here. I figured I owed you a personal explanation."

"Sit down," Rand said, indicating the chair opposite his desk.

"It was kind of a bizarre twist of fate." Hatcher sat gingerly, crossing his left leg over his right, fussing with the crease in his trousers. "I got through a whole skiing vacation without a scratch. This," he said, pointing to his head, "happened at the airport."

Finding it hard to believe Hatcher was the athletic type to begin with, Rand raised a dubious eyebrow. "Go on."

"My plane was canceled. In a scramble to get rescheduled for a vacant seat on another flight, I got careless. I tripped over someone's suitcase and hit my head on the ticket counter. Next thing I know, I'm on my way to the emergency room of the nearest hospital. They kept me overnight but I was at the airport first thing this morning. I didn't realize how long it would take me to get here, or I would have called, I swear." When Rand didn't respond to this, Hatcher eyed him uncertainly. "I tried to call from O'Hare airport at lunchtime to say I was on my way in, but no one answered. I'm really sorry about the extra day, Mr. McNabb. I'll take it without pay."

"I'll accept your explanation." Not that he was satisfied with it, Rand thought, wondering what he'd have to do to check it out.

"This meeting you scheduled with me..." Hatcher cleared his throat. "I hope you're not dissatisfied with my work."

"What I wanted to talk about had nothing to do with your work in data processing." Knowing he had the advantage, Rand leaned back and pinned the nervous little man with his gaze. "Although it does concern Westbrook's."

The manager shifted in his chair. "I—I don't understand."

"Sure, you do. Or you would if you thought about it."

Uncrossing his left leg only to cross the right, Hatcher checked his watch. "Uh, really, Mr. McNabb—"

"I want to know about your deal with Dutch."

"Pardon me?"

"All the details of your stock deal."

"I don't know what you're talking about."

"Westbrook's stock," Rand pressed on. "I've seen the folders my late partner kept in his home safe."

Hatcher's suddenly defiant expression made Rand think the man was going to try to bluff him. Then his eyes shifted to the middle of Rand's chest. "I was a go-between."

"You approached the minor shareholders instead of Dutch."

"And I made the deals," Hatcher admitted. "Cash deals. The buyers didn't know they were selling to me until it was time to sign the papers."

"Didn't you think that was unusual procedure?"

"Listen, Dutch said it was on the up-and-up, that he only wanted to do it this way so they wouldn't raise the price, knowing it was him that was interested." His rapid-fire speech slowed. "He said I couldn't get into trouble." He paused. "Are you going to fire me?"

"Should I?"

"I, uh, n-no."

Let the little bastard sweat out the answer like he'd been doing for almost two weeks, Rand thought. "Who did you contact?"

"Everyone but Althea Westbrook herself and some guy I couldn't find—Stan Horowitz."

"So Althea didn't know about the sales. But Tucker Powers did?"

"Right. I approached him myself. He wasn't interested. Too concerned with his own importance. You know, that tradition stuff he's always spouting when he talks about being associated with Westbrook's."

"Did Tucker know you were making offers through Dutch?"

Hatcher shrugged. "I certainly didn't tell him. Like I said, I didn't tell anyone until they were ready to sign. The only ones who knew about Dutch were the three who sold. Burke, Larson and Wright."

Frowning, Rand recalled his conversation with Tucker. The man hadn't admitted knowing about the stock deal, and yet he hadn't denied knowing, either. He'd talked around the issue in his usual, vague manner. Why?

Either the lawyer really was getting senile... or he had something to hide.

SHELBY PREPARED TO LEAVE the store in a down mood. Nothing had gone right that day—nothing that counted. Rand had said he'd call her about getting together tonight before quitting time, but here she was, exiting the elevators, and still no message. She hadn't heard from him since that morning when he'd canceled their meeting because Hatcher hadn't shown up. If she didn't know better, she might think he was trying to avoid her.

"Shelby, wait up, would you?" called Joy Upton, who was still in the lingerie department but in the process of putting on her coat.

Thinking the manager wanted to talk to her about business, Shelby circumvented her usual route to the employee entrance and made her way over to Joy. "What's up?"

"Have you heard?" the other woman asked, eyes expectantly wide. "No, I see you haven't." She pulled Shelby out of the main aisle and into a currently empty area of her department. In a low-pitched voice, she murmured, "Dutch's will was read this afternoon."

Shelby sighed. Forever a font of information and speculation, Joy merely wanted to gossip. No wonder Rand hadn't called. Curious that he hadn't told her where he'd be.

"The will is none of our business, Joy."

"Come on, loosen up. Wait till you hear! It seems that Westbrook's now belongs solely to Randall McNabb. All of Dutch's shares, that is."

Without thinking that she was encouraging the busy-body to continue, Shelby asked, "Dutch didn't leave his shares to his wife?"

"It wasn't a matter of leaving. It seems the partners had drawn up a contract at the outset of their venture," Joy said gleefully, really getting into her story. "If either partner died, the surviving partner got everything."

A chill shot through Shelby, making her frown. "What are you trying to say?"

"I'm saying that some of us think it's awfully convenient that Rand just happened to return to town the morning *after* Dutch was killed. Or did he? Think about it."

Shelby didn't want to think about it. She didn't want to know that Rand might have reason to murder Dutch himself. "I have to go or I'll be late," she lied. She couldn't listen to any more of this nonsense.

"I'll catch up with you tomorrow," Joy promised.

Shelby kept going without looking back. She tried to forget the other woman's words, because they were fostered by bored people who had nothing better to do than judge others. She just wanted to get home. So intent was she on getting out of Westbrook's that she knocked into a slight man who was also leaving by the employee entrance.

"Whoa, there."

The sight of Frank Hatcher startled Shelby. "Frank. I thought you weren't here today. I mean, Rand...Mr. McNabb said—"

"Don't worry. He knows I'm here. I spoke to him myself." With a shrug, he went on, leaving her staring at his back, her mind in a whirl.

Rand had canceled their meeting this morning on the pretext that Hatcher was nowhere to be found.

Had he lied?

# Chapter Eleven

"I'd like to see Mr. McNabb, now," Shelby told Kristen the next morning. She'd left her office for the executive suite at the first possible opportunity.

"I'm afraid he came in and left again," Rand's secretary explained. "He didn't say where he was going or how long he was going to be gone."

"I think I'll wait."

"I could call you when he gets here," Kristen suggested as Shelby sat in a couch opposite the secretary. "Suit yourself, but I hope you don't mind if you wait alone. I was just about to go downstairs for a cup of coffee with Gloria."

Shelby smiled to put the other woman at ease. "Go ahead. I'll amuse myself by browsing through one of your corporate magazines here."

"All right. If you're sure . . ."

Shelby waved Kristen on to her coffee break with the receptionist. She wasn't sure how she could pretend indifference when she was feeling anything but. Rand had finally called her the night before after nine o'clock. Supposedly he'd been at Pippa's house, once more lending his sister moral support. That's why he wouldn't be able to see her that night, he'd said. He was sure she'd understand.

Well, she hadn't understood Rand's reasoning any more than his fluffing over Hatcher's appearance and the impromptu conference she hadn't been invited to. Rand had assured her he'd detail the conversation when he saw her in person. So, she was here, waiting to be seen. Where was he?—trying to avoid her?

Bothered by the latest rumors about Rand, which were flying along the grapevine and already being elaborated on, she was undoubtedly jumping to conclusions. If only she could prove the truth one way or the other—hopefully the other.

Rand couldn't have anything to do with murder, not even a cover-up.

Wandering into his office began as an exercise to fight boredom that soon presented itself as opportunity. There was nothing to prevent her from doing some investigating of her own, and she could start right here. If they hadn't done the very same thing in Dutch's study, she might not even know where to begin or what to look for.

But she'd had practice.

Of course, if he had a hidden wall safe, she would be out of luck. Rand wasn't the type to use a cutesy combination to jog his memory. And her looking through his things did make it seem as though she didn't trust him. A detached single-minded part of herself wrestled with her conscience; her conscience lost.

Shelby began with a quick look through his filing cabinets, but when they revealed nothing, she turned to the black-and-chrome desk with its single drawer. No file folders in there. Nothing but supplies.

And an airline-ticket holder.

Fingers fumbling with the folded paper, she pulled it out. Inside lay a stub from a trip dated December 14…the night of the fatal Christmas party.

She studied it carefully. The ticket had been made out to Rand McNabb for an early-evening flight from Boston with an approximate Chicago arrival at seven fifty-three. He'd had plenty of time to get to Westbrook's to wish his employees a merry Christmas.

*If* he'd wanted to be seen.

Her stomach churned at the other possibility—that he'd preferred to slip inside the store to confront his partner without anyone knowing about it. What if he'd already found out about Dutch's under-the-table dealings and had decided to do something about them?

Intent on the speculations a mere ticket stub could stir, Shelby didn't immediately hear the shuffle of footsteps in the outer office until they seemed to be directly outside the door. She flew around but didn't see anyone. Quietly she slipped the ticket holder back into the drawer and closed it, then, pulse surging with her boldness, strode out into Kristen's office as if nothing were wrong.

No one.

Nerves jangling, Shelby kept going. The reception area was empty as well, though she heard a door closing and muted voices coming from other offices. She sagged with relief. That was it. She must have heard someone returning to work from a coffee break or a meeting and imagined the sound closer than it actually had been. Guilt had made her jumpy.

But she had nothing about which to feel guilty other than a little prying.

Could Rand say the same?

Shelby took a deep breath and put her imagination on hold. None of this proved anything except that deep down she didn't trust the man she loved as completely as she'd thought she had. If an airline ticket added to gossip could make her suspicions resurface. . . .

No longer in the mood to see Rand for any reason, she decided to leave, but she couldn't avoid looking at the spot where she'd found Dutch's body. Her steps slowed, then stopped. She replayed the scene after the party in her mind analytically as she tried to remember every detail, but no matter how hard she concentrated, Shelby couldn't remember anything more than she had before. Shifting her focus to the tree, she realized something looked different about it, but she wasn't sure what, exactly.

The tree brought her thinking full circle, back to Rand, back to Christmas Eve, back to a possibility she wasn't ready to contemplate. Not only had she made love with a man who might be a murderer, she'd fallen in love with him as well.

A pair of arms snaked around her waist, making her jump. She choked back a scream as she was pulled against a solid male body. "I missed you," Rand murmured into her hair, making her stiffen.

"Obviously."

Though Shelby didn't move a muscle to disentangle herself, she felt as if she were going to explode inside. Her heart seemed to be bruising itself against her rib cage.

"Hmm, you don't sound pleased. Because of last night? I explained what happened."

"That's right," she said with forced calm, wishing he'd let go of her. "You did."

"Didn't you believe me?" Rand's voice took on a teasing tone as he nuzzled her ear with his lips. "You aren't the jealous type, by any chance?"

She struggled out of his arms and faced him. "Don't be silly. You *were* with your sister, weren't you?"

"I said I was." He crinkled his forehead at her, but he didn't pursue the subject. After studying her for a bit, he asked, "What about tonight?"

"What about it?"

"Dinner? I promise I'll explain away all those questions I see lurking in those beautiful hazel eyes." Indicating the other offices, he lowered his voice. "We can't exactly talk here with any privacy."

"Tonight's not a good idea. I was planning on working late."

This wasn't a lie, exactly, since she'd been thinking about doing so. He'd merely helped to make up her mind.

"But you have an in with the boss."

"But the boss isn't going to finish my designs for Valentine's Day," she hedged, "or start the preliminary sketches for the Kuryokhin windows. I have to get going on those as well. The holidays are over."

"If you don't count New Year's Eve and Day."

Shelby gave him an impatient glare.

"So you have to work late tonight," he conceded with an exaggerated sigh. "Tomorrow?"

"We'll see."

It was his turn to look impatient, but Rand didn't contradict her. He seemed to accept her excuse. "I'll talk to you later, then, at home."

Her careless shrug turned his expression from annoyed to something less appealing. "Later," she echoed, making a fast escape.

By the time she raced to the floor below, Shelby had started to hyperventilate. She leaned against the hall wall for a moment to catch her breath and to clear her mind. She had to think rationally. How could she fear a man with whom she'd made love only a few short days ago? She wasn't afraid of Rand directly; not really, she assured herself, even facing the fact that he had had the opportunity to play all those tricks on her.

He could have beat her home from the funeral parlor and left the wreath on her door. It would have been simple for him to send the note via interoffice mail, and just as easy to leave the dead rat on her desk when everyone was out to lunch Christmas Eve. He'd even had the opportunity to play Santa Claus. He'd known she was leaving late and that she'd be heading for the Grant Park Garage—where he'd directed her. And he hadn't been waiting for her at Pippa's.

Even so, she didn't want to believe Rand had done any of those things. She wouldn't believe he was the killer. She told herself she was thinking a little crazy because of the situation, one she'd put herself in when she'd covered up finding the body. More than ever, she regretted her panicked actions. But what could she do to resolve the situation without implicating herself?

She thought about it all day, and late in the afternoon called Tucker Powers. She told him she needed some legal advice and wanted to know if she could speak with him before he left for home. He said he'd be free at five-thirty. Perfect. Westbrook's's lawyer could tell her what would happen to her legally if she suddenly came forward with withheld information, she was sure of it. The only problem was how to get his advice without telling him the exact details of the situation.

RAND RETURNED TO WESTBROOK'S yet again, late in the afternoon, with computer printouts on his employees in his leather attaché. Attending a budget meeting with his vice presidents seemed like a waste of his time at the moment, but he didn't want to shift the schedule around, thereby arousing suspicions. After the interminable meeting finally ended at five twenty-five, he was free to pursue his investigation.

Kristen was long gone, so he locked both her office door and his own. He'd be damned if he'd be disturbed before he got a good look at the printout. Things would fall together quickly now. He could feel it. The chemist should have results for him also. He'd dropped by the lab personally that morning to make sure of it. He quickly dialed the direct number he'd printed on the lab's business card.

A deep-voiced man identified himself as the chemist he'd spoken to that morning. "Sarandon, here."

"This is Rand McNabb. Do you have my results?"

"Right here. Since you're so anxious to get them, I'll use a messenger service—"

"Later. Tell me what you found. Is it something that could be used in the production of cosmetics?"

Sarandon laughed. "Hardly. The white powder is nothing more than secobarbital sodium."

"Try saying it in English."

"A more common name is Seconal. It's a prescription drug, a rapid-acting hypnotic."

"A what?"

"A sleeping powder normally found in a capsule."

Unprepared for this information, Rand slumped back in his chair. His thinking had been totally out of whack, then. "Tell me more about it. Everything you know."

"Like I said, it's a hypnotic," Sarandon repeated. "That differs from a sedative, which is given in small doses at regular intervals throughout the day. Seconal is usually given to patients in full dosage at night and has a direct effect in impairing mental and physical abilities. Puts you out like a light," the chemist explained. "Taken with alcohol, Seconal has a tremendous synergistic effect—and produces a doozer of a hangover. That's about it."

"Not what I was looking for," Rand admitted, "but very thought provoking. Thanks."

Slightly dazed, he hung up. What in the world would Dutch have been doing with a sleeping powder? If only a single Ziploc bag had been found—the one by the body undoubtedly contained the same ingredient—he might have thought the killer gave it to the victim to make his bloody task easier. But the second bag he'd found in his partner's study contradicted that theory. The drug belonged to Dutch, and if he were merely using it as a sleeping aid for himself, it would have been in capsules in a prescription bottle in the medicine cabinet. Instead, he'd hidden it.

Why? Had Dutch intended to give the Seconal to someone else—someone he'd intended to victimize?

Things weren't falling into place as neatly as he'd expected, Rand realized grimly. The computer printout had to be more helpful.

He pulled the sheaf of papers from his attaché and began skimming the report on his employees. He didn't get very far down the list before he stopped cold after reading one of the early entries.

Shelby Corbin had been arrested for assault and battery almost two years before, a fact she'd successfully hidden from him.

And, unless he was mistaken, she'd hidden it from the police, as well.

SHELBY FELT SWALLOWED UP by the massive mahogany furniture that made Tucker Powers's office seem far more claustrophobic than it actually was. Or maybe her nerves were affecting her sense of proportion. Sitting in a high-back chair covered in dark green leather, she shifted uncomfortably, unsure how to begin.

"So, what can I do for you?" Tucker asked from the other side of his sizable desk.

Maybe it was the distance between them that made the distinguished lawyer seem formidable rather than vague. Though the sun had set, he sat in the dark except for the light of a desk lamp—brass with a green glass shade, as traditional as the furniture—which made her focus totally on him, the single bright spot in the room. The atmosphere made Shelby feel as if she were in a library where only hushed tones were allowed.

"This is kind of awkward for me," she said in a low voice. "I appreciate your taking time to talk to me."

"I hope I can be of help."

His smile, probably meant to put her more at ease, made her adjust herself in the chair instead. "What do you think would happen to someone who went to the police with information that person had previously withheld?"

The smile faded slightly. "What kind of information?"

"Say this person stumbled across . . . something that had to do with a crime, but she didn't want to get involved. That's why she . . . this person didn't say anything."

"Concealment of a crime." Tucker's expression grew thoughtful. "Hmm. Could lead to an accessory charge."

"Even if this person had a really good reason for not coming forward at first?"

Rather than answering that, Tucker asked, "Why come forward now?"

Shelby could say that she feared for her life and it would be the truth, but that wasn't the only reason. She admitted another truth, which she'd been denying even to herself. "Because it would have been the right thing to do all along, only she was too afraid to admit it."

Tucker's silvering brows drew together. "The police aren't terribly understanding about personal fears in these situations. Perhaps if you made yourself a little clearer..."

Though Shelby was tempted to tell him everything, something stopped her from being frank. Undoubtedly Tucker knew she was talking about herself, but he'd have no way of guessing she was referring to the murder. He might think she'd caught someone at the store involved in petty theft or something. If he knew the truth, he might run straight to the police with her story before she could make up her mind herself.

"I really can't tell you any more."

"Sometimes not going to the police is understandable," Tucker said. "How often do newspaper and television reports confirm that our justice system is far from perfect? Criminals roam the streets while honest citizens are victimized, sometimes jailed for defending themselves or their property."

Shelby frowned at the lawyer's attack on the system within which he worked. "What are you trying to say? That this person *shouldn't* report the truth?"

He didn't answer directly. "There are times when the truth can be dangerous. In ancient societies, the bearer of bad news was often sacrificed."

Growing more uncomfortable by the moment, Shelby decided coming to Tucker might have been a mistake. Maybe Rand had been right about the lawyer. It was certainly difficult to get a direct answer from him. Realizing she was on her own as far as making a decision was concerned, she decided to excuse herself as quickly as possible.

"I appreciate your advice, Mr. Powers. Thanks so much for your time." Shelby stood. "I know you're probably anxious to get home, so I'll take my leave."

"Then you've made a decision...about what advice to give your friend."

"No, actually, I haven't quite made up my mind, but I'll be giving it serious thought. Thanks again."

Caught by the intent expression in his gray eyes, Shelby suddenly had the oddest impression that he knew exactly why she'd come. She shook off the notion as impossible and left the gloomy room to get her things from her own office. All she wanted to do now was to go home where she could think in peace.

AFTER SCANNING the entire computer printout, Rand re-read the short report on Shelby, which seemed to be the only significant entry. A few other employees had arrest records—for petty theft, demonstrating without a license, unpaid parking fines—but no one else had been connected with a violent crime of any kind.

He just couldn't conceive of Shelby being violent. The report only gave him the bare facts: arrested for assault and battery for breaking a beer bottle over the head of one Pete Wolenski; charges reduced to disturbing the peace; charges dropped by the judge.

What was Shelby's side of the story?

He had to find out. He'd known Shelby had been hiding something—undoubtedly this arrest. Rand couldn't figure out why Lieutenant Jackson hadn't dug up the record. Ripping the perforated page free from the others, he folded and stuffed it into his suit-jacket pocket. Then he went to the wall safe, opened it and took out the Ziploc bag. He had an idea he'd be facing the police before the night was through, so he dropped the remainder of the drug into his other pocket.

Then he checked his watch. Ten after six. Since she'd planned on working late, Shelby would be downstairs. Grabbing his overcoat, he headed for the window-display office.

The place was unlocked but empty, as he discovered a few minutes later. Maybe Shelby was in the ladies' room. He wandered over to her work area. No coat on the wall pegs. She'd left. He'd have to go to her apartment. About to leave, he caught sight of the work on her drawing board—sketches from the Valentine's Day windows.

Unable to help himself, Rand lingered a moment and poured over Shelby's work, somehow feeling closer to her by doing so. Each window had a different approach to the romance theme to appeal to a variety of interests. He picked up the sketch that involved sports. Shelby had included a set of crossed footballs that formed a heart. Smiling, he remembered when she'd been doodling with this one the first day he'd approached her. He'd had such similar reasons for seeking her out that day, and yet everything was different now. No matter what she had to hide, he was in love with Shelby and no computer report could change that fact.

Knowing he had to find her and tell her so, Rand set down the sketch, but it fluttered from the table. As he rose, paper in hand, something else caught his eye—a ragged piece of material caught on a rear hinge of the drawing table. He knew even before he pulled the fabric free that it would be red taffeta.

The crimson cloth lay in his hand, an indictment of the woman he loved. Shelby had to have been the mystery woman. She'd covered up the fact. Why? Not murder. Never murder. He could not—would not—believe her capable of such a deed, not even in self-defense, not even now, holding what the police might say was evidence. She must have found Dutch's body and, because of her arrest record, she'd been afraid to wait around for the police.

A misguided move, he told himself; but running didn't make her guilty.

Rand wanted to hear the truth of what had happened from Shelby's own lips. He would have some answers before this night was finished, he decided, slipping the material into his pocket even as he left the window-display office. He would face Shelby in her own apartment.

Single-minded in his purpose, Rand took the elevator to the ground floor and made his way through the already darkened store, stopping only when he reached the security office where Edgar sat behind his bank of monitors.

"Hey, boss, making a night of it?"

"It's that time," Rand agreed. "Listen, the window-display office was left unlocked. Take care of it, would you? Check the other offices while you're at it. Everyone should be gone by now."

"I was just gonna make my rounds. No problem."

"See you tomorrow, Edgar."

A few minutes later, Rand was on his way to the north side. As he drove, the problem of how to broach the subject of the arrest and the material he'd found grew in complexity. He had to handle this situation carefully or he would lose Shelby, and that was one thing he was determined not to do.

By the time he arrived at the Cleveland Avenue address, he wasn't at all sure he was capable of handling this delicate an inquisition. And when Shelby opened her door to him, obviously distraught and doing her best to hide the fact, he only wanted to take her in his arms and tell her that everything would be all right.

"COME IN," Shelby said, not knowing what else to do. One of these days, she'd learn to ignore her buzzer. She stepped back to let Rand past her, then locked the door behind him. He wandered into the living room where she'd made a fire with the last of her wood. The room was toasty warm and he'd already removed his topcoat and was doing the same with his suit jacket by the time she followed him. "What brings you here?"

"You. What else? I thought you were going to work late."

He undid the knot of his tie and his top shirt button. The result was a mussed look that was endearing. Unable to stand the tug at her heart vying with the doubts plaguing her, she turned away from him and wandered over to the tree.

"I was going to work. I did for a little while. I wasn't feeling too well." The glass heart with the lovebirds caught her attention. She avoided looking at the ornament; avoided the memories of Christmas Eve. "I'm tired from the pressure of the holidays, I guess."

"Yes, they can put quite a strain on you."

"Speaking of the holidays," she began, facing him, "I never did ask you . . . why didn't you come to the Westbrook's Christmas party?"

Though Rand seemed startled by her question, he didn't hesitate to answer. "I had all intentions of being there, but I spent the day in Boston on business. My flight to Chicago would have gotten me in on time for the party if Boston hadn't been fogged in."

"All night?"

She couldn't read Rand's expression as he nodded. "The airline representatives said it might be a matter of an hour or two before the plane could take off, but that was wishful thinking. I spent the night trying to sleep sitting up. Why are you so curious, anyway?"

Because she loved him and wanted to drive suspicion away. A fogged-in airport—she only prayed it was the truth.

"I was thinking about how anxious I'd been to meet the elusive Rand McNabb, and how negative the circumstances were when I finally had the opportunity."

"But we overcame the circumstances and can continue to do so together. If that's what you want."

He was sparring with her. Shelby was sure that all was not right with Rand any more than it was with her. She wondered if he'd followed her from work. Halfway home, she'd had the distinct impression someone was tailing her, though she'd eventually figured her nerves were triggering her imagination. If only she could check on his fog story. Of course she could. All she had to do was call the Boston airport. First, she had to get rid of Rand for a short time.

"I really do want things to work out between us," she told him truthfully. She wanted to lose herself in the comfort of his arms. But she couldn't. Not until she knew about the ticket. "Listen, why don't we relax in front of the fire. I have the rest of that bottle of wine in the refrigerator."

"Sounds like a good start."

Start to what? Shelby wondered. He looked so serious...almost as if he didn't quite trust her.

"This wood isn't going to last," she said decisively "Would you mind going around to Zambrana's on Clark to get a fresh bundle of firewood?"

She could tell he didn't really want to leave, but he agreed. "All right. I'll be back in a minute." He pulled on his overcoat and kissed her lightly on the mouth.

*I love you,* she thought.

But that particular truth didn't stop her from picking up the telephone and calling directory assistance for the number of the Boston airport so she could learn another truth Busy. She tried the airline he'd been booked on. Busy as well. The holidays would make her crazy yet.

Frustrated, she flounced back to the couch and ran her fingers over the brown suit jacket Rand had left there. If only things would work out between them. If only she didn't have this horrible feeling of dread. About to call the Boston airport again, she stopped when a ravel of bright material sticking out of his pocket caught her eye.

Her throat went dry as she slipped her hand into the pocket and pulled out the contents—a small plastic bag and a square of crimson taffeta that she'd recognize anywhere. Where had he found the piece of her dress? Near the body? What was he doing with it? Had he brought it here to confront her?

She stared at the shredded fabric, its crimson contrasting with the white powder encased in plastic. Drugs? Rand? She opened the bag and sniffed. The light scent was somehow familiar. With a fingertip, she took a pinch and touched it to her tongue. Although familiar, too, she couldn't place the odd taste. Trying to decide whether or not to return the items, Shelby slipped both into her pants pocket instead. Then she tried the Boston airport again. Still busy. Her sense of imminent disaster grew.

Something made her check his other jacket pocket. She pulled out a piece of folded computer paper. Opening it, she scanned the information . . . and spotted her name.

He knew. Rand knew she'd been arrested and had found the piece of her dress, but he hadn't confronted her. What kind of game was he playing?

Her doorbell signaled Rand's return. Shelby stuffed the computer report into her other pocket. Edgy, she let him in. He'd barely shrugged out of his overcoat and was taking the wood to the hearth when she realized she couldn't go through with this charade. She couldn't spend a nice cozy evening pretending nothing was wrong until he decided to zap her with what he'd learned. *If* he intended to.

"Did you hate Dutch?" she asked, the words out of her mouth before she knew she was going to ask them.

Rand nearly dropped the wood. "Hate is a strong word."

"Did you?"

He piled the wood neatly in her basket, adding two pieces to the fire. "Sometimes."

"Why? Because he was a lousy partner or—"

"He was a lousy human being, as we have been discovering together."

"Have we? You've told me everything?"

Throwing his overcoat onto the couch, Rand approached her, warily it seemed. "Shelby, why don't we forget about Dutch for a moment. I think we need to talk about—"

"Forget about murder?" she asked, interrupting him. He might have his suspicions, but so did she. "I've tried, but I can't. What about you?" Cornered, she did the only thing she could. She attacked. "Do you want to forget because his death was convenient?" She ignored the escalating fierceness of Rand's expression. "You don't have to deal with Dutch. Pippa doesn't have to deal with him. How desperate was your sister to get out of her marriage, anyway?"

Face white, amber eyes blazing, Rand asked, "What's gotten into you? I thought you liked Pippa and cared about me. I thought we were in this together."

Together. The crimson taffeta burned her leg through her pants, making her want to rip it out of her pocket and fling it at him. "I don't know what to believe anymore."

He grabbed her shoulders, making her shudder. "Why are you saying these things? Why do you flinch when I touch you? Shelby, talk to me!"

She jerked her upper body, twisting her shoulders free. "I've done all the talking I want to do for one night."

"Is that my exit cue?"

"Smart man."

To Shelby's eyes, Rand was on the verge of breaking, of saying something he obviously was holding back, but he didn't. He grabbed his suit jacket and threw his arms into it. Then he did the same with his overcoat.

"If you get past whatever it is that's making you impossible tonight, call me. I can be back here in ten minutes. We have some serious things to discuss."

He stared at her for a few seconds, but when Shelby refused to say anything more, he shook his head in disgust and slammed out the front door. Locking up after him, she steeled herself against the emotions that threatened to make her break down and cry. She was in this alone now and had to figure out what direction to take.

Wedging herself against the doorway, she stared at the tree, the symbol of what they'd shared one special night. She'd never forget that Christmas Eve. Or Rand. Her gaze drifted upward, to the starburst he'd given her. Every time she looked at the tree topper, she'd remember him. Her eyes filled with tears as the colors shifted and changed along the length of the silver metal, creating fuzzy blobs against the darkness of her mind.

Shelby stilled suddenly.

The Christmas tree in the executive suite—it had seemed different somehow, that afternoon. She closed her eyes and focused until the disparity defined itself. Its top had been bare. But the night she and Rand had had dinner in the reception area, she'd seen an elongated silver star there.

She thought further back—to the party. While he'd given her punch with one hand, Santa Claus had held a silver star in the other. The punch had the same taste as the drug . . . and the star looked like the one on her tree.

Suspicions rising, Shelby took down the heavy metal ornament and placed it in her purse. Then she bundled up, planning to head for Westbrook's. She was about to return to the scene of the crime, where she would put the starburst back on the tree in the reception area.

Then she'd know for sure....

# Chapter Twelve

Disgruntled by Shelby's quarrelsome behavior, Rand was halfway home before he admitted he never should have left her apartment without finishing what he'd set out to do. He should have faced her with his discoveries, but once he'd seen her, he hadn't known how to begin. He'd wanted to avoid a negative emotional scene, but one had been forced on him anyway. And still he knew no more than when he'd arrived.

Odd how Shelby had turned hostile on him while he'd been gone, treating him as though he had something to hide, as though he were guilty of Dutch's murder—or at least guilty of covering up for Pippa. That Shelby could think him capable of either of those things had wounded him deeply. What had gotten into her? Something serious must have transpired while he'd been out buying the firewood.

Approaching the driveway to his complex, Rand passed it by, deciding instead to return to Shelby's apartment. He would force a confrontation whether she liked it or not. One way or another, he would clear the air between them by bringing the questions and doubts of both of them into the open. Digging under his overcoat, he slipped his free hand into his jacket pocket to retrieve the material. Empty.

He switched driving hands and checked the other pocket. Empty as well.

"Damn!"

That explained it, then. No wonder she'd worked herself into such a state. She knew he'd found a link between her and the murder. No doubt she'd been wracked with nightmarish fantasies about what he might do with the information.

Rand didn't worry about finding a legal parking spot when he pulled up in front of her building. He left his car next to the fireplug at the corner and ran the short distance to her darkened apartment. He rang the bell several times. When she didn't answer, he dug out the set of spare keys he'd never returned. Using them didn't prove profitable, however, since she wasn't in the apartment.

An uneasy feeling swept through him. Her leaving had something to do with the murder, perhaps with the red taffeta. What if Shelby hadn't gotten rid of the dress? The only other logical place she could have hidden it was at Westbrook's. Perhaps she'd returned there now, intending to destroy the evidence. He'd have to stop her from doing something foolish before she somehow managed to frame herself for murder.

As he quickly set off for the store, Rand could only hope that he and Shelby wouldn't end this night as enemies.

SHELBY USED HER KEYS to cut the alarm and to open the employee entrance to Westbrook's. The darkened store was silent, the only sound the electrical hum emanating from the security office. Shaking off the feeling that she'd been followed again, she took a deep breath and stepped inside, ignoring her stomach's quiver as she thought about facing Edgar. She'd have to make up a story about some nonexistent paperwork she'd forgotten to take home. But if passing the doorway, she saw that lying wouldn't be necessary. Sprawled in his chair, his head rolled toward the monitors, the security guard was fast asleep.

Intuition, and glimmers of soft light escaping from State Street through the display windows, were Shelby's only guides through the store. The faintly luminous red emergency-exit sign over the fire stairs led her directly to the bank of elevators. Hoping the cars hadn't been shut down, she felt for the call button. To her relief, she heard a soft whoosh to her left. She found the opening and stepped in carefully. Sliding her hand up the brass panel on the right, she pressed the button at the top of the row. Another whoosh and she was enshrouded in darkness except for the glowing nine on the wall panel and the strip of changing floor indicators above.

Three . . . four . . . five . . .

After shrugging out of her coat, she dug into her shoulder bag until she found the purse-size flashlight that she always carried with her.

. . . Seven . . . eight . . . nine.

The elevator doors opened once more. Following the thin beam of her flashlight, Shelby approached the executive suite. Every nerve felt charged with negative energy. Now that she'd gone this far, she had to follow through with her plan, yet she couldn't help being reluctant. She didn't want to dash the remainder of her hope that she might be wrong about Rand.

Her hand trembled as it found the knob and opened the door. The inky blackness in front of her gave Shelby pause. She flashed her light in the direction of the Christmas tree, and on feet as cold as ice, she moved toward it. She tried to ignore the sensation of being watched, knowing full well that she was alone. Even so, she peered around her carefully. Nothing.

She threw her coat on the nearby sofa, and after removing the ornament from its depths, deposited her shoulder bag as well. A shuddering breath for courage and she was at the tree. Stooping, she found the electrical switch under the pine branches and turned on the lights.

Colors danced through darkness. Red. Green. Blue. The seductive twinkle of the Christmas lights hypnotized her as she stood on tiptoe, positioned the silver starburst, then moved back to give the tree a long, hard look.

The star was right where it belonged.

She was sure of it.

Memories haunted her: waking in a fog of pain...the tree's lights guiding her...tripping...Santa Claus with staring eyes and a slack mouth. All of it.

A tear escaped down Shelby's cheek as she retrieved the ornament, slid her fingers along its central spire.

Elongated.

Squarish.

Deadly.

A cleaver weapon that would leave an odd-shaped hole to baffle the police....

How ironic that Dutch—the very antithesis of the generosity of spirit associated with Christmas—should have died dressed in the holiday's symbolic costume, killed by a token of hope and magic.

But then she was romanticizing.

Who would have guessed that this lethal weapon would have found its way into her apartment? The idea that Rand might have been trying to frame her made Shelby's chest tighten and her heart ache. Had he made that flight from Boston, he, rather than an actor, could have attended the party dressed as the original Santa who gave her the punch. He might have been setting her up to take the fall even then.

Why else would he have obtained the computer report if not to find some poor soul with an arrest record to take the rap?

Her mind was spinning so fast with the ugly possibilities that she almost missed the faint hum whispering from the hallway. The elevator—someone was coming up! After her? Not willing to wait to find out why or who, Shelby grabbed her coat and shoulder bag and ran out of the executive suite to the fire stairs. It was only when she was two-thirds of the way down the first flight that she remembered she hadn't turned off the lights on the Christmas tree.

Nothing she could do about it now.

*Lights,* Shelby thought again as she followed the beam in front of her. If Edgar was making his rounds, surely he wouldn't do so in the dark. Maybe her imagination hadn't been playing tricks on her when she'd thought she was being followed. Maybe Rand had realized she'd solved the crime and was intent on stopping her from going to the police.

Who else could it be?

She aimed her flashlight on the stairs and continued down to the eighth-floor door, waiting there until she was sure the elevator was ascending to nine. Taking a shallow breath—the best she could manage considering the circumstances—she sneaked out into the hall and down toward her office. She had to hide the murder weapon so the evidence couldn't be destroyed. But where? Her desk would be too obvious.

Quickly unlocking the door, Shelby entered her department. Because she knew the placement of every desk and drawing table, she felt more comfortable in this familiar if crowded dark. She threw her coat and purse down on a chair and made her way to the row of mannequin storage units that lined one wall.

"Esmee, I know you wouldn't mind," she whispered, foolishly believing the sound of her own voice could comfort her.

Actually, Westbrook's owned a dozen Esmees as well as mannequins with other exotic names, each series with bodies in various poses. Shelby picked the least used, reclining Esmee. With fumbling fingers, she opened the cabinet. Her flashlight beam slashing across them made the separated body parts seem grotesque. Shelby pulled out a disembodied hand from the felt-lined shelf separating the upper torso from the legs, then slid the starburst to the back of the cabinet and stuffed a loose piece of felt up against it. She replaced the hand and closed the cabinet, secure in the knowledge that the murderer—Rand?—wouldn't find it easily.

A lot of good that would do if he found *her*. . . .

The sound of the elevator starting once more panicked her into looking for a weapon she could defend herself with. She grabbed a screwdriver from a box of tools on a nearby table and slid it into her belt. Then, leaving her coat and purse, she went flying out of the room and toward the fire stairs as a ding echoed along the corridor and up her spine.

The elevator was stopping on eight.

This could be no coincidence. Someone was systematically searching for her. Heart pounding, Shelby slipped into the stairwell and flew downward, thankful she was wearing crepe-soled boots that whispered along the stairs. She had to get out of Westbrook's before her stalker caught up with her.

Not Rand. Please, not Rand.

Even with what should have been proof positive, part of Shelby wouldn't believe that Rand was guilty of anything but loving her. To think he could use her so cruelly made her sick inside, and she couldn't balance the resulting disgust and fear with the comfort and safety and love she'd felt in his arms only days ago. Her instincts screamed that Rand was innocent, that she was framing him in her own mind, that he wouldn't have formed a relationship with her if he was guilty, that she couldn't have been so wrong about him.

But she'd been wrong about someone, Shelby thought, when a door high above her slammed open against the wall and she heard a whispered, sexless curse.

She switched off her light, knowing she had to get out. The killer was in the stairwell.

The door on six leading into the store proper was an arm's length away. Quietly opening it a crack, she slipped through and held the door until it closed. Then she switched on her flashlight and sped toward the left, to one of the two banks of escalators. She could run down the metal steps, could hide among the displays on any of the lower floors if necessary. But for how long?

Her mind raced along with her heart and her legs as she descended floor after floor. She'd have to make it out of the store and to a public telephone on the street. She didn't want to think about going out into the subzero temperature in nothing but corduroys and a heavy knit sweater, but the adrenaline pumping through her bloodstream was sure to keep her warm for a few minutes.

And being cold was better than being dead, she assured herself.

A noise above and to her right told her she hadn't fooled her pursuer. Trying to control her breathing so she wouldn't give herself away, Shelby finished her race to the first floor and crossed into lingerie. Switching off her flashlight, she stuck it into her pocket and ducked behind a counter just before rapid footfalls stopped at the base of the escalator.

She sneaked to the next counter and the next, all the while holding her breath. Mere feet from an open display window, she grabbed a peignoir, wrapped it around her shoulders and ducked into the holiday setting.

Footsteps crossed in her direction.

*Go the other way!*

But her mind's silent scream was ignored. She listened intently, trying to recognize the light sound of leather against marble. A fruitless task. The footsteps stopped and a wide beam of light swept across her back. Posed like her favorite Esmee, Shelby held her breath and prayed the peignoir wasn't fluttering around to give her away.

The footsteps came so close that cold sweat began to bead her body and her insides twisted painfully. It was then she saw the car—a familiar Saab—turning onto the side street. Her eyes widened. Rand. She could see the car turning into the alley behind the store.

If Rand was out there, then who...?

The footsteps receded and Shelby had to make a quick decision about whether or not to trust the man she loved. He could be in on it; Pippa could be the person behind her. And if not, Rand would be in danger, just as she was.

Shelby followed her instincts and her heart: unable to let him walk into a possible trap, she slipped out of the window and headed for the employee entrance. The lingerie still balanced on her shoulders had other ideas. Catching on a corner, the material pulled over a sign with a loud clunk before she could stop its fall. Even as she heard the outside door opening, a shot rang from nowhere, the bullet whizzing by Shelby too close for her comfort.

"Rand, watch out!" Shedding the garment, she veered to her right and ran for all she was worth.

"Shelby!"

Rand's voice coming from the entrance was followed by the sound of running feet and another gunshot. She saw the brilliant flash from the corner of her eye. Rand caught up to her at the elevators and pushed her into one of the cars. Gasping, she hit nine.

His voice low and urgent, he demanded, "Are you all right?" as the elevator doors slid shut.

"I am now." Blood was rushing through her system at an incredible pace and yet, knowing she wasn't alone, she felt safer than she had since the cat-and-mouse game had begun. "What are you doing here?"

"Later. Do you know who's after you?"

Ironic that she'd thought he might have been the one—but she couldn't tell him that. "No."

"We can lock ourselves in my office and call the police."

That would have been a great idea if the car hadn't stopped with a jerk halfway between six and seven. "The control panel," Shelby muttered. "He's got us now."

"Not necessarily."

"What do you mean?"

"The trap door above us. We can get through it to the next floor."

The words were hardly out of his mouth before she'd found the flashlight and aimed the beam upward. "It looks big enough for me, but I'm not sure about you," she said, visually measuring the opening against his broad shoulders.

He stripped off his coat and jacket. "One thing at a time. I'll lift you."

Rand already had his hands around her waist. Shelby wanted to throw herself into his arms and beg his forgiveness for her idiocy. A sense of urgency stopped her; she'd have enough time to feel guilty later. Instead, with the flashlight on the elevator floor, she concentrated on helping him, finding the rail at the side of the car with one foot so she could push up as he lifted her. Palms flat, she pressed against the trap. The hatch raised and slid out of the way.

"Can you pull yourself up?" Rand asked.

"I don't work out for nothing."

Still, pulling her body weight through a small opening in the dark wasn't easy, and she was glad to get the boost. She used every bit of strength she'd developed on the bench press. Her arm muscles protested but held out. When she scrambled out and on top of the car, she lay flat, the screwdriver wedged in her belt pressing into her hip. Then, taking the flashlight from him, she set it down on top of the car and grabbed onto Rand's shirt, pulling as he struggled upward. His shoulders squeezed through the opening with barely an inch to spare.

Shelby picked up the light and ran the beam up the shaft to the seventh-floor doors that had to be five or six feet above their reach. "Oh, Lord, you can't even lift me that high."

Trapped on top of an elevator car that could move at any minute. Her stomach did a queer dance and she felt suffocated by her narrow prison in spite of the draft of cold air running down the length of the dark shaft.

"There's a repair ladder." Rand took the flashlight from her and pointed out the slender black metal rail that clung to the shaft's wall a foot or more to the side of the opening. "It's our only chance. But we'll need something long and flat to pry open the doors."

Shelby tapped her screwdriver. "Prepared as a Girl Scout," she said wryly.

Rand didn't bother expressing surprise if he felt any. "You go first. I'll be right behind you. I can hang on to you while you work on the doors."

Taking the lead, thankful again for the crepe-soled boots, Shelby clung to the ladder that squeaked and groaned with every step she took. The rail was so close to the wall, she could barely get the ball of her foot on the narrow rungs. Climbing seemed to take forever.

"High enough," Rand finally said. Right below her, he turned the beam to the bottom of the doors. "Once you get the screwdriver wedged in, there's a narrow toehold."

Though she was terrified to let go, Shelby knew she had no choice. She freed the screwdriver and stretched out her upper body and arm. Her left foot slipped sideways and the ladder shifted with a screech of metal, making her stomach tumble. "Aah!"

"I'm right behind you." The length of Rand's body pressed against the back of her leg and buttocks as he stopped directly behind her and hooked a hand through her belt. "Now look straight at the doors this time. You can do it."

Feeling only slightly more sure of herself with Rand steadying her, Shelby stretched out again. The tip of the screwdriver slipped easily between the doors. Holding on to the handle, she shoved until the tool felt securely wedged, then found the tiny ledge with her right toes. She shifted her weight carefully to get as much leverage as she could. Then she pulled on the handle.

"Got it!" she exclaimed as the doors popped open. Curling her fingers around one side, she tugged until the panel slid all the way into the wall. "I can get in."

Thank God she didn't have to stretch too far. She clung to the brass trim and got a better foothold, then shifted her weight and literally tumbled onto the seventh floor.

"Shelby!"

"I'm all right," she whispered, throwing down the screwdriver and reaching for the light.

With his extra leg length, Rand easily followed her through the doorway by the time she rose from the floor.

"What now?" Shelby asked as he wrapped an arm around her and pressed her to him for a second.

"Now you'll have a fatal accident," came a familiar voice that made her head whip toward the darkened store.

The bright beam of a flashlight blinded her for a second. Then it lowered, allowing Shelby to see the gun in Tucker Powers's hand. Rand squeezed her shoulders reassuringly, then let go of her.

"So it was you all along." What a fool. She'd gone to the lawyer for advice that very afternoon, for God's sake.

"I knew you were going to be trouble when I saw you in your red dress the morning after the party," Tucker stated. "Were you hiding in one of the other offices, watching Dutch's death throes?"

Neither agreeing to nor denying anything, Shelby asked, "What did you have against Dutch, anyway?"

Rand purposely moved away from Shelby, putting some distance between them. He could take the lawyer, but he wanted to hear the truth first. And he wanted to make sure that neither he nor Shelby got shot in the process.

"It must have something to do with the stock that Dutch had been secretly buying up through Frank Hatcher, because Tucker refused to sell his shares," Rand said before addressing the lawyer directly. "You shouldn't have pretended that you didn't know anything about the stock sale when I questioned you, Tucker. That was a mistake I caught as soon as I spoke to Hatcher. He said the only stockholders he didn't approach were Althea and some guy he couldn't find named Horowitz."

He could almost feel Shelby tense next to him, but now was not the time to reassure her that he'd meant to tell her everything if only she'd been willing to listen.

"Dutch had to be stopped from turning a quality department store into a junk paradise," Tucker stated matter-of-factly. "The lowlife had been trying to gain controlling interest so he could sell for a huge profit. He was going to hand over Westbrook's to BargainWorld, that no-quality merchandise discount chain. You should be thankful your late partner is dead, Rand, rather than trying to act like some damn vigilante in his no-good name."

"Sorry, Tucker, but I could never thank someone for murdering another human being." Rand crossed his arms and shifted to the right, taking another step away from Shelby and one closer to the lawyer in the process. "Why should you care so much about what happens to Westbrook's? You're only a minor shareholder."

"I devoted my life to this store, as did my father and grandfather before me," Tucker said with pride. "And then, of course, I love Althea dearly."

Shelby shot Rand a look that he took to be significant—as if she was trying to indicate he should go for the man—though he couldn't be sure of much in the half-light.

"So the grapevine was correct, for once," she said, drawing Tucker's attention back to herself. "You and Althea have been having an affair all these years."

"No. Our affair was intense, but sad to say, short-lived and over thirty years ago. I would have given up everything for her, but Althea wouldn't hear of my leaving my wife and children. She halted the affair... then never married as a pledge to our love."

"And in return, you did all this for her?"

"Althea would have been humiliated at seeing the store her father built fall into the hands of sleazy discounters who would trash every tradition that had been upheld throughout eighty years. Dutch had to die. Can't you see that?"

Rand edged even closer while the lawyer was talking. And when Tucker ended his long-winded speech, he demanded, "Are you trying to convince us—or yourself? And are you really willing to kill two more people—*innocent* people—to cover up the murder?"

"What choice do I have?" Tucker looked from him to Shelby. "I saw you coming from the fire stairs in your party dress. I didn't know if you had seen the murder, so I merely sent you warnings and tried to frighten you into keeping your mouth shut. But you ignored them, kept poking your nose where it didn't belong. And when you came to my office earlier, I realized you knew. What were you looking for? Blackmail?"

Jaw clenching at the mention of warnings Shelby hadn't bothered to tell him about, Rand inched forward, all the time assessing the slight tremor in the older man's hand; either Tucker was afraid or not really capable of killing without extreme motivation.

"I didn't know." Shelby spoke directly to Tucker and stepped forward as though she didn't believe he would shoot her, either. "I passed out in your secretary's office and didn't wake up until the next morning. That's when I found the body. Your warnings were for nothing. This is for nothing. I didn't know anything."

"Well, you do now." Tucker pointed the gun directly at her. "I can't let you tell."

Stomach clenching at the danger to the woman he loved, Rand had heard enough. But Shelby didn't have any sense; she took another step toward Tucker.

"You hated Dutch. You had reason to," she said. The tremor turned to a more obvious shake. "But you don't have reason to hate me. I don't think you can do it, Tucker."

At this rate, the gun might go off by accident. Rand readied himself to disarm the lawyer.

"You're basically a fine man," Shelby continued. "A loyal man with a great deal of pride. I don't think you can kill without hate."

Though he'd come to the same conclusion, Rand was not about to take any chances. He downed Tucker with the hardest, swiftest tackle he could muster from a standstill. In better shape than he might have imagined, the lawyer fought him for the gun with everything he had. They rolled over and over, but Rand was driven, and in the end there was no question as to who would win the physical contest. He caught Tucker's gun hand and banged it against the floor.

The weapon went spinning off across the marble floor into the dark. Just as Rand managed to pin Tucker solidly under him, the lights went on. To his surprise, Althea Westbrook stood a few feet away, watching the struggle.

Without taking her eyes off them, she stooped down, and with a gloved hand, picked up the gun.

# Chapter Thirteen

Having picked up Tucker's full-size flashlight, Shelby switched it off as she stared at Althea and the gun, which was aimed at the two men on the floor.

"I—I heard Tucker threaten you just as I arrived," the older woman said, looking from the men to Shelby. "I was afraid something like this might happen."

"Like what, Miss Westbrook?"

"Dear Tucker...he's been ranting on and on about making sure nothing tarnished Westbrooks' reputation," Althea explained. "When he telephoned to inform me he was following you here, Shelby, I felt it my duty to come as well. I suspected he was going to do something foolish again."

Shelby noted that when Rand got to his feet, his eyes never left the weapon. She had the distinct impression that he was edgy, seeing it in Althea's hand.

Tucker wasn't so quick to rise. "Foolish?" His expression confused, he slowly stood. "Again?"

"Killing Bertram *was* very foolish of you, my love." Althea's casually issued statement made Tucker's eyes grow wide with dismay. "I knew he was the murderer all along, of course," she told Shelby, "but I felt it my duty to protect the poor man. He'd been so distraught by Bertram's plan to buy out minor shareholders so he could make a fortune by selling to this BargainWorld company...and of course Tucker has been so loyal to me personally. You can see that I had to shelter him, can you not?''

Shelby shifted uneasily, sensing something didn't ring true. Rand had said Hatcher hadn't approached Althea about the sale, so how had she found out about it? And Dutch had been buying stock secretly, so neither of them should have known about his proposed sale to Bargain-World....

"Althea," Tucker protested, "you know I didn't murder anyone. How could you make such an accusation after all I've done for you?''

Althea's fingers were white knuckled as she pointed the gun directly at him. "Of course you killed Bertram. I followed you back to the store when you dropped me off after the party. I was too late to stop you, but I found your monogrammed handkerchief full of blood next to Bertram's body. I destroyed the evidence to protect you. But I cannot protect you anymore, not when you threaten Randall and Shelby."

Shoulders slumped in defeat, the lawyer shook his head. Hoarsely he asked, "How could you do this to me when I've been the one protecting you?''

Shelby saw the truth of the matter in Althea's tense expression and in the fine quiver of her hand—as if she were merely waiting for the right moment....

"Yes, you protected me and tried to save Westbrook's by killing the one man who threatened to destroy everything you knew and loved."

"I love *you*, for God's sake." Tucker spread out his arms and stumbled forward toward her.

Regret mixed with triumph in the faded blue eyes made Shelby realize Althea was about to shoot the lawyer to shut him up, to hide the truth.

Althea Westbrook was the murderer.

Instinctively Shelby threw the heavy flashlight she was holding into Althea's chest at the exact second the gun went off. Even as she propelled herself forward, Shelby felt a sizzling pain sear her left arm. She rammed the older woman with her right shoulder. Althea got off another shot, but Rand had acted as quickly from the other side and had pulled her gun hand high so the bullet went over their heads. He removed the weapon.

A clumsy shuffle of feet from the store's interior was followed by a shouted, "Hold it right there, folks." Gun drawn, Edgar Siefert panted as he slowed to a stop in their midst. "Back off nice and quiet, now. I called the cops and they're on the way."

Shelby was glad to do as Edgar suggested. Numb with pain, she backed up and leaned against the brass trim surrounding one of the elevators. She cradled her wounded arm next to her body, amazed that there wasn't more blood. She'd always thought you bled a lot from a gunshot wound. Hers merely oozed into the sleeve of her burgundy sweater. No one seemed to be paying any attention to her.

All eyes were on the security guard, whose gun hand was steady and whose balding head was swollen and bruised. "All right. Which one of you knocked me on the noggin?" Edgar demanded to know. He adjusted his pants with his free hand for emphasis.

"I did," Althea admitted with a sigh of resignation. "Tucker telephoned me from the limo to warn me that he was going to stop Shelby. I was the first one here. I owned the store for half of the twenty-five years you worked for Westbrook's, Edgar. You follow a very strict nightly routine. I knew you would be coming back from your rounds within minutes, so I hid in the office until you settled down.''

''You, Miss Westbrook?'' Edgar's expression was shocked. ''But you were always such a nice lady. So refined and everything. How could you do something like that?''

''More important, how could you have tried to pin the murder on me?'' a distraught Tucker demanded.

''Because you were so infuriatingly stupid!'' Althea spat. ''If not for your interference, no one would ever have figured out that I murdered that bastard. Shelby didn't know a thing. She couldn't have. She was unconscious in your secretary's office, knocked out by something that sleaze bag put in her drink.''

''Seconal,'' Rand inserted.

Shelby met his eyes. How much else did he know that he hadn't told her? It seemed they both had a lot of confessing to do. Thinking it, she realized she could never tell him everything. She couldn't stand to see the pain in his expression when she admitted she'd thought he might be guilty. He'd never forgive her for the awful things she'd thought about him. And she couldn't go on with their relationship with another lie between them.

''Bertram admitted he wanted to have a little fun with Shelby while she couldn't put up too great a fight. The pervert even dressed himself in the actor's Santa Claus suit as part of his grotesque game.''

''That's not why you killed him,'' Shelby said, trying not to grimace as fresh pain shot through her. ''Not for me. For yourself. You knew about the stock deal. You knew about BargainWorld. How?''

''Bertram came to me himself when he ran out of sources. He couldn't find Horowitz. Tucker refused to sell.

He had to have more than fifty percent of the stock or the deal with BargainWorld was off. I made him tell me all about it . . . and then I held out for ten times what the stock was worth. I wanted to be wealthy again, as I had been before Westbrook's hit the skids.''

Biting back a moan as her arm lost its numbness, Shelby stared at the fur Althea wore. This one was fox. And the pearls at her throat and ears were real. She had a Lake Shore Drive address. How much money constituted wealthy enough for a woman like Althea Westbrook?

"So why did you kill him?" Rand asked.

"Horowitz crawled out of the woodwork and Bertram no longer needed my stock. He gave me the news at the Christmas party. He wasn't going to pay me a cent. I went back later to confront him. He laughed in my face. Laughed at me, a Westbrook! At that moment I could have killed him.''

"She did," Tucker said, his face sad. "I found one of her lace-edged handkerchiefs near the body the next morning. I couldn't believe she was capable of violence. I figured Dutch must have driven her over the edge.''

And indeed, Althea seemed to be approaching the edge now, Shelby thought. The older woman paced in the small area, her fingers plucking at her fur, her expression vague as though she was turned inward. As though she was lost in the early-morning hours after the party.

She didn't seem to see Lieutenant Isaac Jackson and two uniformed policemen rushing up the escalator—not even when they stopped almost directly behind her.

"It was his laughter that got to me," Althea insisted. "I didn't plan on killing Bertram. The metal star just happened to be there, within reach on the receptionist's desk. Somehow it had been overlooked when the tree had been trimmed. Bertram stopped laughing when I plunged the star's point into his chest." Her expression was triumphant when she added, "He looked so surprised . . ."

"And then you wiped the weapon off and put it at the top of the tree," Rand stated.

"Yes. I didn't mean to kill him, but there I was, faced with going to jail. And I was sure no one would ever guess. We Westbrooks are quite an intelligent and resourceful lot, you know."

"You'll have to tell us all about it, Miss Westbrook," Jackson said. "At the station. You're under arrest. Zimmer, read her her rights."

"You'll have to take me into custody also." Tucker stepped forward. "As an accessory."

Shelby frowned. Something warm and sticky was running down her arm and dripping from her fingers. And she was feeling light-headed. Confused. When she looked at her hand, she swallowed hard.

As the uniformed policeman took a now silent Althea into custody, Rand said, "Lieutenant Jackson, I never thought I'd be glad to see you."

"Me, either," Shelby agreed.

She moved as if to leave her resting place, but there didn't seem to be any solid floor under her feet. And suddenly, someone turned off all the lights again.

THE EMERGENCY WAITING ROOM at Northwestern Hospital was half filled even on a weeknight. There'd been the usual assortment of cases—everything from a toddler's earache to a senior citizen's hip broken by a fall on the ice. But as far as Rand could tell, Shelby Corbin had the sole distinction of being the victim of a gunshot wound.

He still couldn't believe she'd been shot without his realizing it. She hadn't cried out, hadn't said a word. She'd stoically listened to Althea's ravings before fainting from loss of blood. His heart had wrenched painfully when she'd fallen to the floor, leaving a crimson streak on the brass trim next to the elevator opening. He'd been afraid she was seriously hurt.

The paramedics summoned by Jackson had assured him the damage seemed to be minimal—a simple flesh wound. Clean entrance and exit holes. No reason to get too upset.

Were they crazy? That was the woman he loved they'd discussed with such casualness.

His frustration had increased when Lieutenant Jackson had followed them to the hospital, demanding to take his and Shelby's statements separately before they had a chance to talk in private. Rand told the detective everything he knew while the emergency staff worked on Shelby.

And now the lieutenant was with her. Rand paced, anxiety-ridden because he hadn't been allowed to see her first. He wanted assurance from her own lips that she was all right. They had a lot of talking to do—a lot of explaining—but once they cleared the air everything would be all right. He loved her, and though she hadn't told him, he sensed she returned the feeling.

Shelby *had* to love him, Rand thought desperately, raking a hand through his uncombed hair.

When Jackson returned to the waiting room, Rand practically jumped on the man. "How is she?"

"Her spirits are low, but she seems to be doing fine medically, or so the doctors say. They want to keep her under observation. She'll be able to go home tomorrow or the next day at the latest."

"I want to see her right away," Rand said, ignoring the look of concern Jackson gave him. "Are they keeping her in emergency or assigning her to a room?"

"A room, but wait a minute. I don't know how to break this to you, but you can't see her right now."

"What's that supposed to mean, Jackson?"

"Exactly what it sounds like, McNabb. She doesn't *want* to see you."

"I don't believe it." Rand started to push by the detective, but Jackson held him back. The wiry man certainly was strong for his size. Knowing he could win this physical struggle, too, Rand forced himself to relax. "All right. Did she say she didn't want to see me—or anyone in general? I'm not just anyone."

When the lieutenant said "You, specifically," all the life drained out of him.

In shock, Rand slumped into one of the empty seats next to a woman who held a baby and a toddler on her lap. "It doesn't make sense." Unless she didn't love him, after all.

Jackson slapped him lightly on the shoulder. "Give her time, McNabb. She's been through more than one person should have to endure during the past two weeks. Not that she would have had to if she'd been sensible in the first place. Listen, why don't you walk me back to my car."

Nodding, Rand stood and followed the lieutenant outside. To his astonishment, Jackson proceeded to detail what exactly Shelby had been hiding from him since Dutch had been murdered.

WHEN SHELBY LEFT THE HOSPITAL two days later, she was alone. She'd denied the need for a family member to escort her to her apartment. Actually, she'd had an out-and-out argument with her father, who'd tried to bully her into agreeing. He'd finally backed down when he'd seen how upset she'd become, but the worry on his aging face had tied her chest in knots. Even so, she hadn't felt inclined to change her mind.

Part of her—the emotional part—had been hoping against hope that Rand would care enough to defy her de-

cision not to see him. The other, more sensible part had
known that not seeing each other except professionally
would be easiest. But when he'd neither burst into her hospital room in indignation nor been waiting for her when she
was released, she'd been consumed by an overwhelming
disappointment. She'd felt depressed and let down rather
than relieved. Still, perhaps it was better this way.

No scenes.

No tears.

At least, none that he would see.

The cab ride home was mercifully short. She wanted to
crawl into her bed and pull the covers over her head to
make the world go away. Maybe when she was finally alone
with her memories, she would be able to cry for all that had
happened . . . and all that might have been in the future.

Getting out of the taxi, she stared at her front windows,
surprised that her Christmas tree was lit. She'd been in such
a state the other night she hadn't unplugged the lights. She
ought to be grateful she had an apartment to come home to;
unattended trees were always a cause of fires at this time of
the year.

With a heavy heart, Shelby entered her apartment building. She checked her mailbox, but surprisingly it was
empty. The awkward inner door was a trickier matter for a
woman with only one good arm and one usable hand, but
she pushed the door with her hip as she removed the keys.
About to attack the dead bolt on her apartment door,
Shelby almost dropped the key ring when the door flew
open. Her eyes widened at the sight of Rand wearing the
green sweater she'd given him for Christmas.

"Welcome home."

She stood there for a moment, feeling like an intruder.
All the blood seemed to rush out of her, and her voice was
faint as she walked into the living room. "Thanks." Sud-

denly broiling, she unzipped her down coat with numb fingers.

"Such enthusiasm... wait, let me help you."

Shelby continued to struggle out of her coat, not wanting to feel his hands on her. He was quicker than a disabled woman, however. His warmth seared her, even through the cloth. He was so close she could hardly breathe.

"Sit down. Can I get you anything? Hot chocolate?"

She looked around in confusion. A fire blazed in the hearth. The sweet smell of chocolate drifted up to her from two designer mugs on the coffee table. Her mail was neatly laid out next to the mugs. "This *is* still my apartment, isn't it?"

"If you want it to be," he said enigmatically.

Careful of her wounded arm, which was secured to her side in a sling, Shelby sat, muttering, "A woman has to watch who she gives her spare set of keys to."

"She should only give them to a man she loves," Rand agreed, his tone amiable.

Frowning, Shelby avoided the subject... and avoided looking into his heart-stopping amber eyes or at the tiny scar that disappeared into his mustache. She didn't want to be reminded of what she couldn't have. She stared, instead, at the tree. "I guess Jackson wrapped everything up, right?"

"We think so. Althea murdered Dutch; Tucker tried to cover up for her. Simple."

"Poor Tucker," Shelby murmured, still trying to pull herself together while Rand busied himself as though he belonged in her apartment. She was as aware of him folding her coat over one of the chairs and sitting on the couch next to her as she was of the glass heart with the lovebirds that mocked her from the pine branches. "Tucker put himself in jeopardy to protect Althea and Westbrook's, and she was as eager as Dutch to sell out.''

"I found out why he wanted to sell so badly." Rand leaned over and lifted a mug of hot chocolate. "I called Iris into my office and made her talk," he said after taking a sip. "It seems André Kuryokhin is planning to develop a very expensive cosmetics line in the near future. Loretta sold Dutch on the idea through Iris. My late partner agreed to be one of Kuryokhin's major investors. Iris was promised a shining new career working for the line. No doubt they both would have been millionaires if they'd pulled it off. The money in Dutch's safe is legit as far as we can tell. He probably turned assets to cash in case he needed it for a ready sale."

Shelby was only half listening. Her eyes had strayed to the top of the tree, which she assumed would be as barren as she'd left it. Topping the pine branches and touching the nine-foot ceiling sat an angel, a combination of ceramic and fiber art so exquisite it took her breath away.

"Where did that come from?" she asked, her gaze pinned to the fragile ceramic face surrounded by a cloud of dark hair through which were woven silver and gold stars.

"Don't you want to hear the rest of what we found out?" Setting his mug back down, Rand didn't bother waiting for her to agree. "I thought you might be interested to know that Tucker confessed to being responsible for all the nasty tricks played on you during the past two weeks. Being followed, then chased by Santa, the note, the dead rat, the wreath . . . all compliments of Westbrook's former lawyer and vice president."

"Yes, I know that now."

Shelby wondered why Rand wasn't more upset with her for not telling him about all of the incidents. Maybe because he'd neglected to share a few details as well.

"By the way," he continued, "that wreath was merely a copy of one he had sent to the funeral home. Tucker had it made especially to scare you. He got into your hallway by ringing the bell of someone on the third floor. I really think you should speak to your landlord about having a modern intercom system put in. If you really want to stay here, that is."

That was the second time he'd made such a reference to her apartment. Shelby tore her eyes away from the tree and quickly glanced at Rand. "If you have something to say—"

"I have lots of things I want to say to you, Shelby."

He was staring at her with such warmth that he made her want to cry. "There's something I have to tell you first," she said sadly.

"I know all your secrets now."

"No." Shelby shook her head. "Not this one."

She took a long, hard look at the man she loved. His burnished auburn hair, the chiseled cheeks and square jaw, the chip in his front tooth—they very nicely packaged the man she loved, one who could be gentle and funny, strong and determined, but above all, loyal to those he loved. He would expect the same loyalty in return. Once she said her piece, Rand would probably walk right out the door and she wouldn't blame him. And if she was smart, she'd find another job so she wouldn't have to see him professionally, either, she thought morosely.

"So, tell me something I don't already know," Rand said with a challenge in his amber eyes.

"As much as I wanted to, I didn't trust you. When I found out about your getting Dutch's share of Westbrook's because of your contract, I got edgy. I searched your office and found the airline-ticket stub. The one from Boston."

"So that's why you brought up the night of the party."

"Let me finish. Please. When you left to buy firewood, I tried calling the Boston airport and the airline to check on your story, but I couldn't get through. Then I spotted the piece of my dress sticking out of your jacket pocket."

"So you took it and the drug and the page of the computer report Dad had run on all Westbrook's employees after the murder. Sorry I wasn't at liberty to tell you about that. And the reason I didn't mention the drug was because I found it the day you met me at Pippa's, after the Santa incident. Somehow you managed to make me forget about it."

"What about the red material?"

"You were supposed to be working late, remember? I went to look for you to show you the computer report. I wanted to make you talk, to make you share whatever was troubling you. I found the material on a hinge of your drawing board."

Remembering how the dress had caught when she'd been trying to hide it, Shelby flushed under his steady gaze. "All those things added up in my mind, I'm afraid."

"Making you incredibly hostile, which made me undeniably pigheaded or I wouldn't have walked out on you without getting to the truth of the matter right then."

"When you left," Shelby went on, "I stood in the doorway staring at the tree. At the topper. It looked so familiar. I was sure I'd seen the star at Westbrook's."

"I'd been planning on buying you one of those special ornaments for days," Rand explained. "Then Christmas Eve came and I didn't want to come to your place without something that would remind you of me."

Shelby focused on her sling so she wouldn't have to see his face. "Looking at it, I was terrified that I knew..." She couldn't finish. She didn't know how to tell him about her terrible suspicions that had threatened to break her heart.

"You thought I was the murderer."

Startled, Shelby whipped her head up. "How did you know?"

"Your mind is as logical as mine."

"Then you thought I was the murderer, too?"

"No, not once I got to know the wonderful woman you are. I realized you were hiding some secret and that you might have been the woman in red, but I also knew that you could never kill anyone."

"You gave me the benefit of the doubt, while I—"

"Shelby," Rand interrupted, gently touching her cheek, "no one was tormenting me with warnings. No one had me on the edge, afraid of something I couldn't stop. No one had me believing that I might be the next victim. Besides, when it came to the ultimate test, you trusted your heart—and me. When I came into Westbrook's after you, you warned me."

Somehow Rand had managed to move closer. His left hand was wrapped around the back of the couch and tangled in her hair. His right hand was doing unspeakable things to her insides as he stroked her neck. The best part was that he made it sound as if he didn't blame her.

"Let me get this straight. Are you saying that you had it all figured out these past few days and that you don't hate me?" When Rand grinned and nodded, Shelby couldn't keep the indignant tone out of her voice. "The least you could have done was come to the hospital to tell me so. Do you know what I was going through?"

"You probably felt the same way I did when you sent me away through Lieutenant Jackson." Before she could retort, he covered her lips with his fingers. "I promise I wasn't trying to get even. While you were in the hospital, I merely had a lot of details to take care of so I could start taking proper care of things around this place.''

His references to her apartment were getting to her. ''Damn it, McNabb, what are you trying to tell me?'' Shelby asked, praying she wasn't misunderstanding. ''You want my apartment?'' She held her breath waiting for his answer.

''I want you . . . in a slightly larger setting, if you don't mind. My town house would do for a start.''

She could breathe again and her heart began to pound—with joy rather than fear, for once. Everything was going to be all right. ''Are you sure? After all that mistrust between us?''

''We didn't really know each other when we got involved, Shelby. But I'm sure of what I want. And we still have time to end the year right.''

''End the year . . . but this is New Year's Eve.''

''So it is. We have until midnight to get our relationship on the right course. Then we can make some New Year's resolutions about communication and trust. I love you, in case you haven't figured it out.'' Rand paused, then added, ''Well, aren't you going to make a similar confession?''

Shelby knew he'd have to be blind if he couldn't see the love shining through her. ''You could torture it out of me,'' she teased. ''If you have no shame, that is.'' She gave her wounded arm a significant look.

''I'm a football player, remember. We developed special techniques for dealing with disabled players.''

''Why don't you show me a few.''

Before she'd finished the last word, her mouth was engulfed in a kiss that set her holiday right. Rand took possession and ran with the opportunity to show her she was loved and wanted. When he pulled away, she felt thoroughly kissed and slightly dazed.

"The angel," Shelby breathed as she opened her eyes to the beauty at the top of the tree. "She's a real work of art."

"Like you. I bought her because she reminded me of you."

"I thought you likened me to an elf or a grinch."

"All different facets of your personality," he assured her.

"I love you," Shelby whispered with a laugh. "Show me more of those techniques, would you?"

Rand kissed her again, and Shelby knew that their future holidays together would all be bright.

# PAMELA BROWNING

...is fireworks on the green at the Fourth of July and prayers said around the Thanksgiving table. It is the dream of freedom realized in thousands of small towns across this great nation.

But mostly, the Heartland is its people. People who care about and help one another. People who cherish traditional values and give to their children the greatest gift, the gift of love.

American Romance presents HEARTLAND, an emotional trilogy about people whose memories, hopes and dreams are bound up in the acres they farm.

HEARTLAND...the story of America.

Don't miss these heartfelt stories: American Romance #237 SIMPLE GIFTS (March), #241 FLY AWAY (April), and #245 HARVEST HOME (May).

HRT-1

# ATTRACTIVE, SPACE SAVING BOOK RACK

Display your most prized novels on this handsome and sturdy book rack. The hand-rubbed walnut finish will blend into your library decor with quiet elegance, providing a practical organizer for your favorite hard-or soft-covered books.

**Only $9.95**

**Approximately 16" x 8" when assembled**

**Assembles in seconds!**

---

To order, rush your name, address and zip code, along with a check or money order for $10.70* ($9.95 plus 75¢ postage and handling) payable to *Harlequin Reader Service*:

Harlequin Reader Service
Book Rack Offer
901 Fuhrmann Blvd.
P.O. Box 1396
Buffalo, NY 14269-1396

*Offer not available in Canada.*

BKR-1A

*New York and Iowa residents add appropriate sales tax.

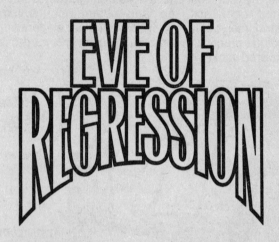